Side Road to Nevada

By Chris Allen Lynch

Printed in the United States of America

ISBN-13: 978-1987464269

ISBN-10: 1987464265

Acknowledgments

Thank you all for taking part in my life's dream to write.

Thank you to my wife, Teri, for your support and patience. We do make a good team.

Thank you to all my friends who gave me feedback, especially Steve who not only makes my day job infinitely better and easier with his incredible mind, but also possesses the most amazing and inspiring moral compass I have ever encountered and who is the inspiration for Sammy. Thanks to Keyan Price, Chris Hopley, Terry Hill, and all the rest of you who helped with ideas and corrections.

Thanks also to Jami of redpengirl.com for your editing, guidance, and especially for your patience with me!

Chapter 1

A FADED RED-GONE-PINK JEEP sits on the shoulder of a desolate Oregon road. The old truck's soft top has seen better days and its tires are so cracked from age and weather that their continued safe use is questionable. Bursts of swearing challenge the insidious quiet of the desert.

Offering to trade God a future of good behavior for a running motor, Trevor turns the key. He pushes slowly against the starter engagement spring. The motor does not run. Extending one hand upward, Trevor raises his middle finger toward the sky, then turns on the radio, tunes in a country station, and sits, sweating, still swearing. The music is surprisingly static free for a point equidistant between nowhere and nothing. The snug-fitting AC-DC tee shirt he wears is stuck to his back. He mutters, "shit," with no enthusiasm and exits the unmoving vehicle.

At the front of the Jeep, he opens the dented hood and looks at the mess of oily motor and bad repair work. Randomly wiggling wires and hoses, he wipes his now greasy hands on faded Levi's. Garth Brooks carries from the sound system, declaring, "We are cowboys, cowboys forever," but refuses to provide insight that would tell Trevor how to fix the broken motor. He slumps down on the dusty shoulder of the road and leans against the tire in the shade of the vehicle waiting for inspiration, or the highway patrol, or God to arrive. Eventually, Trevor decides he should save the battery and goes back into the hot interior to turn the key to the off position, then returns to the warm, dusty ground.

Settling against the tire again, Trevor's ears pick up a low frequency whooshing, undulating sound. He looks around and realizes the ground is shaking. Being from the west coast, he has felt tremors before but this spasm is short and lacking in significant ground motion. It's more like a being in a school bus going over washboard than experiencing a typical earthquake. The experience makes the hair on the back of his neck stand up and then, suddenly, the shaking stops. There is no fade, just a five mile-an-hour impact with no bounce. Done and over, thanks. The freaky event is scary for its unusual nature, but does nothing to alleviate Trevor's sweating against the tire of the Jeep.

With nothing else to do, Trevor's gaze wanders. Twelve distinct peaks are visible from this spot where his backside is becoming one with the dusty Earth. Thirteen, if you count the little hill thing off to the right. Trevor thinks the small peaks are generally in a circle, arranged like the rim of a giant asshole with him in approximately its geometric center, fitting. There are no trees, a lot of sage brush, and apparently a Bonneville Power Substation, or so the only sign within sight claims.

More time passes, enough time, Trevor thinks, that all the world's glaciers are now gone and the sea level has risen its projected one hundred and fifty feet. More than that, enough time has passed for humanity to have thankfully killed itself off. This is probably the case or else, even here, which is actually nowhere, a car would have passed. At least one.

Trevor hears the rhythmic crunch of footsteps on gravel.

Looking to his right, he sees a figure approaching from about a hundred yards away. The individual is walking on the shoulder of the road. This strikes Trevor as odd; what is this person doing here at all, and why, in God's name, is he walking on the shoulder of the desolate road. There are no cars. Walking in the middle of the road, even deaf and unable to see, makes more sense for its flat surface, as opposed to the canted and dusty shoulder. To say death here by car seems implausible is an understatement. Being killed by rabid penguins would be more likely, if one consulted the actuarial tables relevant to these options. The more enigmatic question, though, is where did this person come from? Trevor knows the closest habitable place is a long way away and absolutely not one single car, truck, or UFO has passed by.

As the walker nears, Trevor sees it's a young man wearing a cowboy hat and possibly a backpack, or is a horribly disfigured hunchback, and is carrying what appears to be a guitar case. Trevor hopes the guy is mechanically inclined.

"Is that a six or twelve string?" Trevor asks as the young man nears the Jeep.

"It's a Takamine twelve. I'm Samuel Houston, Sammy." A thickly drawled answer as he finishes his approach to the still-sitting Trevor. There's a slightly uncomfortable pause and then, "Do y' all play?" asked over a hand thrust out, thin wrist exposed from the sleeve of a fully buttoned dress shirt. The buttoned-up shirt is a contradiction to both the temperature and the down-the-middle-of-the-back length hair.

Looking up at the thin-faced newcomer, Trevor takes the outstretched hand and shakes it briefly. "I don't play. Trevor Tavish and nice to meet you. I do know that Takamine makes a sweet acoustic. Where did you come from?"

The newcomer looks away. "I hitched out of California yesterday and spent the night in the desert. I came out here to look at some of the southeastern Oregon wildlife and hunt down some historical sites. I was camped out on that little knoll back there near the substation, about a half mile back. My next stop is an old homestead I want to check out."

There's a peculiar southern upturn at the end of his sentences that give these statements a questioning quality.

"Are you a mechanic, Sammy?" That would be amazing if it were true.

"No, but my daddy taught me a little bit about cars. I could look at it if you like?" The Texas drawl is very thick.

"Oh Jesus, please do." Trevor rises to his feet. "I can't pay for a repair, but if you feel like exercising a philanthropist streak, by all means, look."

"Okay." Sammy puts down his guitar and starts to shed the large backpack onto the ground.

"Throw that stuff in the Jeep. If we get this thing running, I'll definitely give you a ride as far as I can."

"That would be great." Sammy unzips the crusty canvas door to do so. He walks to the front of the vehicle and carefully and methodically unbuttons and rolls up his sleeves. Leaning under the hood, Sammy fiddles with some of the parts inside. "Gasoline is getting to the carb anyway. Would you mind turning the motor over for me, Trevor?"

Trevor returns to the driver's side and flops open the soft door of the removable top. He settles himself again into the driver's seat and turns the key to the start position. Billie Currington's singing can be heard briefly, but is immediately overcome by static as the motor turns over. Trevor snaps off the radio and then turns the motor over again. It does not start.

"Would you mind turning the radio on, but not starting the motor?"

Perplexed, Trevor does this.

"Okay, now turn up the radio a bit and try to start the motor again."

Trevor does as Sammy asks. He's unsure why he is so willing to comply with this stranger's unusual request. Maybe because there doesn't seem to be any potential harm, but mostly, because the young man seems both unassuming and competent at the same time. Trevor thinks these are usually exclusive attributes.

"Okay, hang on for a second with the key off."

Trevor complies again and can feel the Jeep moving slightly as Sammy leans over and does something else with the motor. They go through another start attempt and then Sammy pokes his head around the upturned hood of the Jeep.

"Do you have some sandpaper or a nail file, maybe clippers with one of those little files on them?"

Must require an emergency manicure, Trevor thinks as he turns to riffle through his gear. He finds a small clipper set with a file on it and maneuvers back out of the Jeep to hand the clippers to Sammy. "Hang nail?"

Sammy smiles at him and says enigmatically, "Points."

Trevor has an idea that 'points' are some part of the car, but can't help picturing the young man filing his nails to sharp talons. He steps out and watches as Sammy takes something off the motor and then leans in and files for a bit.

Sammy puts the parts back on. "Try it now."

Trevor climbs back into the Jeep and to his amazement the vehicle starts.

"How the fuck did you do that?"

Sammy lowers the hood over the sweetly running motor. "It was you having the radio on. After I heard the interference when you were turning it over, I had a good idea what it might be. Since I'd already ruled out fuel as the problem, it had to be something like the points. Thank God you had that nail file to resurface them."

Trevor somehow feels like a hero. Sammy seems to have implied that having the radio on and owning a pair of nail clippers are inherently brilliant things to do.

Sliding into the passenger's side, Sammy joins Trevor in the hot car. As he pulls away from the shoulder of the road, Trevor really looks at Sammy for the first time. The cowboy hat is now in the back with the gear and Trevor can't help but notice the angular nature of the young man's thin face. He watches as Sammy adroitly latches the door, something that is an unusual feat for an uninitiated passenger of a 1968 CJ5 soft top. Made decades before the word "ergonomics" was ever thought of, most passengers have to be shown where to pull and which way to twist the archaic latching mechanism before mastering that art. As they speed up, the loose canvas top begins to flap in the breeze.

Trevor is impressed by his passenger. "Your diagnosis by radio and repair by nail clippers was pretty amazing."

"Well," in his slow drawl, "it is a little self-serving."

"Yeah, still impressed. Where are you heading anyway?"

"A place called Nye, Montana. Where are you going?"

"I'm also going to Montana, but mostly, I'm going away from Grants Pass, Oregon, and a pissed-off girlfriend."

A smiling Sammy asks if they're expecting unfriendly fire.

Unfriendly fire; Trevor's imagination conjures up recent ex-girlfriend Shawna. An image of her standing in the middle of the road comes too easy. His mind adds a large caliber revolver along with a gun belt hanging low on her hips. He can picture her standing, wearing her usual uniform, those sweet, ass-crack loving shorts and a mostly un-button-up shirt and shooting vehemently in Trevor's direction.

"No. We're okay. She's about two hundred miles behind me, and…" pretending there's no guilt, "on foot." Until she gets a car to replace her Jeep. "Nye, Montana? Is that a big, ah, acoustic guitar place?" Trevor tries to envision what might be interesting in a placed called Nye. "Lots of bar

5

gigs there?"

A crooked smile softens Sammy's face. "One of the world's biggest palladium mines is there."

"Oh, okay." Trevor stops himself short of caustic. Isn't Palladium some gunslinger guy? "You're a miner?" Sammy's long hair and very thin build leave Trevor pretty sure that Sammy is not a miner.

"Well, I'm fixing to see if I can help with the palladium refining process."

Trevor looks Sammy full on, hands on the wheel, but attention not on the road. He again assesses the hitchhiker: clear blue eyes, no tinfoil cap. "So," speaking a little slow, "you're going to Nye and help the Nyeans do a better job with their palladium?"

Sammy nods in affirmation and then nods directionally, forward, toward the road. His demeanor suggests that this is a normal conversation.

"Palladium sounds like," Trevor barely brings the Jeep back onto the pavement and away from the shoulder, "a venereal disease. And you're going to tell them how to do what they do, only better?" He shrugs. "No offense, but do you really have something to offer the palladium producing world?"

Shy smile in place below a fuzzy near-mustache, Sammy says, "I just finished with a stretch of schooling and palladium was the subject of some of my research. I wrote a thesis on palladium mining and recovery."

Trevor is skeptical. "What kind of schooling, college?"

"I went to an engineering school for a few years: Massachusetts Institute of Technology. I did some research and teaching. Palladium is an element that's used for jewelry and for some catalytic processes."

"So, engineering, jewelry, and teaching? You look pretty young to be a teacher, and at a college, even if it is jewelry. They paid you to be there?"

Nodding, "I like research, it's relaxing and fun. What I'm fixing to do is use palladium to validate some other theories I have. I want to see if those ideas work in the field before I go any farther with the rest of my thesis. Part of my hypothesis depends on easy access to palladium."

Trevor likes research, too, and thinks back to a recent investigation, conducted inside a pair of panties, light blue and sporting, for some incomprehensible reason, stegosaurus images. "So, you're a research scientist and professor?" Trevor tries to not measure his own shortcomings against this kind of success but can't quite shut out that familiar voice.

They keep driving, top flapping, across the arid landscape of eastern Oregon. Trevor watches the desert go by, admires the dry countryside and tries to sort out Sammy's story, fill the gaps. "Massachusetts is east and Montana is less east and you are west, going east...?"

"I spent the early part of the year hiking through the redwoods. Have you ever seen them?"

"My uncle took me down through the redwoods once. They're huge. So, you headed out west from MIT, camped in the trees, and are now heading to work in Nye?"

Sammy considers this version and nods in agreement. "Yes, camped in the forest for a few months. I got chased out more than once by some rangers. Mostly I walked around with my mouth hanging open. I was there last month when that big storm came through. Those trees were amazing. I kept remembering that Disney cartoon where Mickey gets all the mops dancing together by casting a spell on accident." He giggles. "It was kind of wild and exhilarating, but crazy cool. I could have never left."

"Then it's time to move on to palladium experiments?"

Sammy nods again in agreement. "So how about you? Besides angry girlfriends, what are you running from?"

Trevor winces at the wording, unintentionally truthful in its ugly accuracy. He thinks about the lies trailing behind the Jeep like oil dripping from a leaky motor and even considers giving a more honest answer, but the opportunity slides on by. "A place up in Montana is giving me a job. They do agricultural spraying and I am in as chief ground grunt."

"Chief of the grunts?"

"Of one. I'm the crew, too."

"Crop dusting for the summer?"

"For me it's hopper filling, chemical truck driving, Av gas pimping, probably coffee getting, and all around powerful and respected gofer work.

Crop dusting for some cocky somebody I haven't yet had the opportunity to hate."

"How'd you get a line on that?"

"Years of being a ramp rat and pilot connections."

Sammy giggles a little. "What's a ramp rat?"

"An airport hanger-onner, one of those obnoxious kids with an airplane boner who washes airplanes for free so that they won't make him go home." He glances at Sammy. "Home wasn't really safe and the Grants Pass airport was only about a half mile away. Airplanes fascinated me so that's where I spent most summer days and weekends as a kid and then off and on ever since. I met some people and a few weeks ago made a phone call. Now, Montana bound."

With both hands on the wheel of the wandering car, Trevor revectors the vehicle once again as he tries to connect the dots. Struggling for common ground, he says, "I had a couple of buddies when I was a kid. One was slow enough to be considered retarded, a sweet and extraordinarily dumb kid. We called him Bibs because he always wore bib overalls. The other one was pretty much the brightest person I've ever met until he OD'd at 15. They both got beat up on a fairly regular basis. Truth is, the three of us got pounded on regularly, me by virtue of my acidic personality, but mostly just proximity. I never could sort out why people hated them. When we weren't busy getting beat up, or trying to talk our way out of it, or running, we had a great time together. Our conversations were always a little weird. I sure as hell never knew what was coming next. Bibs was really slow, probably diagnosable as mentally disabled. The thing was, buried in that messed-up wiring was a crazy sense of humor that was beautiful and amazing. I probably spent half my youth with snot spraying from my nose and sore abs from laughing. He almost made it fun to get beat up for all of the smartass shit he came up with about the bad guys."

"It's amazing how much people fear difference and things they can't sort out. I get that. Are you still friends with the overalls guy?"

"Bibs? Also dead. Walking to his job as a dishwasher and got taken out by a drunken guy in an old Camaro. Bibs knew how different he was. I always wondered about that. What it was like to live in a brain that is so much of an outlier. I never got that it was fun. He always seemed lonely."

Sammy looks out the window. Trevor argues with the worn steering. Miles tick off as the fascinatingly uninteresting landscape of eastern Oregon moves slowly west, attached to the planet and forcefully rolled away from under them by the Jeep. A few miles before the town of Juntura they see a coyote loping across the dry ground near the highway. The animal stops and turns to them, watching their passage.

"He's pissed off that he doesn't have opposable thumbs and a way to jack the car."

"Wouldn't matter, he's got no driver's license anyway."

"Do you know what it's called, the scientific name for it?" More curious about Sammy's ability to answer than the actual answer.

"Canis Latrans."

Trevor suppresses the familiar wave of insecurity as the desert rolls by them with no judgment of its own.

Passing through town, three houses, a small gas station and apparently for rush hour, one traffic light, they see all the buildings are dark. The traffic light is not lit. A hand-written sign on the gas pumps read: "No gas, power out."

"The economy got them and they couldn't pay the bill?"

"Something like that." Sammy's face is turned away from Trevor, looking out the opposite window.

About forty-five minutes later, Sammy tells Trevor that the abandoned homestead he's looking for is another four miles down the road and he'd like to wander around it a little bit.

"So you want me to drop you there?"

A few minutes pass before Sammy answers, "You could look around with me. It's in the book Ghost Towns of Oregon."

Trevor gauges the possibility that his thin passenger has concealed weapons, thinks the fully buttoned and tucked-in shirt make this is unlikely. Besides, the guy doesn't throw that vibe… mostly. "Sure, I'd like to. What's your interest, though?"

Back at watching the desert on his side of the car, Sammy shakes his head and shrugs. "Nothing really, I read about it in some old land records. At one time the original settlers who built the place thought they might claim the whole area. After a while I guess they figured out that even all of the east side didn't have much value and that was the last they were heard from."

"You read about that in land records?"

"I started with the land records, killing time some evenings at school. I found a lot of info on the archived pages of the Eastern Oregon Gazette, too."

"Excellent bathroom reading. Why this place?"

"It sounded cool, but mostly because it is relatively undisturbed for a historical site. Apparently, it's not much and it's also so far from civilization that it's not yet filled up with condoms and beer bottles."

"Always a plus."

After a few more minutes, Sammy points ahead and to the right.

~

Trevor is surprised there's no trail from the main road. There is a weathered farm house about a half mile off, back near a bluff. He looks his company over again while they walk, calculating his odds. He guesses Sammy at one-fifty. He's a pretty buff two-sixty, husky but well-built.

Fortunately, they both have boots, making the scattered sage brush more passable and they cover the ground in a leisurely half hour. The house is in surprisingly good shape. There are missing shingles and no windows, but with a few days and some materials it could probably be made livable. It seems like an odd waste.

"When did they build this place?"

They are standing directly in front of the old building. "Thomas and Becka Worthington came here in eighteen forty-three and started building and farming. They had seven kids right here."

Trevor thinks it looks like very tight quarters for nine people.

"Only three of the kids lived past birth."

Trevor looks at the arid ground. "Did they starve to death? Not too many

Safeways back then."

"They might have. I never found that in the archives."

"We aren't going to find bones sitting at a table in there, are we?" They make their way inside the dusty building.

Trevor watches Sammy look around at the small room.

Without turning to him, Sammy says, "I can't get enough of the last century. I ran some calculations once, came up with an algorithm that nailed eighteen seventy-two as the optimal point from which the world could have been changed."

The world did change, and a lot. "Not sure what you mean, bro?"

"It was the perfect intersection of world awareness, population density, and technology that would have allowed educating our race about the need to limit population and carbon output. There were trains, telegraph, and lots of printing presses. The American Civil War was over and the world population was still small enough that the right group could have gotten that information out, if they had it."

Trevor follows as Sammy slowly explores the interior of the homestead. The path seems less than random.

"Are you saying the world is lost now?"

Sammy's pony tail bounces as he shakes his head in front of Trevor. "Nope, I don't think it's lost yet. It would have been cleaner back then and a lot of natural resources and species could have been saved."

"If somebody could have informed the population?"

"Yeah, maybe, that's what my calculations showed. Besides that, it would have been an incredibly cool time to live."

Walking out the back of the building, Sammy still seems to have a destination.

Looking in a small window set in the end of the building, Sammy steps back, smiling. "Check it out," he inclines his head toward the window.

Trevor looks at the ground around that end of the building. There are no footprints in the loose dust. No other shoed feet have walked here in a while, maybe even a really long while and they are definitely leaving footprints now. He scoots around the weirdly amused Sammy and looks in through the window.

He can see into a very small room, probably a pantry or something. Everything in it is extremely dusty. There are a few broken jars and something that looks like it might have been a pie tin a thousand years ago. No bleached skulls though, thankfully. "I don't see anything amazing in there. Are the voices telling you to do anything?"

Sammy hasn't stopped smiling. It's a little unsettling.

"I think I saw something off to the right, almost around the corner on the shelf that's about shoulder height."

Trevor looks back at the smiling Sammy. The young man is standing, on the balls of his feet and is about eight feet back. A reasonably safe distance. Trevor looks again at the shelf Sammy has described. Something gleams back there. He glances back again at the unmoving hitchhiker. Sammy nods, a clear 'Go on.'

Trevor reaches in and grabs the shiny object. His fist closes on something round, thin, and fairly flat. He withdraws it and opens his hand in the sunlight. There is a dusty gold pocket watch in his palm. He looks at the ground, unmarked except for their footprints, back up at Sammy. "How did you know that was in there?"

Sammy's smile slips, he looks away. "I just saw it, that's all."

Trevor holds the watch out to Sammy.

Sammy's smile rebounds and he shakes his head. "It's yours, you found it."

What is that about? "Okay," Trevor nods, still watching, closer now. "Where do we look now?"

Sammy shrugs, "You want to get rolling?"

"That's it? We are done with our forensics?"

Sammy shrugs. "I just wanted to see what it looked like." The smile is still tilting his mouth slightly.

They poke around for another few minutes and then walk back toward the road and the Jeep.

~

As they near the more populated area closer to Boise, a sheriff's car is parked alongside the road, on the opposite lane. Trevor is, as he usually is, doing the speed limit. He notices Sammy watching the officer's car as they pass it.

A bright blue sign proudly welcoming them to Idaho flashes past. Trevor glances at Sammy's pack in the back of the Jeep. "I was thinking about going up Idaho-52 past Emmett and then do a loop through Garden Valley and Stanley. It's a whole lot slower than I-84 but it's pretty country. I can either drop you at the Interstate and you can catch somebody going a more direct route to Nye, or you can come with me through the backcountry. I'm planning on camping along the way and might take a few hikes to look around."

"Well, if you really don't mind, I'll stay with you, if it's all the same."

Trevor steers the Jeep into a gas station, shuts the motor down, and hops out to pump gas. Sammy steps out on his own side and reaches for the sponge and squeegee and begins cleaning the windshield. "Alright if I check the oil?" He pronounces it 'Ol'.

"Great, probably ought to," Trevor agrees, he's liking the Texan. Sammy's company is distracting him too, if ever so briefly, from the nagging emptiness that seems to be his life.

Like always in the flat lands of Idaho, a breeze is blowing. The wind is strong enough that when an older guy on the other gas island takes money out of his pocket, two bills skitter across the parking lot. Trevor watches, realizes the man didn't notice and waits. He simultaneously tracks the trajectory of the money and monitors the progress and attention of the guy. He realizes the man has a handful of cash so big that its size is as much the cause of the lost bills as the wind. Another second ticks by, Trevor hangs up the fuel nozzle, then he trots down wind, snags the bills, turns and walks into the store.

Trevor's pace slows as he walks by the old guy but he continues on past to the cashier. He pays for the gas with the twenties, turns and nods to the elderly gentleman and then he's out the door.

Driving through the flat land going east from I-84, They stop in Emmett at a pizza joint. They discuss the warm summer air and Sammy explains a little bit about theories on the jet stream and its effect on North American

13

weather. Trevor explains his theory on why the waitress most likely has large areolas but small nipples, citing anecdotal evidence from which he has concluded that all brown-haired girls with blue eyes are so equipped. Sammy quietly observes that, of the dozen or so customers in the restaurant, there are abnormal similarities between them and that, considering the relative isolation of Emmett and the probable lack of higher education, they may all be more closely related than is strictly beneficial from a health standpoint. He further speculates that too many familial parings could potentially skew Trevor's excellent nipple-to-areola research, if conducted here. Sammy then adds that Trevor might consider applying for grant money to do PHD research into the nuances of this often-overlooked area of science, but would, of course, best be conducted somewhere with more genetic diversity and, said even more under his breath, better pizza.

Chapter 2

LEAVING EMMETT, they follow the wandering road along the Black Canyon reservoir. Late in the day they come to an outcropping that juts into the lake and on which the Bureau of Land Management has put a small campground. Trevor and Sammy pick one of the sites close to the water's edge and Trevor backs the Jeep into the spot.

Stepping out, they stretch and admire the scenery of the lake. The afternoon air has stilled early for an Idaho mountain day and the surface of the lake perfectly mirrors the ridge of ragged peaks on the far side. Trevor wonders how to navigate the issue of two more-or-less strangers and an overnight with a tent. He pulls his lightweight back packing tent out of his gear and rolls it out on the grassy area near the water's edge. Sammy removes a tent from his own pack.

Later, thinking that few things are better than sitting right here, beside this fire, beside a lake in the Idaho Mountains and drinking one of the three beers they have between them, Trevor considers this a good day.

Sammy gets up, drags his guitar out from the Jeep, and sits back by the fire. Looking out over the lake, his fingers wander over the strings.

Trevor watches the reflection of the mountains in the glassy lake as the sky turns slowly to night. Coyotes are calling in the distance. He sips his beer, squinting his eyes so the night blurs, but the firelight is still there, reflecting off the trees and water and teasing the shadows dancing around them, flickering across the hitchhiker's angular face.

Trevor picks out pieces of songs as Sammy plays, but can't define the transitions between them. After finishing his beer, Trevor gets up to rummage in the back of the Jeep and take an inventory of his supplies. He returns with a propane stove, a pan, and a single freeze-dried meal but waits before lighting the stove. "I'm happy to warm something up if you like?"

"Yeah, if you're going to boil some water, I'd be much obliged to share a bit." Sammy makes his own trek to the Jeep. A minute later he returns with a food packet, a spoon, and an insulated cup.

"Hey," Trevor says then, lying, "Don't open that, dude. I just realized this meal is for two. If you want to share this, I think we'll come out okay."

Sammy nods, "That'd be great. Thanks."

~

Waking to the deafening noise of his stubble rasping across the nylon sleeping bag, Trevor looks out on the tent tinted glow of morning light, and smells of bacon cooking. He suffers a furious but brief internal struggle between his lazy side and his hungry side and finally accepts the inevitable fact that no human being can continue sleeping in after smelling bacon being cooked. He unzips the tent.

"Hey, good morning. Are you hungry?" Sammy says as he flips pancakes in the pan. "I was about to wake you. Pancakes?"

"Pancakes? Pancakes sound wonderful, but it's your bacon I want. Feed me bacon and I will keep driving you east. Refuse my need and your body will be floating face down in this lake while the coyotes wait until you make landfall."

Sammy laughs. "So that's how it is."

"Sorry, man, I like you, but I am a confessed bacon whore and can no longer be held responsible for my actions."

~

After they load their gear, Trevor guides the Jeep back onto the winding road. Their conversation wanders, and after an hour or so coalesces onto Sammy's life.

"Alright, dude. You started college young?"

"Yes. I was ten when I graduated from high school."

Even though he had known roughly where this conversation had been likely to go, Trevor is shocked, ten, and in college.

"Was that totally weird for you?"

16

Sammy shrugs, "That's what normal is to me really. I've never known anything different so, no, not weird. It was okay. There were some mean people, but there always are. There are a lot of people who are desperate about their need to be The Smart One and once in a while they turn ugly when that need gets challenged. I've never understood that. It's not a zero-sum situation."

"I see what you are saying, your being smart doesn't detract from them being smart. What degrees do you have?"

Sammy doesn't answer for a while, long enough that Trevor assumes he might simply ignore the question but eventually, he does answer, "An MD, a PHD in physics, and a bachelor's degree in chemistry."

"You're a doctor, too?"

"Sort of. I never completed my residency. The reception to my age was embarrassing. I was a little afraid that it might be like that when I was going into it, but I had a scholarship and the time so what the heck."

Trevor wondered how many times in the history of modern medicine anybody became an actual physician because, 'what the heck, they just could.'

"What the heck," Trevor says quietly.

"What's your future looking like, Trevor? I mean after the job with the Ag place, what then?"

There is no trace of condescension. Trevor tries pushing away the gray doubt, the lurking voices with their eternal, shitty assessment of him. He considers Sammy's apparent straightforward nature, takes his own less self-pitying path. "Maybe a life of crime and some debauchery. For now, it looks like my main assets are a strong back and a small mind. Those will get me through the summer at least. Same to you, what comes after the fall of Nye?"

"I haven't exactly decided." Sammy drags the words out in his drawling cadence. He laughs a little too, like there's an inside joke. "The thing I would most like to do is find a new band and play. That's when I feel the best, jamming along with a bar full of folks kicking to our music, feels like God himself is there with us tapping his foot."

17

Trevor waits for clarification from Sammy, but nothing comes. The obvious contradiction probably doesn't need stating. There are not a lot of bar bands with a guitarist who has a PHD. He waits Sammy out for a while but eventually gives in to his own impatient nature. "Are you on a poster in a post office somewhere?"

"Not yet." Sammy shrugs. "No more schools, though."

"The ivy league crowd not your set?"

"Not really. I'm a small-town guy. The competition wasn't my thing."

"Publish or perish or just too many big heads?"

"Something like that, a lot of weird competition too. The one good friend I thought I had ended up being on the FBI payroll."

"That actually sounds kind of cool and I would imagine that even FBI employees still have friends?" Do lots of hitchhikers have friends in the FBI, maybe even most of them? Probably so. Shit.

"It went a little deeper than that. I didn't have a clue until agents showed up and started asking about my stuff. That was when I realized my buddy Paxton had to be the source."

"All right, PHD boy, no offense, but what amazing thing were you dabbling in that the FBI would want to know about anyway?"

Sammy shrugs again and sighs. "Time travel and cold fusion reactors."

Oh fuck, time travel and cold fusion reactors and friends in the FBI.

"I did my thesis work on cold fusion. That was the beginning of how I ended up heading for Nye. The time thing was completely theoretical until very recently. Nobody else actually knew anything about that side of my research, but Pax, my friend at MIT, had enough info to get the bureaucratic monster looking my way."

"Sorry, bro, that's rough." He is staring at the road. The comment is completely disconnected from his real thoughts.

Sammy goes on, "My initial research was with fusion reactions. There was already a theory that a fusion reaction could be created and sustained using palladium. Basically, palladium rods could be submerged, then charged electrons covering the palladium would combine with hydrogen atoms and kick out neutrons. Those neutrons would stick on the lithium molecules and make them emit radiation. The electrons would absorb the radiation and reemit it as heat in a low-energy nuclear reaction. I added to the existing theory with a way to enhance that reaction using focused high energy magnetism and came up with a new reactor design."

"You're thinking that would work, your reactors?" Trevor allows himself a glance at the guileless face beside him.

"I am certain it'll work. I've done it."

"You have made a reactor? And it worked?"

"It worked beautifully and made almost free energy. If my ideas on palladium extraction work out, the fuel will be cost effective too. The reactors would be simple, small, cheap, and completely nonpolluting. There isn't even any nuclear waste."

"Wow." Trevor is trying to wedge some acceptance into his resident doubt. The implausibility and scale of what Sammy has just told him is more than a little bewildering. No way.

"Thanks for listening, even if you don't believe me. I think playing guitar is the moral way anyway, the right thing to do."

Trevor's head snaps away from the road. "You just lost me, dude. How does that work. You can seriously give cheap or free energy to the world and you think it's the wrong thing to do? How do you not do that?"

Sammy looks away. "That's where the problem is, I don't believe the outcome would be good. I believe that unlimited energy means unlimited population and many new ways to cause damage to people and the planet. So, for all the time I've sat and thought about this, I don't see that it's an actual benefit for the world to have free energy. I just don't feel like the human race is responsible enough to deal with that."

"But you're still heading for Nye?"

Sammy's shoulders drop a little as he turns back to face Trevor. "I will let you know when I figure out why that is. I just wish I really knew what the right thing to do is but right now for Sammy, the right thing is to eat a granola bar."

"I like those morals. Maybe you could teach guitar if you're going for the low hanging fruit."

Sammy chews and thinks a second. "There are more chicks in the bar band scene."

"And it does skew the whole save-the-world debate when you throw the possibility of getting laid into the mix."

The two-lane paved road becomes one lane, with just enough room for a game of chicken when encountering oncoming traffic. They talk about childhoods. Sammy grew up in a strict, religious, traditional Texas home. His father was a God-fearing man who changed mufflers and shocks on cars during the day and cleaned the local elementary school at night. His mother was a kind-hearted, stay-at-home wife and mother of four boys, one of whom was Samuel, on the younger side of the middle. The whole brood had been birthed during a stretch of about thirty-nine months, a revelation that, after doing the math, brought a sideways glance from Trevor. Sammy went on to say that his family was warm, considerate, and kind to each other and that none of them had any idea what was wrong with Sammy. They especially did not know what to do with him.

It was mostly strategy on Sammy's part and a little bit of luck that had them "accidentally" run into the dean of the local college and then to some very early SAT testing. The following faculty interviews turned into a relieved sigh from his parents, a forty-dollar bus ticket to Austin, and a free ride through the University of Texas at an unprecedented young age.

Trevor's story was shorter and involved much less kindness, none really. He'd grown up an only child of a millworker and a truck stop waitress, both of whom seemed to share a deep fear that he might do better in his life than they had done in theirs. The one iota of harmony in the home seemed to come from their uncanny ability to undermine any, however minor, success Trevor was able to wring out of his troubled teen years. At about fifteen, Trevor got a job loading trucks at a local warehouse. Shortly after that, he moved into an apartment of his own. A fact which, despite his being an only child, his parents failed to notice for several weeks. From there it had been a string of crappy jobs, mostly in the timber industry, and a string of crappy relationships, often with the wives of other men working in the timber industry.

They stop at a turnoff alongside the road. The mountain scenery is breathtaking, a misty waterfall is a beautiful backdrop to the rest of the sub-alpine countryside. Getting out of the Jeep, they separate, wandering in different directions. Trevor is thinking whizzing in some artistically perfect spot is one of life's greater pleasures when he notices, through a gap in the foliage, that Sammy is standing very near the edge of the tall waterfall. He's close enough to the precipice that Trevor wonders how far down he would have to go to retrieve Sammy's body, or if he would bother. Sammy takes something from a pocket.

Trevor remains still and unzipped as he waits out the scene and is surprised when Sammy hauls back an arm and heaves an outfield-to-home-base throw, propelling the object in a high arc over the spray of the water and out into the swirling vapor below. Trevor sees the thing glinting in the sunlight as it tumbles through its parabola. It looks like it's metal, maybe hour-glass shaped, but Trevor can't be certain as it cartwheels down and into the obscuring veil of the waterfall. As Trevor continues watching, Sammy climbs down from the rocky outcrop and walks out of sight behind some rocks and trees. Trevor takes advantage of the moment to return himself to normal without getting caught in the zipper, then heads back to the jeep.

Later in the day they find another roadside campground. This one is also small, four sites. Their second evening goes mostly as the first with Sammy playing his guitar and Trevor watching the stars passing slowly overhead.

"You ever think about what the distance is that the arc of our view takes as we watch out there?" Sammy says, looking over at Trevor between songs. "Do you wonder how many million miles would the radius of our field of vision travel through the galaxy during one night? We think of it as finite and it's really not; that darkness goes on out there forever and what we are seeing in our field of view as we spin around, happened billions of years ago and very far away."

"Hmm." Trevor thinks about that for a moment before confessing silently to himself that, no, he has never pondered that particular question. "I think mostly about where to find new chicks that will put out."

~

The next morning Trevor wakes before Sammy. The sky is light, but they are still on the west side of the mountain range and there is no direct sun on them yet. He hears Sammy stirring in his tent. "Dude, there's a restaurant down the road, in Garden Valley. I'll buy you breakfast if you get your lazy ass out of bed!"

"Do you owe me bacon?"

They get camp broke and their gear stowed quickly and then are kicking up dust down the gravel road. The restaurant at Garden Valley is a small log cabin. A sign above the door tells them that the cabin has been in this exact spot for nearly a hundred and twelve years and had originally served trappers from the high Idaho valleys.

They settle into one of the six booths, directly under a large buffalo head mounted on the wall. Other examples of taxidermy are scattered around the inside of the building. A cougar guards the cash register from a shelf.

"That's Ben," the waitress says as she walks up to the table. "He was the last wild buffalo in the state of Idaho. They took him in about fifty-two."

Trevor can't resist, "He introduced himself before they took him?"

The waitress laughs lightly. "No idea where the name came from. It's funny, I've been here for a long time and never thought to ask."

Sammy asks if Trevor is a hunter.

"No, but not for any real reason except maybe to avoid further violence in my life."

"We humans are pretty hypocritical, aren't we?"

"What do you mean?"

"Just that we are our own deepest fear. There are a lot of scary stories about the boogey man, the creature that wants to take us. He might eat us, but our true fear is that he wants to harm us for the sake of harming us. Don't get me wrong, I'm a carnivore, and from Texas where only sissy faggots are not hunters. But it does make it a little harder to have faith in us humans."

Chapter 3

WAKING UP EARLY after another night spent camping, they load their gear. It's a little before nine when the gravel road takes them into the town of Stanley. Turning right onto Eva Falls avenue, Trevor remarks about the ambiguous phrasing, "Wonder if Eva's inspiration was regarding gravity and water or just gravity and Eva?"

Sammy gives that comment an eye roll, then points, "What do you think about the lodge there for a night? I haven't had anything more than a scrub in a stream for too many days now. A shower has some amazing appeal. I can spring for a room if you don't mind sharing."

Trevor pulls into the gravel parking lot of the log building. A sign says, "The House, Restaurant." They pull up and park under another sign proclaiming, "Good food, lousy service."

Stepping out over dried horse turds, they walk around a weathered hitching post and into the combined motel lobby and dining room where they are greeted by a middle-aged woman with a handsome, weatherworn face. She stands behind a large rustic desk, mostly looking down at a computer screen. She glances up briefly, gives them a distracted, "Howdy," and points to a table. "I'll be right with you if you want to go and sit down, darn computers."

They sit at one of the tables in the direction she'd indicated. Surprising them, after the horseshit in the parking lot, the building is beautifully furnished and elegantly built. It is finished with grainy marble floors, clear fir trim, and abundant windows and skylights. The tables all look to be antique, mostly polished and gleaming oak. A few overstuffed and tapestry upholstered chairs are scattered around at the dining tables and by the large fireplace.

The woman approaches their table saying, "Dear God, I hate computers.

Coffee?"

Both men nod and as she hands them menus, Sammy says, "I have some training with coding."

She looks at him oddly, like she he had just told her he was Elvis.

"Computer coding, programming. I could take a look at your PC if you like?"

Trevor thinks this would be too forward an offer from most people and that he could never pull that off without somebody being uncomfortable. She simply nods toward Sammy and says that any help would be great. Sammy follows the woman to the desk then sits as she points at the screen and talks. Sammy asks a few questions, smiles up at her and then bends to the computer. As the woman watches, Sammy massages the keyboard for a few minutes and then rests his hands on the desk. There is a little more conversation, then Sammy stands up to a hand shake that becomes a hug from the woman. Smiling, Sammy returns to the table.

Sammy nods his head in the direction of the departing woman, "Claire."

"What did you do to save the day?"

"Restarted her computer." Sammy smiles wider and shrugs.

"Seriously. Without benefit of either FM radio or nail clippers?"

"She had some malware that was trying to bust through her firewall and her anti-virus stuff was working, but not very well. It wasn't a hard fix, though. It's funny, people will hand you their computers and trust you to fix them and then they will mostly let you charge them whatever you feel you are due. Fortunately, most geeks are honest, at least with people's money. Hacking challenges use a different set of situationally appropriate morals, though."

Trevor nods and is about to ask if Sammy has been on that side of hacking when he notices a red-haired girl has entered the dining room. Carrying coffee cups and glasses of water, wearing tight-fitting blue jeans and a tee shirt that says, "Geology rocks," she breezes up to the table. Her smile is stunning.

"Hi guys. Welcome to The House."

Trevor is somewhat blindsided by her, but in well-practiced form, hides it. He is used to catching the attention of women and gives her a smile.

Sammy reaches out his hand to shake with her. "I'm Sammy."

Have I ever shaken a waitress's hand? That lack seems somehow significant.

"I'm Amy. My mom says breakfast is on us as you two traveling wizards saved the day."

Trevor points at Sammy, "Wizard. I'm the non-wizard, Trevor," Debating an offer to shake, he notices the freckled Amy has golden colored eyes, they are show stoppers. She's stunning and laughing at something Sammy has said. She glances Trevor's way. He wants to bask in those eyes, to have them looking at him. Never mind the skinny Texas kid.

"Well, Mom sure is happy. Apparently, all the accounts receivables and tax records are on that machine."

"We talked a little about backing up files and virus-protection updates."

"Mom is a technotard. Cool mom but not hip with the changing world. I'll see if your lunch is ready." She turns to go.

There are no other customers in the restaurant. "You want to eat with us?" Sammy's smile is putting out some wattage.

Trevor is surprised by this forwardness on Sammy's part. He had assumed that Sammy was shy, at least around girls.

"Sure. I'd love to. Be right back." She heads out the door she had come in through.

Still mildly surprised, Trevor looks at the less handsome young man across the table from him. They have spent several enjoyable days together. It's unusual for him to be comfortable with another person for that long, especially another guy, and particularly one who claims that the FBI is interested in him. Past that one little bit, though, Sammy is definitely a cool and amazingly bright person, but much like himself, he doesn't think Sammy feels like he belongs much or often.

Amy returns to the table and sets down three plates. She sits exactly between them with an empty chair on either side of her. They chat about the remoteness of Stanley and each other. She was born and raised in

Stanley but has been away the last three years studying geology at the University of Washington.

Trevor watches as Sammy and Amy talk. He's mildly surprised that Amy seems interested in Sammy too. That Sammy is an amazing person, he gets, but this conclusion on his part is after days of getting to know the skinny southern genius. Being attractive is the one thing Trevor feels actual confidence in and he has rarely lacked for opposite sex attention. He has struggled to maintain depth or to hold women's interest, but rarely has to work to spark a blip on their radar screens, at least initially.

With no prior discussion, the two help Amy clear the table, follow her into the kitchen, and begin washing dishes as they continue chatting. Trevor fills the sink with sudsy water in which he scrubs while Sammy rinses and dries.

Claire leans in through the doorway, watching for a moment. "Amy, we have another table and do you boys want to work for the day?"

Amy dries her hands and heads to the dining area.

"If you can you tell me how the meals are supposed to be made, I can cook." Sammy dries his hands and turns toward the stoves.

"I bet I can figure out the dishes."

Amy's mother smiles, "I'll take it!" and turns back out through the doorway.

After the table of six hunters has been fed and the dishes have been cleaned and put away, Sammy and Trevor are back at the sink. Amy's mother is again at the doorway. "I really can't pay much in wages, but if you two want a free room and food in trade for some cooking, Alan and I could get a few things done. If not, your help has sure been appreciated."

Trevor looks at Sammy and shrugs. "Up to you, bro. I don't have to be anywhere for a few more weeks."

Sammy turns to Claire, "We would be much obliged to you, ma'am. That'd be really nice."

"Well, hope you enjoy our little town. We'll fix you boys up with a room."

Later in the day, Amy breezes, "Hey guys, how about hot dogs and beer later, after we close?"

~

They turn the restaurants lights off at nine p.m. Traffic is rare by that time on the remote mountain road. Trevor and Sammy toss their gear into the shared room before meeting Amy at the rear of the main building.

"Beer, buns, and dogs are sitting right there," Amy tells them as they enter the propped open back door. "There's ketchup packets and stuff on that rack."

Sammy, wearing his guitar strapped to his back, grabs the basket and the six-pack.

Trevor scoops out a handful of condiment packets. "I've got the heavy lifting." He pushes the packets into the pocket of his hoody.

The three head out the door with Amy leading the way through the near dark, winding down a trail toward the river. "There's a fire pit on the gravel bar and there's already wood so we should be good to go. The locals call it Central Park."

"Hey, about that," Sammy asks Amy. "Is Stanley an actual incorporated town? Like mayor and property tax?"

"Not exactly, no. We don't have a mayor or taxes or any of that, but we do have a chief of police." This is delivered with some odd undertone that Trevor thinks he catches but can't quite identify.

"A police chief?"

"Yeah." Amy's voice clouds with some emotion. "We elected her last year for her seventh birthday. It was kind of a make-a-wish thing. She has leukemia. We had a little fundraiser and got her a real uniform; she looks great in it, beams like crazy when we call her Chief. Her folks bring her in to The House pretty often. She has leukemia."

"Acute lymphoblastic?" Sammy asks her. They step out onto the small pebbly surface of the gravel bar.

"I think so. They call it A L L." She pronounces each letter. "That's kind of a weird thing to know."

Trevor looks at Amy. "He's an MD."

Amy looks at Sammy who shrugs. She looks back to Trevor who nods slightly and also shrugs. Past the doubts, Trevor feels oddly proud of Sammy.

"I never finished my internship though."

With the fire throwing off enough heat for them to be comfortable in the cooling evening, Sammy is seated on a log. Trevor, across the fire from him, is in his normal sprawl, butt on the gravel and back against a log. Amy is also on the gravel and leaning against a log. She has taken a spot between them and chats with Sammy as he tunes the Takamine.

Trevor is attracted to Amy, more importantly, he wants to know she is attracted to him. As they took their places at the gravel bar, Sammy first, Trevor next and Amy last, he was initially relieved that she hadn't favored either of them.

Sammy plays the Tak, rolling through some sixties folk songs. Except for the river and Sammy's music, the night is quiet. Amy kicks back and smiles. Trevor watches the stars and hopes a cue is out there somewhere, regardless of how infinite the distance of the arc is, that will help him navigate the complexities of life.

Amy asks if Sammy has a favorite song.

Sammy is silent for a second, smiles shyly, and starts out, looking into the distance as he plays. Trevor recognizes, "Go for a Soda" by Kim Mitchell. Amazing Trevor and Amy, Sammy stands up and starts singing.

"Might as well go for a soda,

Nobody hurts and nobody dies,

Might as well go for a soda,

Nobody drowns and nobody dies…"

By the time Sammy bangs out a final chord and then kicks out a full-blown rock and roll split to the sandbar, he's sweating. Both Trevor and Amy laugh like crazy. Amy claps. It's not every day you see a brilliant scientist jamming to old rock and roll on an Idaho sandbar; he can now check that one off his bucket list.

Amy and Trevor give Sammy a hard time about the wild performance as they discuss finer points of his choreography.

"What's a nineteen seventy-four song by the Pure Prairie League, Alex?" Trevor knows this is an obscure reference, but would be fun if Sammy caught it. He is rewarded as Sammy tilts his head slightly for a moment and then breaks into a huge smile.

Sammy's fingers begin to pluck out the old country hit and sings,

"I can see why you think you belong to me.

I never tried to make you think, or let you see one thing for yourself.

But now you're off with someone else and I'm alone.

You see I thought that I might keep you for my own.

Amy, what you wanna do?

I think I could stay with you,

For a while maybe longer if I do."

Amy claps again and then holds folded hands to her chest as Sammy sings. Sammy's voice is clear and true and Amy rocks herself gently. Trevor wishes he hadn't suggested that song after all.

"Hey guys!" Amy's tone smashes the mood. There is alarm in her voice. "What is that?" Pointing toward town.

Sammy and Trevor snap their heads in the direction Amy pointed and see a flickering glow reflected on the roofs of some of the houses. Amy hops to her feet and heads off at a fast trot toward the light. Trevor and Sammy jump up and flank her, Sammy is holding the Takamine one-handed as he runs. Trevor is trying to guzzle his Corona without breaking out his teeth as he keeps up with them.

Sammy veers off and sets the guitar gently on the boardwalk as they trot past the restaurant, then sprints to catch up with Amy and Trevor. They can clearly see that there is a building on fire several hundred feet away.

"Fuck," Sammy says as they break around the corner and come onto the large cleared lot of the burning home. The roof of the two-story structure is burning through in at least one place and a bright glow can be seen in the windows of most of the upstairs rooms.

Trevor doesn't remember hearing Sammy swear before and thinks that "fuck," with a drawl, has a lot of U's in it.

29

"Mack's place," Amy yells as she heads for the front door. She grabs the doorknob, finds it locked, and begins banging on it, shouting, "Mack!"

Sammy says, "There are bars on the windows!"

Amy continues banging on the door and shouting. Trevor picks up a rock and is about to break the window, but Sammy grabs his arm.

"If we can't get in through the bars and we don't wake them up, it could provide more oxygen for the fire. We have to get in there!"

"Gotcha." Trevor looks around, there is a backhoe parked next to the shop behind the burning house. "Door key." He runs toward the machine. Amy continues to pound and yell.

At the backhoe, Trevor swings into the cab, and thanks God and the mindset of small towns when he finds that, despite having bars on the nearby windows, the keys are in the tractor's ignition. The diesel kicks over and spews a brief cloud of black sooty exhaust into the night and then runs smoothly. He jams the gear selector into reverse and smashes the throttle as the tractor lurches back away from the shop building.

Seeing what Trevor is doing, Sammy grabs Amy, pulling her aside. As they jump off the front porch, Trevor maneuvers the tractor and stops with the back end a few feet from the front steps of the dwelling. He jumps from the front seat into the rear operator's seat, grabs hold of the levers and the backhoe arm reaches out, skims the floor of the front porch, and smashes out the door of the burning house.

Trevor jumps out of the back of the machine, meeting Sammy and Amy as they race in through the ragged opening and into the burning building.

Amy screams "MACK!" as they all start frantically scanning the smoky room, then split up to check the rest of the first floor.

Sammy disappears behind them through a doorway and shouts, "Nothing in this room!"

Amy grabs Trevor's hand and pulls him toward the back of the house, yelling, "Let's look back this way, quick!" Visibility is almost gone and they are coughing.

Running with Amy, Trevor is about to yell for Sammy when Sammy inexplicably charges out of the smoke from the direction they're headed and screams at them, "Do NOT go that way! Go back! It's too hot!" He pushes Trevor hard toward the front of the house and then disappears, yelling. "GO, right now!"

Amy is staring toward Sammy as Trevor virtually picks her up, half carrying her toward the front of the house. He is turning to find Sammy when a hand wraps around his arm, he is incredibly relieved to make out Sammy's face through the smoke. Amy looks sharply at him, then they all turn as one and run to the next doorway.

Stumbling through the door, there is the sound of deep snoring coming from inside the smoky room. Trevor pulls Amy with him and Sammy begins shaking the man. The situation is critical, the house is extremely smoky, they can hear the crackling roar of flames from very close by. They are down to seconds. Amy screams and slaps the snoring man.

"Amy, we have got to get out of here!" Trevor yells. "I'll grab his arms; you guys try to get his feet!"

As they wrestle to lift the large man, Trevor looks around the room at the bizarre collection of guns and knives scattered everywhere. The walls are virtually a hanging arsenal and weapons lean against the furniture and on top of all horizontal surfaces. He realizes the figure is wearing full length, military style clothing. "Go figure," he mutters to himself as he grunts to lift the large Mack.

Trevor has the man under both arms, Amy and Sammy grapple with his limp feet. Coughing, the three of them carry-drag him out of the weird bedroom. The fire is raging as they struggle to breathe in the thickening smoke. The smoke and heat are getting unbearable but they manage to get Mack around the corner.

The fire is closing in, closing in fast. There's a sudden deafening roar and it sounds like the second story just came down on the first floor in the back of the house, where they had been going before Sammy chased them out. A wave of embers and black smoke explodes into the main room as they scramble frantically out under the backhoe arm sticking through where the front door had been. Coughing and profusely sweating, Trevor follows with the bulk of Mack as Amy and Sammy carry his feet, and they skid down the bare wooden steps of the porch. Trevor ends up on his ass, cradling Mack's head while getting his own back side beaten as he slips down the last few stairs.

At the bottom of the crash-landing, Amy and Sammy struggle to lift the burden and Trevor fights to regain his footing with Mack. They manage a few more yards of coughing, hurried shuffle into the sweet night air and onto Mack's sketchy grass and then collapse for a minute.

After Mack is moved a safer distance from the house, Trevor returns to the still-running backhoe and hurriedly extracts it from the building. Flames have fully engulfed the lower floor. The fire is shooting fifty feet into the air through the section of the house that had collapsed. He parks the backhoe well away from the building, shuts it down, and rejoins the group.

Several locals come out of their houses and gather around the prone Mack as Sammy checks the man's pulse. As Trevor approaches, one of the new bystanders enthusiastically sticks one hand out in Trevor's direction and claps him on the back with the other.

"I'm John, a neighbor." He nods his head in the direction of one of the nearby houses. "Holy shit, Thanks, man! Mack would have been cooked. He is really heavy into sleeping pills. I've tried to wake him before at night. Good thing you got around his burglar protection system."

"Why don't we bring him into my house?" a woman says.

Some of the men lift the still unconscious Mack and carry him into a nearby home.

Trevor looks over and sees Amy's mother trotting up to the three of them. Other neighbors are gathering garden hoses or other tools.

"Wow and holy crap, you guys. Fry cook and dishwasher by day and rescue crew by night? Is Mack okay?"

"Looks like he's all pilled out." Sammy says. "I think he'll be fine when he wakes up."

"I guess Lisa and John are going to load him into the car and take him out to Boise to the hospital to make sure. You guys want a cup of coffee or something? I can open up The House." Claire looks toward the growing fire and the group of people still stringing hoses together to wet the surrounding ground. "Opening up might not be a bad idea anyway."

The four of them walk back down to the restaurant and Sammy retrieves his guitar. Claire turns on lights and Amy heads for the kitchen. Trevor and Sammy take a table, sit, and with shaking hands, Sammy starts picking at the guitar. Claire takes a seat beside him.

Amy returns with coffee cups. She looks around at them slowly, displaying a measure of surprise.

Sammy looks up from the guitar, "There was a pretty big growing operation in his spare bedroom and maybe his wiring went south or a hot light fell over or something. I saw some tin foil and maybe hydroponics stuff back there before it came down."

Trevor nods in agreement, he feels, a little exhilarated and weirdly proud, not so much of himself as of the three of them together. "So, maybe that's what all the guns and bars were about? Mack is paranoid about losing his crop to bad guys. I'm just glad we got him out. I don't know what we'd have done without the backhoe. The whole thing did get your heart going, though, didn't it?"

Claire looks around at the three of them, "I could hear you down by the river, the singing, but even the talking, too. I really enjoyed listening to you all. It sounded like you were having fun. Amy, I've always loved hearing you laugh, and Sammy, you sound good, even from a distance. Is that what you do when you aren't being conscripted as a cook, rescue worker, or fixing computers, are you a musician?"

Sammy looks at his fingers at the neck of the guitar for a second and then sips his hot coffee. "I paid for some of my school by playing and teaching guitar and I've been in a variety of bar bands, but no, that's not really what I do. Up until now I've been mostly a student."

"And teacher." Trevor smiles at Claire. "He has been teaching too."

"What did you teach besides guitar?"

"Particle physics."

"Where?" Claire's eyebrows are raised and she is looking at him closely.

"I taught at MIT for a few years."

Amy circles her coffee cup around and around in her hands. Claire looks at Trevor with a question lingering on her face. Realizing that Sammy must know they don't believe him, Trevor watches the scene with interest, wonders about truth. "Sammy does have a fault. He thinks we're as smart as he is and has no idea how far off the mark he is." The easy thing for all of them would be to let this drop, not to call Sammy on it.

Amy is apparently not willing to take the easy route. "Are you on the faculty directory?"

"Yes, Department of Physics."

Trevor wants to show his confidence in Sammy, but fears that Sammy actually is full of shit. He is holding his breath as Amy gets up from the table. Trevor finally looks at Sammy but sees only a smile.

Amy returns a half minute later and sets a laptop down on the table, flips up the top, and looks to Sammy.

"Web dot M I T dot E D U."

Thirty seconds go by while the satellite internet slogs through the information, then, "There you are!" Amy spins the laptop around for Claire and Trevor to see. Sammy's picture is on the second row from the top, with the entry "Samuel Houston, MD, PhD" below his photo.

Claire reads and nods, then closes the laptop. She smiles at Sammy and raises both hands in a gesture of question. "So, what are you doing?" There is no malice in her voice.

"Beyond enjoying the day and the company," he shrugs. "I don't know. It's a kind of long story but for now, the whole, real answer is, I really don't know. I'm cooking for you today and tomorrow hasn't arrived yet. My research led to some developments that have potential to be weaponized. When I left MIT, I destroyed all my data. There's nothing left that isn't with me or in my head."

Claire nods slowly. "Well Sammy from Texas. You are welcome to hide here in Stanley for as long as you want." She stands up and moves the half step toward Sammy. Her hands go around him and she pulls him into a warm hug. Her head settles onto his for a moment. "It'll be okay Sam. I think you will make it be okay and we will be here any time you need backup. Are you guys going to be able to sleep tonight after all of the adrenaline and coffee?"

~

Later that night, after showering off the smoke, the two young men sprawl out on the beds. Trevor looks over at Sammy. "Is it hard for you, being that smart and carrying this struggle over the deeper right and wrong and trying to figure out what to do with your theories?"

"I don't think about it that way. I like people and try to fit in like everybody else and otherwise don't worry about who is smart or not. The other struggle, the question about what to do with my theories, is with me all the time, though. When I'm hunting for the right path, I always come around to the same old place: why do we care what happens to each other?" Sammy pauses for a moment and looks at Trevor and then continues.

"Is it God, written into our DNA, or is it possible that there really is something just fundamentally good about being good? I guess I keep hoping that's the answer, but sometimes I lose faith and then I'm just a skinny, long-haired kid who doesn't really belong anywhere. If there is no purpose and I'm just a statistical outlier and since we humans aren't all that good for the rest of the world, then bar gigs sound like a great way to pass the time until I don't have to worry about it anymore."

Trevor lies back on the motel bed thinking about what Sammy has said. He fires off a pillow in Sammy's direction and is rewarded with the "oof" of a well-aimed shot.

The pillow sails back a minute later, but is high and flops against the wall, then slides on top of Trevor, who collects it and replaces it under his head.

Chapter 4

THE DAYS EVOLVE into a contented routine. Sammy and Trevor are in The House every morning for a quick cup of coffee and some breakfast.

The sixth evening, after closing the restaurant, the group, along with Amy's mother and father, are sitting in a circle around the fire on the sandbar. Their conversation ranges to global warming and Alan suggests that additional taxes should be added to all fossil fuels.

"Dad! I'm a geologist! Don't you go taxing my industry; we love our fossil fuels!"

"Okay, young people," Alan looks around, appraising. "Where are you on that issue? Do you agree that global warming is caused by humans and what should do about it?" He looks at Amy for the first answer.

"I really don't think there's any doubt that humans are contributing to global warming. I think some gigantic effort should be made to limit use of fossil fuels, I guess that I should have picked a different major."

"Okay. How about you, Trevor?"

"Honestly, Alan, I don't know. I'm not sure any of it really matters. The world is a changing place, I guess."

Alan nods, his expression neutral. "Sammy?" All their heads swivel in Sammy's direction.

Trevor realizes this is probably the real intent of the original question, to hear what Sammy has to say about this issue. He ponders the dynamics of their group and realizes that Sammy has become, in a weird way, their alpha. He finds himself a little surprised by this epiphany. Alan and Claire are bright, capable people and are obviously senior to the rest. Trevor is used to becoming a sort of default leader by virtue of his size and looks, but here, he has no doubt, Sammy is the core.

"Well, sir, as your company, I wouldn't mind skipping political discussions." His tone suggests that he has an answer but prefers not to share it.

"Son, I respect you quite a lot and all the more for that sensitivity. But if you are willing, I would really like to hear your thoughts." Alan gives him a reassuring smile.

Sammy nods. "Well, sir, my answer is not a popular one, because I believe that limiting population is the only answer that can work. The math says that if you cut each person's carbon footprint in half and then double the population, you have arrived nowhere." He looks around at them. "I believe there is incontrovertible evidence that we are causing global climate change and pushing other resources toward the tipping point. My math says there has to be fewer people or more pollution."

They are all silent. Amy, directly beside Sammy, leans into him a little. "Okay, assuming your version is accurate. What next? How do we fix it?"

"Really? Go back in time and educate the world." Sammy's smile tilts a little more than usual. "Other than that, I believe the internet is a powerful tool and we can use it to spread the word. If all of the world's governments and corporations are willing to spend resources on getting information out, we can create enough social inertia to turn the world's population growth around in a generation or maybe two."

"I was a child of the sixties," Claire says, looking out into the night. "I thought the whole population thing would be in check by now. There was a lot of talk about it back then."

"There was a decline in US population in the late sixties, and then there was economic stagflation in the seventies. That was when governments and corporations realized that population growth equals economic growth and when we shifted to encouraging emigration to drive the economy."

"Is it really like that?" Amy asks. "Are we really just responding to economic growth trends without any connection to the rest of our future?"

Sammy's gaze sweeps around them. "It looks that way, yeah."

"Are you taking requests?" Trevor asks, looking at Sammy and letting go of the breath he didn't know he was holding. "Do you know how to play Crazy Train?"

38

~

The next day in the restaurant, Sammy is finishing some cooking and Trevor is washing dishes when Amy walks into the kitchen. Her face catches his attention.

Trevor asks first. "Is something up, Ames?"

"Yeah, it's a little weird, the sheriff was just in, said they found bones in the back of Mack's house. I guess they are thinking that maybe somebody broke in, like maybe they were trying to steal some of Mack's stash, and stumbled or something, hit his head maybe and that's how the fire started. It's so weird that we almost stumbled on a body."

"That's messed up. I wonder if we could have saved whoever it was if we'd have gone a little farther back in the house?" Trevor looks at Sammy. "You were back there. I never asked how you got there anyway."

Claire pokes her head around the corner. "Sammy, can you look at my computer again? It's doing something goofy."

Sammy turns, without answering and walks toward Claire's desk.

Amy and Trevor exchange a look. God, he loves those eyes, tries to read her face as he sends her mind rays, willing her to step toward him, but she turns and walks away. He starts cleaning the grill.

~

Ten days after arriving in Stanley, Trevor and Sammy are in their room after closing the restaurant, Trevor kicks back and thinks how odd it is that until now, nobody has mentioned them leaving. He wonders how that happens, the tacit omissions that can be maintained without a single word being exchanged. It seems to him that he and Sammy are finding the situation comfortable and something more… safe, maybe. Willing himself not to, he asks quietly, "So, Sammy dude. What are we doing?"

Sammy sighs, "Seems like a bit of a crossroads, doesn't it?"

"Maybe more for you than me, brother. I'm not faced with the 'save the world versus being a rock star' struggle. I like Stanley fine and fry cookery is fun, but some other future is out there for me. You could potentially stay and marry Amy and have ginger babies and inherit The House from her folks and never have to feel guilty about spending your life's nights out there on the sandbar. That would solve the 'whether-humanity-is-good-or-bad' conundrum by default."

"I was thinking she has eyes for you, bro. Besides, I have to go, too."

"Why?"

"I feel like I owe something to somebody. Or maybe it's only an excuse and the real answer is that I am compelled to finish what I've started, to find the end of that trail."

"Wouldn't MIT be the better place for that?"

"No, it's not!" Sammy says with a rare flare of exposed emotion. "There is an amazing amount of government spying on our campuses. I honestly believe that the fastest way for me to have gotten my ideas used to create weapons would have been for me to lock my desk drawers with my research materials in them. My work would have been on some FBI desk the next day."

"You have to know how weird and paranoid that sounds?"

Sammy looks serious. "I caught them, several times. I set software traps and busted them. I even confronted the department head who, it turned out, knew all about it. The entire faculty management told me flat out that it is pretty much SOP for every university and that would be a condition of my tenure as it is a condition of the school's funding. All I had to do was not openly acknowledge anything was going on. They said it worked out best for everybody that way. The school and I still got credit and the government had immediate access to any new potential weapon."

"So, they blackmail the school and you really think they would make weapons out of your stuff?"

"I'm certain they would."

"And you think your research might take you in a direction that, if exposed, would give our government bad guys a better way to be bad?"

"A really insidious way to be bad, yes." Sammy sits up on his bed and turns toward Trevor. There is distress on his face. "Trev, my problem is that I really can't let it go, I just can't back away and I can't go on either. What if it gets out?"

"What comes next?" Trevor asks, wishing he had something funny or brilliant or even remotely relevant to say.

"I really don't know." Sammy lets out a long sigh. "Are you ready to head out tomorrow?"

"Yeah, bro, tomorrow is fine."

~

The next morning, meeting in The House for coffee, the table is full; Sammy, Trevor, Amy, Claire, and Alan are all there.

"One day after a party at my house I found a pretty good saying on a refrigerator magnet: 'Hot coffee, like sex, is a healing gift of the gods'." Trevor raises his cup in a toast. He sips and goes on. "Sammy has been begging me to stay, but I really have to move on." Trevor looks around the table at them and wishes, not for the first time, that he could let this be home. "I've enjoyed being here more than just about anything I can remember, but I do have commitments in Montana, so…" He shrugs.

Claire looks at Sammy and then Trevor. "I wish there was a way we could keep you two."

"We'll work through the day and head out after closing, if that's alright with you guys?" Sammy does not make eye contact.

Trevor thinks no one is happy, but that all understand. He sure as hell isn't happy and he isn't even sure why not. This kind of belonging is good but he's never had it before and it's probably better not to start having it now. He looks at the clock, "Got to open in ten minutes." and pushes his chair back from the table.

The familiarity of the routine has been comforting, but today Trevor never gets too far from a sense of loss. He realizes he is willing the clock to slow down, but it stubbornly refuses to do that.

As the day winds down, Amy enters the room. Sammy and Trevor are putting away the cleaning supplies. Amy looks at each of them. Sammy shrugs. Trevor can't think of anything funny to say, can barely think of anything to say at all and brilliantly comes up with, "Our gear is in the Jeep."

Amy nods. "Okay, sit down for a last cup before you go?"

"We'll be in there in a few minutes," Sammy says, watching her closely.

When the group is at their usual table, Claire turns to the men and holds up two cell phones. "We had a few of these for Amy and her friends, but now she's home, and apparently, never leaving. Ours, and Amy's, numbers are programmed in. We are sure you both have friends you can call, but now you have us, too."

They stand for a round of hugs. Trevor wraps his arms around Amy and gets a kiss. It's a real kiss, on the lips, a girly, sweet, wet kiss. He is elated. Then she steps to Sammy and gives him the same thing, full on and lingering. Without another word between any of them, Sammy and Trevor turn and walk out the door toward the Jeep.

They climb in, both watching The House, slightly dazed, like sailors heading to sea and gawking at home port knowing their eyes won't set on it again for a long time. Trevor starts the tired motor and they roll back and away from the hitching post, the restaurant and Amy, Claire, and Alan. Trevor pushes the gear shift into first and they clatter onto Eva Falls Avenue, picking up at the point they'd turned off so long ago. Accelerating, they drive into the night.

"You good with an all-nighter?"

Sammy nods and plugs his MP3 player into the Jeep's stereo, turns up the volume, turns it up again, competing with the noise of the Jeep's top. The first song is country. "Too loud?"

Trevor gives a head shake and works at keeping the horrible steering in check.

~

As they pass the signs for Big Hole National Battlefield, Trevor turns down the music, breaking the conversation hiatus. "You said your experiments involved some sort of, time manipulation?"

"The Palladium is just the start. I think I explained already, it's a means to an end."

"I got that from before."

"You know much about the Higgs Field?"

"Yeah, they grow corn there, right?"

"Corn-ee." Sammy smiles. "It's a long story, but the concept of the Higgs field has to do with mass… sort of. I have a theory about how the Higgs field affects other things besides mass."

"Okay, like?" Trevor asks, trying to decide if this is serious, or crap. As is often the case when a conversation with Sammy gets deep, Trevor has a weird sense of disbelief bordering on distrust.

"My research has led me to believe that the Higgs field affects time and that there is a way to use it to influence time."

"So you're saying that you can time travel."

"Kind of, but in a weird way; it's possible we could project a copy of something across time and space."

"A copy. This is on the level, right?" He risks taking his eyes off the road long enough to look directly at Sammy.

"All on the level. And the government's actively looking in all the schools for ideas that can be weaponized. I need to be out of sight to sort it all out and finish my research and prove to myself that it's real on a larger scale and still keep it a secret. I couldn't live with myself if my research was used to cause harm, especially on a military scale."

"Sam, you aren't crazy, right?"

"Not crazy, Trev. Maybe a little paranoid, but I don't honestly think even that. I might be crazy and think I am not, that's always possible except I do have proof. My real problem is that I can't not finish what I've started. I have to finish it." He doesn't say anything for a minute and then adds, "I have never been kissed before."

"Holy shit, Amy was your first kiss?"

Smiling hugely, Sammy confirms that, in fact, she was.

"Jesus, dude," Trevor is struck first by a feeling of loss and then by an overwhelming sense of absurdity. He fiercely hopes that Sammy's brilliance is carrying him on the right path and what a path it is. Can the young man sitting beside him in his crappy old Jeep really be on the verge of bridging the energy gap for the world or allowing us to affect time somehow? No way. Meet a nice new friend and he turns out to be crazy. Go figure. Trevor turns up the stereo again.

~

Nye, Montana, consists of about seven buildings. A NAPA parts store, the ubiquitous diner of small western towns, a post office, a few houses and the large Smith Bros mining company offices and dorms. Trevor stops the Jeep in front of the mining complex and shuts the motor down.

"They really are expecting you?" It's the middle of a windy day. The Jeep is noisy, even sitting still.

Sammy turns and looks at his backpack and guitar. "Yeah, they really are expecting me. I made them a good offer and my credentials are good and they took me seriously enough. There should be a dorm room waiting for me and best of all, I get to eat at the cafeteria."

"So, that was the deal you made them… you share your brilliance and they give you all the institutional mashed potatoes you can eat?"

"I improve their extraction process by fifteen percent and they pay me one hundred thousand dollars, and yes, most importantly, free spuds."

"Holy shit, that's serious money, dude! What does fifteen percent gain them?"

"In dollars? About ten million a year."

"Sammy! A hundred grand is a lot of money, but ten million a year is a lot more. Did you sell yourself short?"

"There is mutual benefit. I traded a bunch of emails with them, and then talked on the phone quite a bit with the mine's owner, Mike Smith. I gave them enough to convince them that I had something, but without giving out the something I had. Mike agreed that if I can produce, I would get my hundred thousand, that it wouldn't be taxable or traceable, and most importantly, there would be no news. They will also set up a scholarship fund for miners' kids with five percent of the extra from then on. Their cooperation on those few things is worth a lot."

"So the scholarship is guilt buy-down?"

Sammy smiles and nods and then sticks out his hand to Trevor. As the handshake ends Sammy's smile slips and he looks out the window of the Jeep. "I'm not really sure how this next part is going to go, Trev, but I would be much obliged if you would let me buy you a beer when this phase is all over."

"You're on, buddy," Trevor answers back as he watches his friend. "You have my number, right?" He holds up the pre-paid cell that Amy's folks had given him.

Sammy nods and holds up the other phone. "So, see you in a few months?" He climbs out of the metal frame and canvas door of the Jeep.

"I'll look forward to that beer, Sam."

As Sammy closes the door Trevor wonders about the weird way the world works and backs away from the mining company building. He likes it when Sammy calls him Trev.

Chapter 5

EVEN WITH THE ROAD NOISE of the Jeep, the trip from Nye to Billings seems like about ninety miles of quiet and it's a different quiet. When Sammy was sitting here not saying anything, it was a whole lot less quiet than this. He wonders if he will ever see his friend again, wonders, if Sammy's claims are true and if it is possible that Sammy is who he says he is, that he can "influence" time? That belief is a heavy lift.

Trevor thinks about time, about the perception of time, and the idea that it is supposed to be a linear construct. Science is all about even measurements. Atomic clocks are built around the precise metered decay of some particle and the whole precision thing is flat out a line of shit when it comes to people stuff. When we are dealing with each other and with our perceptions of what is real, time is not linear. Time is, in fact, clunky, congealed in spots, stretched thin in others, and anything but homogenous or even. It feels like about half of Trevor's life has been condensed into the last stretch of a few weeks.

Amazingly, in the current world, Trevor's new cell doesn't have an app for foot massages or a moving map, leaving him with the ugly choice of either stopping to ask for directions or being lost. The cute girl at the convenience store seems both happy to flirt and to tell Trevor how to get to his destination; he mentally marks that store as having future potential for providing entertainment. As he drives under the sign for the store, the "Kum and Go," he thinks there's a certain irony in that thought. A few minutes later he sees signs for the Billings Airport.

Driving along the fence, Trevor looks for the entrance. He finds the gate, keys in the code, and drives onto the airport tarmac.

The airport is a little confusing as, once on the property, the yellow line becomes the middle of the taxiway instead of the division between lanes. Trevor wonders how often pilots leave the airport in their cars and have head-on collisions.

Trevor finds the spray business, J D Ag, and walks into an office where an attractive thirty-something woman sits at a cluttered desk. The office obviously isn't set up to make an impression on the public. Shelves are full of loosely bound magazines and periodicals. Papers, books, and manuals are scattered everywhere. Three propellers are propped in one corner

"Hey." Trevor thinks that's a stupid opening shot to a new employer, especially when the employer is represented by a cute chick.

"Hey yourself."

He sticks out a hand. "Trevor Tavish."

"Mattie," smiling, she shakes his hand firmly.

"Hi, Mattie, I talked to Jake a month or so ago about coming to work for you guys."

"I remember that. Jake said you'd be coming around. Let me find your stuff."

Mattie gives him employment paperwork, clears books and papers off a chair, and sits him down with a pen. Trevor puts all the relevant information on the forms using the back of a Cessna 100 series manual as a desk. Eventually he hands the stack back to Mattie. She gives it a quick scan and tosses it on top of the mess.

"Okay, let's go show you to Jake."

Trevor follows her out of the office through what looks like a parts area and out into an open shop. They wind their way to where a man is working, at least to where a lower body protrudes from an open panel on the underbelly of a large yellow airplane. A grinning, tail-wagging golden retriever sits mostly at the feet attached to those legs. Mattie sticks out an index finger, gun-like, and puts it in the middle of the man's exposed lower back.

"Give me all of your money and the dog lives."

"Jesus Mattie, you know better than that! I pay you too much and you already have all my money and please, kill the dog! His farts are making my eyes water!" The voice is muffled from inside the airplane.

To this comment the Golden's tail thumps faster, perhaps with pride.

"I have your FNG," Mattie says.

"Trevor?" The man says, bending down and extracting himself from the aircraft.

"Hi, Jake." Trevor extends his hand.

"Hi, yourself, and good to see you. The furry gasbag is Jinn."

They spend twenty minutes discussing the basic schedule for the next few days and some of the fundamentals of Trevor's new job, and then Jake says he needs to finish working on the aircraft he's repairing in order for it to fly the following day.

Trevor follows Mattie to another section of the building and up some stairs and can't help noticing the sway of her nice-looking backside as she leads him. "These are the crew rooms. Right now, it's just you and Jinn. I'm not sure if any of the other guys will be bunking here or not this season. The dog's reputation may have scared them all away."

She shows him through the complex. There are three small bunk rooms, a bathroom and shower room, and a simple kitchen. Aviation periodicals are on most of the surfaces, including the beds.

"Pick whichever room you like and make yourself comfortable. Swing back by the office and I'll give you the keys you need and there you are, an employee of J D Ag!"

"So, is Jake the J and who is the D?" He is trying to stall her departure, liking her company.

"Nope, Jake grew up a John Deere tractor fanatic. That's it. And," she smiles at him, "don't forget to be rolling by four in the morning." turns to leave.

As she is walking through the hall door out of the dorm area, Trevor calls after her, "That's not morning. That's still tonight!"

Mattie smiles over her shoulder and leaves Trevor on his own.

The next weeks pass in a whirlwind. Trevor gets up every day, fuels the trucks, fuels the airplanes, loads the chemicals, gets coffee ready for the pilots, and completes all the tasks that need to be performed to maintain the aerial spraying operation. The business goes seven days a week, sun up to sun down when there is an active season, and this is the beginning of a very active season. Trevor is surprised to find that while he doesn't mind the work, he also isn't really becoming immersed in the culture. The aviation bug is not biting him. He does get to know the pilots. There are currently three flying for JD. Two are the main full-time employees and the third is a relief pilot. Mostly, though, he's busy, dawn to dusk. It's early July when he hears again from Sammy.

"Hey, bro," Sammy drawls from the cell phone one exhausted evening.

Trevor is surprised at the depth of his relief in hearing Sammy's voice. "Dude! How the heck is the world of palladium mining?"

"Well, Nye's a little boring. Outside of some very good pancakes at the local diner, there isn't much to do here besides work."

"Wow, I'd trade you, man. The word on the street is that there's a ton of shit to do in Billings, but since I'm working from about an hour before dawn to about an hour or two after dusk, there's no empirical proof of that from my end. You talk to anybody in Stanley?"

"Traded a few emails with Claire. That's about it."

"So, how is the whole mining process thing going? You get your extraction enhancement ideas working?"

"I did. We have set up a very small batch system and it's working like crazy. The results are better than I had thought they'd be. Mike Smith, the owner, is pleased."

"So, you're going to get your cash?"

"Well, it's kind of funny. I've gotten to know Mike pretty well and he's agreed to endow my slush fund with some extra money. After the full-scale process proves itself out, he's actually going to double what we originally agreed on. He figures the additional extraction will benefit the company by a huge amount. He also offered me pretty much lifetime employment."

"Holy Christ," Trevor groans. He wonders what life is like when your pulse doesn't go up discussing sums over a hundred dollars let alone hundreds of thousands. "Dude, you are golden. Are you thinking about the jib offer?"

"Not really. Mining isn't my thing and I've got other fish to fry."

"And now you are funded to carry on with…" he pauses, not really sure how to phrase the question, "the other thing?"

"Yeah, and to that end I was thinking that me and the Tak might check out the big city for a few days soon. Do you think I could stay with you for a few days?"

"I think Jake wouldn't mind you staying. He's an amazing guy." He is pleased by this.

"Do you have to know some secret code words or a special hand shake to get along with the fraternity there?"

"No, they're great people, they just really like their flying stuff. It's like some kind of religion to them. Those cups that say 'I love the smell of jet fuel in the morning'? They mean in the cup."

Sammy laughs a little. "I'll stay out of your hair, I just need to spend some time dealing with equipment contracts."

He is not sure what Sammy means by that but really doesn't care, he is just anxious to see his friend. "Okay, dude, give me a call when you're headed this way. In the meantime, I'll talk with Jake. Hey, want me to come down and get you? It's only a couple of hours."

"No, I think I'll just hitch. You meet some crazy people that way."

He laughs, "Don't I know it. See you later then, bro." They end the connection and Trevor ponders the call. Wondering about the 'equipment contracts,' he heads for the shower to finish the day and enjoy the brief respite before starting another.

~

The next day he remembers to ask Jake about Sammy staying, tells him that Sammy is on some business of his own, and is pleased when Jake seems at ease about accommodating his friend.

Until then, there's the continuing blur of long days of chemicals, fuel, coffee, and repair work.

"You work your ass off, Trev. I'm impressed," Jake says one day between loading the big yellow Air Tractor 602s. "If you're interested in making a long-term thing out of it, we'll find work through the winter for you. I can train you as a mechanic and you could work off your time to become an A&P, an airframe and power plant mechanic. If we find the time to get off the ground a little and you have the aptitude and interest, we could also work you up through your private pilot and commercial and right on into a seat as well."

Trevor had learned enough of the idioms of the industry to know that 'a seat' was a job flying in the aerial application sector. The money is good as well. It's a good offer. Enjoying the validation, he shakes Jakes hand and thanks him.

~

It's the middle of August when Sam calls again. "Hey, dude, you still up for some company?"

"Absolutely! Jake's cool with you staying in the bunk house. I told him you'll be recruiting a string of underage hookers for porno work here in the hangar and he agrees that is important work so it's all good. I'm the only crew living here this year anyway. I guess the other guys are long-term locals now. The best part is that things have slowed down a little, so I'll have occasional stretches when I can take time to breathe and we can catch up. When do you think you'll be here?"

"I'm leaving in the morning. I have a ride up to the interstate with one of the managers. Then he heads west, so I'll find somebody heading east. I should be in Billings sometime tomorrow."

"Okay, Mattie will be in the office and is expecting you."

~

Trevor parks the big chemical truck, climbs down from the cab and finishes off his workday by tossing his fast food trash in a twenty-foot lob into an open garbage can. He heads up to the bunk house and is pleased to find Sammy sitting at the kitchen table with a laptop. They spend some time catching up, how the hitching had gone, a nice older lady picked him up and took him right to the airport gate. Trevor gives Sammy a somewhat disengaged two-minute rundown on his day ending with the McDonalds lunch bag swish as the point of his greatest excitement.

"Jake offered me a full-time thing," Trevor says. "Year round. I am not making two hundred grand in a few months, but it's not bad either. Since

I'm living here in the heaven of aviation magazines, I've bankrolled almost every penny I've made this summer. It's pretty sweet. I've got about twenty-two thousand bucks sitting in Billings First National."

"Seems like a good thing. Are you learning to fly, too?"

Trevor shrugs. "Not really. I think the whole aviation thing is cool. Jake is the best boss a guy could want, but I feel a little bit like an agnostic hanging out with a bunch of churchies. These guys eat, sleep, and drink airplanes. They have all these formulas in their heads for calculating fuel burn, density altitude, and useable load… and probably estimating the weight of their poops and analyzing the effect of it on the number of acres they will spray tomorrow. I'm not taken with it that way. I'm not shining on the inside to do this."

"Okay," Sammy says. "That's kind of good, because I have this thought. I spent a lot of time in Nye working on their extraction process, but I was also thinking about my life, too." Sammy pauses and then, in a way that is unusual for him, switches subjects without finishing where he was going. "Y'all up for a beer and maybe some food? I'm starved!"

"Sure," Trevor answers, confused. "Jake keeps telling me about a bar out on Lindsey Avenue, it's supposed to have good steaks. I have tomorrow off, my first whole day down since I came here, so I can stay up past eight. Give me five minutes to shower?"

~

They head out through the hangar building, winding between two of the sleek yellow airplanes. Tool boxes and pieces of equipment are scattered all around the large open space.

"You have this all to yourself?" Sammy asks Trevor as they close up the building.

"Yup." Trevor takes a sideways glance at Sammy. "It kind of struck me, too. I walked in off the street and they handed me a key. The air tractors are about a million and a half a copy. The tools, tool boxes, and all that shit look pretty pricey. It's the zealot thing here; you're either an innie or you're an outie. That makes me a little bit of a poser but I'd die before I'd ever rip off Jake or let anybody else do it."

"I forgot how damn noisy this engineering miracle is." Sammy raises his voice to be heard over the flapping canvas of the Jeep as they pull out of the airport property onto the road.

Trevor smiles and reaches to the stereo and twists the knob up.

They pull to a stop in front of the Naked Dixie Chicks Bar. Sammy looks at the sign as the tired engine clatters out sounds that might be its last death rattle.

Trevor looks at Sammy, "Don't know, bro. When Jake told me the name I thought I'd heard him wrong. He did seem pretty clear about the good food part."

They push through the doors and enter the noisy room. The tavern is set up in a traditional saloon layout, a long, dark wood counter with stools distributed along the length of it. The bar's ornate backdrop is cluttered with a variety of liquors, dishes, glasses, and miscellaneous crap. Booths are set along the outside wall with roughhewn tables scattered throughout the open space in no obvious pattern. Groups or pairs of patrons sit in various configurations around the room. Trevor waffles between relief and disappointment after discovering that the waitresses are clothed. They buy beers, find a booth and sit. Sammy puts a laptop out on the table.

"I've been thinking. I have this idea that might keep us busy and in food and spending money. I'm going to set myself up to finish my research project, but that is not going to take all of my time. I'd like to fill out the rest of my life a little with other things, like living. I was thinking that if you aren't going to be an aviation junkie you might be looking for another career path, so what would you think about going into business with me?"

Trevor is weirdly struck by the realization that whenever he is uncomfortable, the southerness in Sammy's drawl amps up and he is sounding really southern right now. Watching Sammy watch him, Trevor is pretty sure he's serious but asks anyway. "You serious?"

"Very."

Trevor, uncertain, shrugs, "Hit me, dude."

"There's an old building for sale here in Billings. It's being offered on an owner contract with good rates."

Sammy spins the laptop around so Trevor can see the brick building on the screen. He scans through other photos of the building while Sammy watches. The ad shows what looks like an old bank with a very dated lobby, teller stations, and a vault, as well as several other rooms of various sizes.

"The building sat unused and unchanged for about sixty years, stuck in a some hinky estate struggle. It's been kept up somewhat, but has been mostly empty for a really long time. I think it was an antique store off and on and was lived in by some family member or other, but otherwise is mostly a large dust collection center."

"Cool." Trevor looks at the pictures, feeling confused. "An unused building. Is it a safe house for spiders you're thinking about operating there? It's got a good start going."

A fully clothed but cranky waitress appears and asks if they want food.

After ordering, Sammy turns to Trevor. "I'd like us to open a pub."

Trevor looks at Sammy. There is something missing here. Brilliant Sammy co-owning a pub with a no-future, loser guy doesn't really get all the bright lights flashing. Depressed by this insight, Trevor hides his lack of enthusiasm, waves a hand at the room. "We could definitely steal over this clientele just by being less mean. A pub, you and I would be pouring beer and cheffing and all?"

"With a small stage for jamming."

Thoughts do an end run around Trevor's filter and come out of his mouth. "Why with me? You have a lot of other options Sammy."

"Trev, one of my favorite things is people. I like people. That's why I hitch. It's a cool way to meet random folks and spend some time getting to know them, to find out who they are and why they are. I can't get enough of it and a pub would be a perfect place to make a kind of career out of people. As for why you, I know you've got your struggles, but you've become a great friend, one of my favorite people I've met. I feel like we run on the same wave length. We all have our difficulties, but I trust you. You have a good heart and I think we make a great team."

People are milling around and the din of voices presses into his head, he wonders about trust and teams. Does he trust Sammy? Is he, Trevor, trustworthy? Can he be a reliable team member? Does he trust anybody? Not really. "Okay. A stage for jamming, do I get to play bass?"

"Do you know how to play bass?"

"No, but I can look really cool. Besides, all you do is pick at one of those fat strings every once in a while, right? You really want to do this? It seems like a weird stop along the way of your life."

"I want to do this for the reasons I said. Also, I enjoy your company and your thinking. The time we spent in Stanley was great. I know it was a short representation, but I think it was valid especially after we went through the fire. That can't be faked. Besides that, I know you don't mind working your butt off. The bigger deal is, I do trust you. As for me, I definitely want the opportunity for some connections while I do my research."

Trevor looks into his glass, searches hard for wisdom but finds only beer. Coming from anybody else he would treat the suggestion lightly and blow it off. Coming from Sammy this is a solid thing, one step away from reality. "We could call it 'The Malt Vault'."

Sammy rolls his eyes.

"Just saying. So, as I slide down this slippery slope, I feel compelled to ask what your thinking is about the whole money thing. What are they asking for the building, how do we come up with whatever that is, and then further, how do we fund all of the turn-a-bank-into-a-bar things?"

"Well, I have a bunch of cash, but after I get my lab set up there isn't going to be that much left. I think I'll have about forty or fifty thousand to throw toward this project. You have your twenty-some thousand saved, maybe a little more by the end of the season. The building is ninety and they're offering great owner financing."

"So, like ten grand down and you think we could do the remodel with the rest of the cash?"

"I think finishing the inside of the building would be tight on that, but my daddy taught me a whole bunch about construction and remodeling. Our family never paid a dime to any contractor and our stuff seemed pretty solid to me. I was thinking we could buy the building now and when the season runs to a close, we could start ripping up stuff." Sammy pauses for a minute, maybe letting Trevor absorb this, and then goes on. "It needs to be only in your name, though."

What? The Oh-Shit-ometer slams into the red arc. Sammy is watching him closely and reassures him with a self-aware smile and slight shake of his head.

"I know we don't have a long history. And I gather your personal history isn't awash with things that make you a big believer in the natural righteousness of folks, I get that. So, here's my idea to set your mind at rest. We go forward, you buy the bank, and I put my forty thousand in your account. You hold all the cards, no strings."

"No cashier's check for twenty thousand more and I refund you the difference in cash?"

Sammy laughs a little. "And no African address for corporate headquarters."

On the one hand, he thinks Sammy is sincere, but also wildly optimistic. On the other, it seems possible that he could lose whatever he has in the business regardless of what the source of the money was if big brother comes in for some kind of government smack-down on Sammy. Feeling around that, 'in your name only' thing, is what genuine crazy looks like and could actual law enforcement people be after professor Sammy Houston's ideas? He realizes he's humoring himself, "Okay."

"Want to go look over the building? We can't get in, but we can check out the outside and get a feel for the neighborhood."

Their food shows up. They thank the still fully clothed waitress, and Trevor checks out her ass as she walks away, thinking it's too bad the circumstances don't fit the name better after all and says, "Sounds great."

They finish dinner and pay separately. Heading out the door, Sammy glances back. "I'm glad they don't live up to their name."

"Nah, I'd go for cranky and naked over plain vanilla cranky any day."

Sammy tells Trevor the address and helps guide him as he navigates the combative Jeep through the streets of Billings. The bank building is on the corner and has an ornate, crenelated top and fancy brickwork across the two exposed faces. Stopping the truck at the curb, they get out to peer in through the tall windows in the front.

Trevor cups his hands to the window to see into the dark building. "Nice high ceilings."

"According to the ad, the lobby area is fourteen feet high and there is a basement with an extra vault for our overflowing millions."

The adjoining building is a fishing shop that looks to cater to upscale fly fishermen. The bank building goes back to the alley on the side that's exposed to the street. Most of the surrounding buildings have what appear to be viable, long-term businesses in them.

"Parking is good." Sammy points to the fairly wide street with angle parking on both sides.

"Yup, good access. I like it. Had you already seen it?"

"No, bro, not until now." Texas upturn at the end.

"You're a bright guy with questionable sanity, Sam." Trevor looks at his friend and tries once again to fit the pieces together. "But do you think we can get a realtor to show it tomorrow?"

"Real estate sales being the way they are, you could probably get somebody out of bed to show us right now."

"You mentioned that it's some estate thing. Do you think that might be a problem?" Trevor asks as they wander the neighboring area. "Like we'll be fighting relatives or something?"

"I don't think so, it was apparently in some kind of weird trust from way back. The original will specified that the building wouldn't be sold out of the family until this exact date. Nobody seems to know why the old papers got written up that way. Death brings out greed in folks, but it usually doesn't bring out patient and bizarre."

"Okay, I'm game for tomorrow. For tonight, I'm about wiped out. This getting up at three-thirty shit sucks. This feels like the middle of the night for me."

As they drive back to the airport, Trevor is still trying to make the puzzle pieces fit. "So, bro, I got a question. When we were driving up through the boonies in Idaho, right after we'd met, we stopped one day to take a leak and I saw you throw something away. You gave it a kind of ceremonious chuck out into a waterfall. What was that all about?"

Sammy looks silently out the window on his side for a moment before he turns to Trevor. Surprisingly, he looks surprised, even pale. "That was a

prototype device that came out of some of my ideas. I had t
the week, overloaded it, and it wasn't viable any more. The
could be reverse engineered if it was ever found and the
waterfall looked like a perfect place to make something like
didn't mean to come across as sneaky or anything."

That seems reasonable, or at least consistent with Sammy's other craziness
that he was getting used to. The only odd bit was the pale face. What was
up with that?

They come to the gate, enter the code, retrace their path to J D Ag, and
park. Walking to the building, they stop to watch as a large airplane makes
its approach and lands. The night is calm and warm.

"I really thought this would end up being your calling."

"I thought it was, too until I figured out that it's not like a normal job,
though. Like I said earlier, flying life is more like being in the military or
joining a cult. It's something you become. I saw a guy wearing a shirt that
said 'I'm a pilot, what's your super power?' I get it, these people Zen
through the air. I think they're born with it and instead of training for it, it's
more like they erase the not-knowing veil or something. I'm sure I could
learn it, but not that way. In my core, I just don't feel that lift or whatever it
is these folks have."

"I get both the Zen thing and the pun." Sammy looks straight at Trevor.
"To thine own self be true. That's good shit, a worthy axiom of life."

Trevor thinks that 'axiom of life,' said with a thick hick drawl, seems like a
contradiction. He inserts the key to the office door. "I guess I need to tell
Jake I'm not going to be a lifer."

They lock up and wind through the office and hangar areas to the crew
dorms. Trevor dives onto a neatly made-up bed in one of the bunk rooms.
His muffled voice tells Sammy to take either the Amelia suite or the Hoover
suite. "The Hoover suite has the best bed, even without a hot tub, wet bar,
mirrored ceiling, and lap pool."

Chapter 6

TREVOR'S UP at his normal, still dark outside, time. Remembering that Sammy is both a late and light sleeper, he makes coffee as quietly as possible. After fixing a cup, he grabs his laptop and heads down to the hangar where Jinn greets him with a soft chuff and an exuberant tail wag. After giving the golden a good head rub, Trevor picks a spot against a wall and sits on the floor, setting the laptop, appropriately, in his lap. He stretches out his legs and Jinn flops against him, laying out on the floor, strategically, with his head at a perfect arm's reach from Trevor, just right for petting.

Trevor opens the laptop, deletes the usual ads for Viagra, along with the claims that FedEx is trying to deliver valuable packages, and reads his few uninteresting emails. Of course, the head of the FBI is, unsurprisingly, trying to verify that he actually is deserving of the previously unclaimed multi-million-dollar prize money. He closes his mail program and pops up the Google home page, then stares at it while he pets Jinn. The page stares expectantly back asking him to "Search Google or type URL." His hands lift to the keyboard and nothing happens with them, they hold there, poised. Eventually he gives in and types, "Samuel Houston, MIT."

There are many scholarly articles, some authored by and some about Sammy. He scans several pages. Most all of what he finds is centered around physics. Some of the blurbs cite Sammy's impressive credentials. A few are more social in origin and talk about goings-on at the MIT campus, and none of them mention either fusion reactors or time travel.

"That doesn't mean too much, does it, Jinn?" Trevor's hands leave the keyboard to pet the dog. He doesn't really know what he was looking for. As he's about to shut off the computer he remembers that it's been a while since he checked his old email address, the one from before the debacle with Shawna. He logs in to that account.

It's not another Viagra ad, but another notice from the FBI. More millions, no doubt. Just before hitting the delete key, Trevor notices the sender, G.Paxton@FBI.gov. He stares for a moment and then closes the screen, email unopened. It's odd sometimes, he thinks, that not knowing can feel okay. There is, after all, that whole line about ignorance and bliss.

Trevor spends the rest of the morning daydreaming about the pub and success, his thoughts drift back to his parents. He fantasizes about flying them out from Grants Pass. Not that he wants to see them really; they are too frequently shitty to enjoy that. Mostly, he wants to rub it in that he's successful, or going to be. Pretty juvenile point of view, not that he minds being juvenile, they're assholes.

Sammy catches up with him about eight. "Hey, good morning. Do you want to set up something with a realtor to check out the bank building?"

"The Malt Vault?"

"You really like that name?"

"No, it's just that Hooters is already taken."

"Okay, I'll make some calls and see what I can fix up for a realtor. How would you feel about loaning me the Jeep a few days when you're at work?"

"Sure, on the Jeep, the keys are securely hidden in the guarded safety of the ignition. Help yourself. Have you been making headway on your lab stuff?"

"I'm doing pretty good. A few things are ordered and most of the drawings are delivered to the different fabrication shops. I'm gaining some ground."

"Sounds good." Trevor debates asking more, decides he isn't that interested. "I'm going to knock around in the hangar for a minute. Let me know if you get something set up with the realtor?"

The Montana sun is warm and friendly. As Trevor is taking the top off the Jeep and stowing it, Sammy comes out of the office with a cup of coffee in each hand.

"I don't care if you turn out to be a brilliant business partner or not." Trevor takes a cup. "I will keep you around simply because you understand the underlying truth to the order of the universe, coffee is everything. I'll get the dog."

During the drive across town, they again discuss the potential business plan. Sammy tells Trevor about the accumulation of information he has hunted up regarding pubs and business start-ups in general.

"You ever study business in your line of college careers?"

"Not yet I haven't. But I've always believed that the world is a pretty open place. People really enjoy sharing what they know if you ask politely. Throw in the internet and it makes it almost difficult to fail if you're willing to work at it a little bit. If you read it right, the internet is a great oracle. It's almost literally our collective consciousness."

"Yeah, I get that you might see things in there that others can't, but you've got an amazing mind too." Trevor holds out his now finished coffee cup and turns it upside down. "This is my brain, pretty much empty." A drip runs falls onto the floor of the Jeep.

Sammy smiles. "There isn't so much difference between us, Trev, we're just people and we all need each other and the whole spectrum of being together as humans with all our many messy personalities and differences. We each add what we add and take what we take, and in the end, all any of us really has to offer is our hard work and a smile."

Trevor senses that Sammy believes what he's saying and appreciates that. He thinks this is the core of how Sammy views humanity. Trevor's darker version does not share this naiveté.

"That works for me I guess. Who's our realtor anyway?" They pull up in front of the brick building.

"A gal named Cheryl, I think."

Trevor reaches back to give Jinn a good head ruffling before stepping out of the Jeep.

The four come to a collection point on the sidewalk. Hands are shaken and Jinn is introduced. Not to be left out, he raises a paw to Cheryl, who takes it, bowing formally, and shakes with this introduction. Laughing, Cheryl guides them to the old, but elegant, front door.

Trevor can see there's work to be done to the building, but it isn't in bad shape for being a hundred and some years old. His assessment is that a coat of paint and maybe a little window glazing should work a lot of magic.

Otherwise it looks pretty good. Cheryl unlocks the large front door and ushers them in.

The floors, and most surfaces, are dusty but nothing immediate catches Trevor's attention as needing major repairs. He can see tables scattered around with patrons laughing and talking and likes the image. "What are we going to do for the stage?" The question is mostly tongue-in-cheek.

"Don't know bro, let's look." Sammy walks toward the back of the building. The lobby area takes up about one quarter of the first-floor area.

"What are you guys planning for the building?" Cheryl asks as Jinn walks beside her, tail fanning the air.

Waiting a beat to see if Sammy will answer first, Trevor says, "We want to open a pub."

"This would be a great place for it," she agrees. "A lot of younger people work in this area, definitely potential for a pub crowd."

~

They spend a few hours looking the building over, then end up in the lobby.

Sammy nods, "You interested still?"

"Okay, Cheryl, we are but we need to think it over a little. Do you think they'd take seventy-five? We really like the building, but we need to stretch our dollars."

"My impression from the family is that they've finally gotten to the sales date specified in the will, and now all they want is the building sold."

Sammy, Trevor, and Jinn hop back into the faded Jeep and start out for their return to the airport.

Sammy, looking out his side of the Jeep says, "Hey Trev. I need to pop down to Houston for a couple of days. I just heard from my folks. It sounds like they are some legal issues I need to help them with. Is that cool?"

"Yeah, all good. I will get by without you for a few days."

~

It's interesting, having Sammy gone for a few days. It does give Trevor some time to think this whole thing over. The pub seems like it could be a good opportunity, the best part of which is that he can use it to mess with his parents, a clear win. The one big upside is being teamed up with Sammy. Then again, the downside is being teamed up with Sammy if Sammy turns out to be mostly or completely full of shit.

On that, how not full of shit could his friend be? There hasn't been any outright bragging on Sam's part but when you give the whole thing a twenty thousand foot over view, there are some major grand claims in it, aren't there. What it really comes down to is the risk versus benefit and if it comes right down to that, he can cut Sammy loose, turn him in to the feds or somebody, maybe even make a little coin on the deal. There is that.

~

Trevor opens the squeaky office door. He finds Jake sitting at the still cluttered office desk, talking with Mattie and greets them warmly. "Hey, guys."

"Hey, Trevor," from both.

Trevor sniffs, wrinkling up his nose. "Did Jinn just leave?"

Mattie crosses her eyes at him and smiles. Trevor thinks she's really attractive. He asks how they're doing, gets asked in return. Eventually he goes on, "Hey, I was wondering if I could come in late tomorrow. It looks like it's a fairly short day. I think we're only flying one plane and John is the pilot. I don't think it'd be too big of an impact if he loaded his own plane for a day." Mattie's button-up sweater strains at its fastenings and Trevor tries not to notice the lacey fabric or the contents within.

Jake nods, his curly blond hair bobbing as he does. "Sure, I was going to tell you that you were the record holding FNG for the most days worked."

"Wow, is there a trophy?" Mattie would make a good prize.

Jake fiddles with some papers. "I usually don't ask until the end of the season, but we're impressed by you, Trevor. Think you'll stick around?"

Trevor's shoulders slump a little. What he really wants to tell Jake is that he would love to stay but that he is a poser, a faker among the zealots. "Well, yeah, no." Damn, it's hard to go on. "Sammy and I are looking at starting a business in town. We made an offer on a building here and we're roughing out a plan for it. We are hoping to hear if they've accepted our offer soon. I appreciate a whole bunch that you were going to make work for me through the winter, but this is maybe not my calling." Feeling like a total shit.

Jake sticks out his hand and nods. "Not a problem, Trevor. I want the best for you. You and Sam can stay in the dorm through the fall and winter if you're willing to feed Jinn and deal with the aftermath when I'm not around. It's yours until I need it for the next FNG or my seasonal guys."

"Thanks, Jake." Trevor shoots Mattie and him a smile. "That would be a huge help."

Trevor winds through the hangar, stops to bend under the Air Tractor and trade Jinn a rub behind the ears for a tail wag. He heads up the stairs and finds that Sammy is back from Texas and sitting at the table in the kitchenette. The aviation magazines are now neatly stacked along the wall, the rest of the horizontal surfaces are clear of clutter. The laptop is out and Sammy looks up at Trevor. "Hey Trev."

"Hey, dude. Did you find stuck-together pages when you moved the sacred scrolls there?"

"You're just jealous that you don't get an airplane hard-on is all."

"Yeah, maybe, sexual freak that I am and preferring girls and all, speaking of, did you see Mattie's sweater? Lotta boob, not so much button. That's a rough way to hold a conversation. Have we heard anything from the realtor?"

Sammy shakes his head. "No bro, sorry. No word yet."

"The suspense is murder. So, how goes the science project? Are you getting ready to launch any outhouses or anything?"

"Negative, the density and design of most outhouses is unlikely to retain structural integrity under the stresses of accelerating sloshy blue poop at thirty-two feet per second, per second, so no outhouse launching today."

"You are a regular comodian. You are shopping for lab equipment with our money, then?" Convinces himself that the phrasing was funny. "Is the Vault in danger, because I kind of just quit my job. Although, since I am the only person who can endure the application chemicals and Jinn's daily gassing. They would take me back."

"No worries. We're still afloat. Do you mind if I take the Jeep tomorrow?"

"Sure, I can always drive the fuel truck. You want a cup of coffee? I think there's some left in the office."

Sammy looks up for a beat, shrugs. "Sure."

"Okay, back in a minute." Trevor walks back out of the kitchen trying to think about the world outside of himself and mostly comes back to the truly important things like those gaps in Mattie's button. Navigating the aircraft, tools, and equipment opens the office door and breathes a sigh of relief and perfume to see Mattie and her breasts, are still there.

"Hey, Mattie," Trevor says, quite proud of his current, but wavering, ability to look into her eyes.

"Back again so soon? What are you up to?"

He thinks her voice is soft and sexy and he notices that Jake is gone. "I thought I'd get the last of the coffee out of the pot before I have to run it through the blender to drink it."

Mattie waves a hand distractedly in the direction of the coffee.

"What are you still doing here anyway?" Trevor pours two cups, raises one and asks, "Want some?"

"No thanks. That stuff will put hair on your chest. In a general sense, I'm here because I need a job and I like working for Jake. In a specific sense, because Jake asked me to get the Wilber Ellis report done." She holds up a folder. "I think he's trying to negotiate better prices. They're meeting for lunch tomorrow."

Trevor nods as he pours cream into both cups. He really wants to ask if she's married but all the ways he thinks about phrasing the question will rat out his true, horny guy nature. For now, his plan is to keep up the pretension of having moral depth. "Okay, if you want to come and hang with Sammy and me, we'll be up in the dorm for a while."

"Okay, thanks but I have ladies' bible study tonight."

Trevor sees a smile with a hint of devious tugging at the corners of her mouth. She's not looking at him.

As he backs out through the door, without looking his way she asks, "Are you going to invite me to your new place when you get it open?"

Oh Jesus, he thinks, and backpedals to look at her, tries not to be clumsy and is anyway. Hopeful, he tries to read her face but finds it inscrutable. "You, and whoever, will definitely be on the VIP list."

He gets nothing but a calm look and a half nod in return. "Okay, thanks. Probably catch you in the morning."

He scoots out the door. "Good night, Mattie," and can't help but notice she is smiling as he catches a last glimpse before the door closes.

Sammy is still at the table, bent over the laptop.

"Searching eBay for cheap brain wave controllers?"

"I'm massaging the DMV files." He does not look up.

"Erasing traffic fines from millions?"

"Not today. I'm checking for software traps attached to my name. I'm a little worried about driving and the possibility of getting pulled over."

"When you get done hacking the government, you want to go grab a beer?"

"Yeah. Let me finish writing a little more code to get around their firewall and I'll be ready to let my program run while we eat."

"Are you really doing that?"

Sammy flips the hair out of his eyes and looks, not unkindly, at Trevor for a long moment. "Yes, I am, but the world is still solid, dude."

"Let's go get that beer." Trevor is watching the floor.

A few minutes later they have the tail-wagging dog in the Jeep and are backing away from the building. Trevor shifts into first and pulls away, then stops the car, turns to his passenger. "Sammy, do you really know what you're doing, I mean are you really hacking the DMV?"

Sammy takes a breath, reaches back and pets Jinn. "On most days I think I know what I'm doing. Some days I have my doubts. I am hacking into the DMV." There is a long beat before he goes on. "Do you want full disclosure on everything Trev? I will tell you anything you want to know."

Trevor is silent as he lets out the clutch again, continues away from the building and into the Montana summer night. Plausible deniability, don't ask don't tell. Plausible deniability works fine. "Nope, I'm good."

They sneak Jinn into the bar where he takes up position sweeping a visible triangular patch of clean floor under the table. Sammy and Trevor leave him in charge of being petted to head for the bar to order beers.

"No dogs allowed," The bartender says as they belly up to order.

He looks in Jinn's direction and sees that two girls are feeding him pretzels, thinks they shouldn't do that, that the pretzels will give him gas, then realizes breathing probably gives him gas and shrugs it off.

"He's not really a dog," Trevor says.

"No?" she looks bored.

"Definitely not a dog. He was recently reincarnated from an ancient Chinese man."

"Really, that's four bucks."

"It gave him gas, too. The being reincarnated, bad farts."

"Okay, well you may have some choices to make if I get complaints."

"Thanks." Smiling, Trevor lifts his beer to the bartender. They return to the table and get a few giggling comments from the departing girls, but no phone numbers.

They discuss their potential business plan. Sammy has several spread sheets showing the demographics of Billings. He explains the numbers to Trevor, who is happy that he stays successfully engaged in the animated discussion. He's proud that he is even taking notes and stabbing question marks next to scribbles. The business talk winds down and Trevor is feeling bright and alive, likes that. Sammy has that effect on him.

Jinn considers himself to be a central point of this discussion as well, a good facilitator. Another pair of young women approach the table.

"Can we pet your dog?"

Agreeing that would be fine with all parties, Trevor asks them questions, where are they from, Billings, what they do, they both work at a bank and, yes even with, or possibly because of, the hint of a horny young man, he gets the blonde's phone number.

"It's for the dog. Have him give me a call? I'm Suzy."

"I'm Trevor." He holds out a hand to shake.

"Mike," Sammy says.

The other girl introduces herself and then the two head out the door.

"Mike?" Trevor looks at Sammy with a half-smile.

Sammy slides a perfect Montana license across the table. Without picking it up, Trevor sees that it has Sammy's image and the name 'Mike Johnson' on it. He considers things to say or ask Sammy. Plausible deniability, settles on the safety of a subject change. "Cute girls. I think Suzy took a shine to you, Mike." He pauses and bends to pet Jinn. "Okay, dude. I'm in on the bar thing." Before straightening from the dog, asks, "When do we make the offer?"

"Does tomorrow sound good?"

"It sounds terrifying, but doable. I already told Jake that I thought we'd probably be doing something in the morning so he's expecting me to be late."

Driving them back to the airport, Trevor tries not to wonder too much. There's a comfortable lack of conversation.

~

The next morning, Trevor makes breakfast and then wakes up Sammy. "Bacon, eggs, and waffles, dude. Gotta get up to eat it, though."

He dodges a thrown pillow and makes his way back to the small kitchen and the art deco table. A few minutes later Sammy stumbles in. His long hair is barely contained in a frizzy ponytail.

"Morning; thanks for breakfast." He sits.

"You all ready to make our offer today?"

Sammy nods as he chews waffle.

"Seventy-five, right?"

Sammy nods again.

Trevor scrubs his face with his hands. His stomach is feeling sketchy. "You want the Jeep for the rest of the day or do you have other, indoor, mad scientist things planned?"

"I think I'll hang out at the dorm and cruise the net. Mike Johnson is looking to rent a place off the grid and off the books."

"Like a house or something? Sammy, you're about the craziest thing that's ever happened in my life." He tries to sound offhand. But in the back of his mind he wonders about aiding and abetting laws and if domestically arrested prisoners can be taken to Guantanamo Bay and tortured.

"Like a house; I think I'll be okay. Our realtor told me about a remote place off Ingomar Road out east of here. Apparently, it was part of the same estate as the bank building."

"What kind of place?"

"I guess it's an old ranch house, but she said there's a mine shaft that goes back into a hillside. I think I can get one of those storage boxes set back into that."

"Very prepper dude, with a box in the hillside. So, you've been talking to the agent about renting or buying that place, are you going to live there?"

They're finishing up breakfast and start washing up dishes.

"Not really. I'll probably stay there on occasion as I work, but that's about it. And, yeah, it's all through the same realtor."

"Okay, so we are both going to bunk at The Vault?"

"I guess. Are we back to calling it that?"

"I don't know. It's growing on me and maybe sounds okay. For now, it's something anyway. You like it?"

"I don't know, it's kind of growing on me, too." Sammy laughs. "I'm afraid it's going to stick."

"It might." Trevor laughs, too. "Tell me about your lab, bro." They walk out through the hangar.

Sammy is silent for a minute, then smiles sideways at Trevor. "I kind of thought you were going with the less knowledge is better theme?"

There is a moment and Trevor can't decide if he is more worried that Sammy will go on or that he won't. Sammy does go on.

"It doesn't need to be very big. I just need space for a small reactor and then a few other things and some computers, mostly I need to make sure it's secure, that's my bigger worry and part of why this place with the mineshaft sounds so good. Short of someone with dynamite, as long as the one door is solid, nobody can get in."

Trevor is silently praying that Sammy will stop talking. Bro, you are seriously eroding my plausible deniability. Maybe Sammy reads that in his face. He does stop.

"Okay, Sam. If I visit, will I need a tinfoil hat?" They pull away from the hangar and Trevor notes that there are no black Suburbans following them. He actually was checking.

In front of the building, they meet up with the real estate agent.

"Still good?" Sammy asks, looking at him quietly.

Without meeting anyone's eyes, Trevor offers up a check as earnest money. They ask her to let them know if she gets any feedback from the estate lawyers and head back toward the airport.

~

They pull up to the airport gate and Trevor keys in the code and then straddles the yellow line with the Jeep as they roll across the tarmac to J D Ag. "Okay, Sam, Jake wanted me work the last half of the day and somebody has to work for a living because this somebody does not have a sexy brain to pimp out. I'll catch you after work?"

When Trevor arrives back at the Billings airport at the end of the day, he keys in the code and guides the truck to the fuel island, refills the tanks, then parks and then enters the office.

"Hey, Trev," Mattie greets him.

She looks great and smells of sweet lilac perfume.

"What are you slaving over now?" He tries not to notice that the two top snaps of her western shirt are not done up.

"Working on some financial performance data for Jake."

"More lunch dates for him tomorrow?"

"Nope, just didn't have anything going on at home and didn't feel like leaving in the middle of what I was doing."

"I understand that." He turns and smiles at her. "No bible study or is your... boyfriend out of town or something?"

She looks up at him. Trevor isn't sure what he would call her expression, serious maybe. He hopes that general good humor is lurking behind whatever it is.

"I have bible study tomorrow night," smiling.

Trevor wonders what that statement means, can't decide but finds encouragement in the positive lack of a negative. Besides, that smile must mean something. "Okay, for today then." Trevor heads out through the door into the hangar area. No acknowledgement of a boyfriend, that's not a bad thing.

~

"Hey, bro." He finds Sammy working at the keyboard, hunched over the kitchen table.

"Hey." Sammy looks up from the kitchen table and his computer. "We close tomorrow."

"Okay. Want to head out for a beer?"

"Yeah. I would like to do that. Give me five minutes to finish?"

"You aren't hacking the government again? Messing with somebody's centrifuges or changing the nuclear access codes?"

Sammy smiles as his fingers go back to their dance.

Trevor would have felt more comfortable with at least a head shake.

~

After Trevor showers and Sammy has finished his computer work, they head out through the office where, to Trevor's disappointment, Mattie's not still working. Loading Jinn, they make the short drive across town to the Naked Dixie Chicks where they have now been enough times that they get in without verbal threats about the dog. Sammy sits down at a table and

Jinn settles comfortably onto the floor.

As Trevor returns with beers, a middle-aged man boldly approaches the table. He's wearing an apron and his hand is oddly outstretched, as if it is being pulled by an invisible wire that is leading him along. It takes Trevor a moment to realize that the guy is offering to shake hands with them. The man is pleasant looking and smiling broadly. When he speaks, his voice is bold, almost brash, but oddly flat, his demeanor is not timid but his speech is largely void of inflection. His attention is directed toward Sammy.

"I'm Ford. What's your name, I like your dog, what's his name?" The words are strung together with almost no definition between the statements and questions. His attention is very focused.

Seeming completely at ease, Sammy takes the outstretched hand and smiles warmly back at Ford. "My name is Sammy. Pleased to meet you, Ford," in his slow drawl. "The dog's name is Jinn."

"I like Jinn," He continues to shake Sammy's hand for a while and then abruptly pulls away and turns the still outstretched hand toward Trevor. "I'm Ford, what's your name?"

Without waiting for either a hand shake or a reply, Ford bends down to pet Jinn and laughs as he is greeted by a lifted paw.

Ford takes the offered paw and shakes. "Hey! That's really cool! He is a smart dog! He can't talk though, right?" Ford looks up at Sammy for an answer to this profound question.

"No, Jinn doesn't talk, but he only shakes with people he really likes and he is super smart. Dogs are funny that way, they can tell who good people are." Sammy says this without any trace of condescension.

"Wow. I like dogs, especially smart dogs. I have a job here. I wash dishes. They pay me."

"That's great, Ford." Trevor smiles at him as Ford continues to pet the dog. "Maybe if we're still here when you have a break, you could come out and have a soda with us or something." Trevor's having a hard time assembling the moving parts of this encounter. That Ford is mentally impaired is clear, but the juxtaposition of the clear, handsome face and the very low IQ is oddly jarring.

"You guys are nice. I'd better go back to work. Thanks!" Ford turns and heads back to the kitchen.

Sammy and Trevor discuss how they will go about the next bits of navigating the health department paperwork and investigating permitting issues when Ford shows back up with their plates. He also carries a third plate with a sandwich on it, which he sets down near Sammy.

"I'll be right back." He hurries back into the kitchen.

Trevor catches the eye of the bartender and smiles in her direction as he nods slightly and shrugs, trying to convey that Ford's presence at the table will be welcome. The bartender does not smile or shrug back.

Ford returns with three glasses, again says, "I'll be right back," and returns for the third and final time with a bowl of water and a dog treat. These he gives, almost reverently, to Jinn. "There you go, buddy." He scoots into the chair beside Sammy and looks up at them, first Trevor and then Sammy, "I like you guys." He begins eating but stops, looks up suddenly and tells them, "P B and J." holds the sandwich up to clarify that he wasn't talking about a new brand of auto or a political party. "My momma said it'll make me grow smart."

"Dude," Trevor pats Ford's back, "you seem pretty smart already."

"Momma said sometimes people can be mean and sometimes they are mean, but not very often and if you are smart they will be less mean."

"Do you live with your mom?" Sammy asks.

"No, I live in a grope home. Mom went home to be with the Lord and Daddy. I live with my buddies in the home. That's a house full of retards, a grope home is, in case you didn't know."

Trevor debates actually pinching himself. He pulls in a single, long, not laughing breath and manages to speak clearly. "You live in a group home?" Out of the corner of his eye Trevor notices that Sammy might actually be biting his own cheek. "I always heard that group homes were places for a bunch of regular guys to live, guys like you or us. Sam and I kind of live in a group home of our own."

"I'm a regular guy?"

"You're as regular as we are," Sammy adds.

Trevor is thinking Sammy phrased that comment about as close to the edge of truth as his Christian upbringing would let him. "You're a good guy, Ford, and that's all that matters."

They chat as they eat. Sammy and Trevor ask the enthusiastic Ford about his life. They learn that he grew up in a loving home where Momma was the best and Daddy got down in the grumps once in a while. Ford felt happy until Daddy went up to have a long meeting with God and then he missed him a lot, and then Momma went after that and he missed her, too, "Like the dead kids." Then, having eaten his smart making peanut butter and jelly sandwich, Ford tells them goodbye and goes back to the kitchen before the dishes stack up so much that, "he'll be here until Hell breezes over and maybe tomorrow, too."

"Like the dickens?" Sammy looks at Trevor after Ford is back in the kitchen.

"That would be my guess," Trevor agrees.

Jinn gives Ford a farewell fart and Sammy and Trevor pick back up on their conversation about their business plans.

"Hey, guys." Donna, the cranky bartender approaches their table. "You guys alright with Ford? I asked him to stay in the back, but he's got this soft spot for dogs. Speaking of which, yours stinks and shouldn't be in here."

"Ford is great," Trevor says. "No worries, we really don't mind."

"Okay, that's great. He's my best friend's cousin and after my last dishwasher quit, I thought I'd give him a chance. He's really, really slow, but he's sweet for a retard."

"He's welcome at our table any time, Donna," Sammy adds.

Trevor thinks there's some subtle menace in that statement, something he's never heard from Sammy before.

"Okay, and thanks." She wrinkles her nose and turns to head back to the bar. "What do you feed that gasbag anyway?"

Ignoring her, Trevor asks, "Are we going to sign papers tomorrow?"

Sammy nods his head.

~

After they turn in at the dorm rooms, Trevor picks up his laptop. He pretends, mostly successfully, that there's not a voice in his head telling him not to look at the damn email. He logs in.

The note is brief. "Transformer, if you know the whereabouts of Samuel Houston, you need to contact me immediately. There can be legal consequences for failing to do so. My credentials can be verified by calling 202-324-3000. Please do not delay. Sincerely, Agent Garwin Paxton."

Trevor sits, watches the computer for a while. He reads the email again, an even forty words. He tries to imagine how big those forty words might be. Are they infinite, like the arc of our view in the night of the turning world? Maybe. On the screen they are not very big. In the real world the potential of those words is, if not infinite, is at least extremely large. Forty words. With very little additional thought, none really, Trevor closes the laptop and goes to sleep.

Chapter 7

THE MEETING is scheduled at Billings First National Bank to get the documents notarized and then the former bank building is theirs and waiting for its next incarnation as a pub. Trevor thinks about this unexpected turn of his life as they walk back out to the Jeep where Jinn waits for the news.

"We got it, buddy," Trevor tells the dog as they start driving. After a few blocks asks, "Were you an up-and-comer in the academic world Sam? Are you famous?" From his internet searches, he has a good idea that Sammy was on the road to fame of some sort.

Sammy's crooked smile stays comfortably on his thin face. "Outside of the physics world I'm not. I was starting to get some media attention. Some of my theories were being leaked out to the press and there were some questions being asked in the larger forums, social media and regular news both. That's part of why I dropped out when I did."

"Wow, we should theme our pub as a mad scientist laboratory or something. We could put Tesla coils around and have steam vents and waitresses in lab coats? Really, really short lab coats, ooh, and garters. Lab coats with garters." They pull to the curb in front of their new building and Trevor shuts off the engine.

"Hiring hookers is not in the current business plan, dude," Sammy says, but he's smiling as he looks out the window. "It's going to be some work."

"The hookers would be easy. Pun intended. I should get back and see if Jake or Mattie need anything else from me today."

Trevor gets a congratulatory hug from Mattie who seems genuinely excited. He tries telling himself that it's an excuse to hug him but even his hungry ego can't quite choke that down. She requests that he repeat his promise of a dinner when the place is open and he's blown away when, in response to his clumsy repeat of his query about who she would be having dinner with, she answers, "You!"

Later in the evening, standing in the kitchen of the crew dorm, Trevor pulls out the prepaid cell, hits one button and puts it to his ear.

"Hey, Ames, it's Trevor."

"Hi, Trev! how's Billings? How are you doing?"

"All good, Sam's here with me. We just bought a building and we need you to come to work for us." Trevor watches Sammy as he says this and can't help but smile at the raised eyebrows.

"Okay, what sort of business is going to be in your building?"

"Mostly Sammy is going to rock out, but we're going to sell beer and food, too, and we need you! Here's Sammy." He hands over the phone.

"Hey, Amy, he's on the up and up. We really are doing that. And we really do need you to come and work for us. You can be boss of something."

"You guys are really serious?"

"We are. Everything good there?"

"Yeah." Amy pauses a second, then, "They still can't figure at who died in the fire at Mack's place."

"That's weird. Mack isn't in trouble about it, right? It was just some pot stealer?"

"That's the way it looks. In Stanley, that's big news."

"I imagine. Hey, Trev started the phone call so I better let him have it back. Hopefully I'll see you soon."

"I'd like that."

The smiling Sammy hands the phone to Trevor.

"Okay, Ames. We'll be working on the building for a month or two. Let us know if you're really up for it and we will come and get you. There should be dorm space here by then."

"Okay, Trev. I hope to see you guys soon."

Trevor ends the call and looks at Sammy. "Sorry man, little spur of the moment there."

"I'm on board. Are you working tomorrow?"

"I am. I have a few more days as the season winds down and then Jake is going to let me go remodel a shitty old building, full time for zero pay." He smiles, turns, and heads for his dorm room. "Definitely an opportunity any smart person would take."

~

Trevor runs through the routine of another day, filling and mixing chemicals, but his mind is not there. The email thing eats at him. Now that they've signed on the dotted line, it really is his ass hanging out there so if he looks into this thing, he is actually not being disloyal. He is wondering how he might word his response to the Paxton guy.

~

As Trevor walks from the big Ag truck back toward the office in the evening, it occurs to him that on the current path, he's going to run out of excuses to talk to Mattie. He isn't sure what to do with this moment of panicked realization and is surprised, and disappointed, to find that Mattie isn't in the office anyway. Pondering, he walks through the hangar maze, looks for Jinn, and is more surprised to find him also missing. Trevor thinks about UFOs and Sasquatch abductions as he goes up the stairs and into the weirdly dark crew dorm area and is completely blown away as the lights come on and a collectively shouted "Surprise!" pours over him from a room full of people.

"Wow." Trevor is completely stunned. "Wow." Mattie is there, so are Jake and his wife, Sammy and, more by nose than sight, he detects Jinn. He sees all the pilots as well as Cheryl, the realtor. "I am surprised and have to admit to being a little confused. What are we celebrating?"

"It's your birthday!" Mattie yells out.

Trevor is dumbfounded. He has literally never celebrated a birthday before, that much focusing of attention on a non-parent child was definitely taboo in the Tavish world of Grants Pass, Oregon. There was a time when he had been acutely aware of his birthday, as it had remained an annual reminder of his lack of value to the world. Somewhere along the way. though, he had convinced himself that he had forgotten he had one. "Wow," he says and sits down in one of the nearby chairs, amazed. "Thanks, you guys."

"Mattie looks worried and a little shocked. "It is your birthday, right? It's on the copy of your driver's license."

"Yeah, it is. I don't usually celebrate it, is all."

"Oh shit, do you belong to one of those religions where birthdays are bad or something?"

"No, definitely not. Do they make religions where birthdays are bad?" Trevor looks up at Mattie and grins then gets up and hugs her, kissing her on the cheek as she giggles. He shakes hands around the room, thanking people for coming. Beer is taken from the fridge and one of the pilots produces a half gallon of Crown Royal from behind a false wall in the back of a cupboard. Trevor makes a mental note to knock on the back of the other cupboards in case others had the same idea.

At the end of the evening, after everyone but Sammy has gone, Trevor feels better than he has in a long time. Sammy is sitting at the quirky table in the kitchen area watching him.

"You know, bro, people really do like you. I don't think you see that for what it's worth. I see it all the time when I'm around you. People are drawn to you and enjoy your company, but I sense you have no idea that is the case, like maybe you have some conspiracy theories of your own?"

Trevor looks at Sammy wishing that his friend would stop talking. Sammy stubbornly does not pick up on that mental broadcast.

"You are a good person, Trevor, people respond to that. They trust you and enjoy you. I trust you and enjoy you. I would trust you with my life."

Realizing his hands are actually sweating, Trevor cuts off his friend. "Sammy, thanks, I trust you, too, now shut the fuck up. You're making me uncomfortable." His tone is mostly light, but Trevor is pretty sure Sammy knows it's not an empty statement. He doesn't understand this reaction in himself and is happy not to think about it too deeply.

Sammy continues to look at Trevor for a moment until Trevor, wiping his palms on his pants, gets up and looks down at the still-sitting Sammy. "I appreciate what you're saying, Sammy, but it doesn't really work like that for people like me. You're a super smart guy, but you can't read inside of me, bro. If people do like me, it's for some reason that isn't really there. I'm a poser." He pauses and wipes his still sweaty hands on his jeans. "Sorry, man. No pity party tonight. Thanks for the birthday party. You ready to go to work tomorrow?"

"Yup," Sammy says. "Get me up whenever you get up."

"Alright, and really, Sam, thanks."

"You do know that it wasn't my idea, right?" Sammy says to Trevor's retreating back.

Trevor stops, surprised, and without turning around, asks, "Who's idea was it?"

"Mattie's, I believe. It might have been Jake, but I think it was Mattie."

Chapter 8

AFTER HIS LAST DAY of employment with JD Ag, life goes by in a blur of cleaning and garbage runs, more cleaning and more garbage runs. There are a multitude of sketches drawn on napkins and trips to City Hall for questions and clarifying future permit issues. Laughter is constant and one-liners and jokes are abundant. Sammy frequently gets out the Takamine and jams into the dusty space at breaks or when they quit for the day

It takes Trevor another three days of work to stop ignoring the laptop and his email but after they return to the hangar one night, he sits up and waits until no sounds come from Sammy's room, waits another fifteen minutes, and then starts the machine. He quickly scans the almost sixty emails. One is from G Paxton. It takes Trevor almost a half-hour to carefully wade through and respond to or delete all the other crap until only one unopened email remains.

A few more minutes pass slowly while that email, the one with a blue bar still next to it, waits him out. Feeling like he's lost a game of chicken with the gods, he opens it.

"Transformer, the Federal Bureau of Investigation is aware, through NSA channels, that the user of this email address has been repeatedly searching for information on Samuel Houston. If you know where S Houston is, it is imperative that you contact the Bureau, specifically me, Garwin Paxton, immediately. This is an issue of national security."

Trevor sits still and wondering. This was the guy from MIT Sammy mentioned. What the fuck does that mean? Is the guy trying to track Sammy down for some gooney revenge thing? Way too weird right here.

Trevor does not respond to the email. He also does not delete it.

~

Trevor is pleased to find Mattie is occasionally still in the office when they return to their bunk rooms at night. He looks forward to talking with her after his days of hard work and takes pride in his new proficiency at navigating around the gravitational draw on his eyeballs.

Trevor finds reconstruction to be satisfying and rewarding. As they transition from the cleanup stage into the construction phase, he and Sammy team up to put up and finish new wall board.

"You look pretty good with white hair," Sammy tells Trevor. Along with the two of them, white dust coats everything.

"I feel like I'll be happy to have any hair by the time this project is done."

"As in, not pulled out? It does feel kind of slow, doesn't it?"

"I wonder if Amy will actually show up when we get closer to opening?"

"Are you hoping I'll have less hair by then?"

"It wouldn't hurt my side of the cause." He can't see Sammy's mouth because of the respirator but is fairly sure those are smile lines around his eyes.

"Besides, you have Mattie all hot on you."

"Not hardly, bro. I haven't figured her out yet and besides, while Amy kissed both of us, Mattie sure as heck hasn't kissed either one, so nothing is ruled out."

Sammy leans toward Trevor and through the respirator says, "Okay," and repeatedly smacks one hand against the sanding block in the other, creating a huge cloud of white sheetrock dust that engulfs Trevor.

~

Sammy and Trevor eat lunch at a diner a few blocks away and often head there for a break. "It looks to me like we're about ready to move into the building and give Jake his dorm back," Sammy says as they walk over one day.

"I really don't think he minds our being there."

"What about Jinn? Is Jake working at the hangar all winter or do they take him home?"

"You want a mascot?" Trevor asks as he opens the door to the café.

Sammy shrugs. "Worse things could happen."

They sit at a booth and a now familiar waitress approaches, greets them warmly, gives Trevor an extra big smile, and takes their order. They spend time going over materials and expenses and planning the project. Trevor is surprised when he realizes that he always feels smarter with Sammy around. How does that work? "Speaking of scrimping, what all is going on with your lab?"

"I got one of those shipping containers and there's a guy modifying it a little and setting it up for me. He thinks I'm a doomsday prepper and this is all to get my place ready for the zombies. He also thinks he can get the box into that mine shaft I was telling you about. The whole prepper thing really works in my favor. It's like a secret society and anybody who has that mindset is one of them. Plus, it makes it much easier to deal in cash. I'm kind of enjoying the group on the fuzzier side of rationality, it's way more sane than academia."

"How about the parts you're having built. Are you spinning that to be doomsday stuff, too?"

"Mostly; my supply chain is complicated."

"So, your paranoid side is having a heyday?"

Sammy raises his eyebrows a little, takes a breath, and then sighing, says, "I've set up a series of blind hand offs where the parts get delivered to one party and are then shipped off to another. It's all cash so delivery is to a storage unit by the first shipper. An independent person picks it up from that unit and moves it to another. It's then picked up from the second place by another shipper. This process happens a couple of times with each piece."

"Holy shit! You are a therapist's dream come true! How do you find these people and how do you know they won't rip you off?"

"For starters, they're mostly former or current cops. I've found most of them through online sites and have background checked each of them. The deal I've been offering is straight up. The money's good and they're free to look inside the crates. It's guaranteed to be legal and as a prepper, I'm looking out for my constitutional rights to disappear and be ready."

"You believe that your super-secret stuff will stay out of bad guy hands that way?"

"I do. As long as I can stay under the radar."

Trevor nods as he considers this. "So, for the dots to be connected, somebody would have to have been watching every machine shop or custom electronics shop and then would have to track the pieces while literally keeping them in sight, that's your theory?"

"Mostly that's it. I believe there's no phase of the project that can be easily traced. The only weak link I can see in my scheme is that the NSA and FBI computers could have picked up the emails that I sent, but I spent a lot of time making sure those messages didn't have any of the flag words or phrases that might get tagged, and I never use my real name in any way on the internet. So, there's that."

Trevor looks out the window. "They could really do that? Pick up emails from the zillions out there by key words or your name?"

"Yeah, they could. The whole thing is a lot like writing virus protection software. You can't really stop a hacker from hacking; there's always a way to get in. The real goal is to make it use up too much in the way of their resources. That's the theory I'm using with the parts for my equipment. I make it such a total pain in the ass to follow any of it so that, without a solid lead, they will never focus enough energy on any of the crumbs left behind."

"Are you ready to go back to building a pub?"

Sammy shakes his head, tossing his long hair over a shoulder, producing a small cloud of white dust. "Ready, let's go apply calcium carbonate with vinyl polymer and hydroxypropyl amylopectin phosphate additive."

"Sheet rock mud?"

Sammy nods as they make their way back toward their bank building. The rest of the day is spent generating dust as they sand and finish the hallway walls. They decide the effort produces reasonably satisfying results. Sammy runs his hand over the expanse of wall. "It's pretty good for a low budget operation."

~

As they roll up to the J D Ag building, Trevor notices Mattie's car out front, despite it being almost seven. He looks forward to seeing her and as he walks into the building he's surprised to see her wearing a suit.

"Hey, Mattie, what's up?" Trevor asks, disappointed in the dress code.

"Hi, Trevor. Are you guys ready to go have a drink?"

Surprised, "Sure," Trevor answers as Sammy steps into the office beside him. "Are you okay?"

"I spent the day with some idiot attorney going over contract stuff for Jake and I'm about done for, is all."

"Oh, man, sorry, Mattie. That sounds about like being water boarded and, yeah, we would love to buy you a drink!"

Mattie looks up, there is a remote suggestion there, like an echo of an echo, of a smile. "Can I meet you guys at the Dixie Chicks. That's where you've been going, right?"

"Yep, we were just grabbing some stuff and checking to see if Jinn wants to go and then we're heading out." He lies.

"Okay," Mattie says. "I'm going to run by my house and then come and find you."

"I can drive you if you like. Sammy could meet us there," Trevor suggests.

Mattie shakes her head. "No, I'm okay. Go get your dog." Mattie tilts her head toward the hangar door.

Trevor steps through the door with Sammy. They see Jinn lying mostly sideways in a packing box under an aircraft. "Hey buddy, do you want to go get a beer?"

Jinn, in full agreement, hops up and wags that yes, going to the bar is a solid idea.

Trevor and Sammy bound, like a well-trained SWAT team, up the stairs, shower and change clothes in a mere five minutes and then head back down the stairs to collect the dog.

They coax Jinn out of his shipping box with promises of pretzels and phone numbers, gather in the Jeep and make the drive to the Naked Dixie Chicks where they get a weirdly mixed smiling-scowl from the bartender. They let Jinn pick a table and then slide easily into the familiar discussion about plans for the building and business. Within minutes Ford materializes from out of the kitchen carrying a plate with a neatly trimmed sandwich and four dog treats.

Ford hunkers down and solemnly feeds each individual biscuit to Jinn, then sticking to his ritual, straightens and thrusts out his hand. "Hi Trevor, hi Sammy. Can I sit with you guys? Donna said it was probably alright and you wouldn't bind."

Trevor can't help himself. "We rarely bind, buddy, and definitely not when it's about you."

"It's nice to see you guys! I'm going to eat my sandwich now. I only have some minutes and then I gotta be working."

Sammy pats Ford's shoulder. "No worries, buddy."

As the PB&J disappears, Sammy and Trevor continue their discussion.

"So the math favors natural gas forced air," Sammy says, "though the environment would benefit more from an electric heat pump, provided that electricity comes from a hydro source. Coal fired is a little iffy. If it's from an updated plant with a scrubber, it's kind of a toss-up, about the same carbon footprint either way."

"Sorry, dude," Trevor says. "You're already saving the world so we are squared up on guilt payments. The natural gas furnace is about eighteen hundred dollars cheaper. What do you say we just go with that and let somebody else worry about the environment?"

Sammy pauses a moment. His face is mostly neutral with subtle hints of complicated lurking. "Okay, we can go with that."

They talk a little more about energy cost, the potential of higher natural gas costs, and the impact that would have on the business. Ford has finished his sandwich and glass of milk and is raptly focusing on the conversation. He watches each person intently as they speak and then, like a spectator at a tennis game, switches his head to focus on the new speaker when the topic is volleyed between them.

Besides finding this behavior irritating, Trevor also has a difficult time concentrating as his focus keeps getting drawn back to bobble head Ford. He wonders what would happen if they both started talking at once. He considers trying this and decides that it would be fun, but also cruel. After a few minutes, though, it's driving him crazy. Stopping mid-sentence, he turns to Ford. "What do you think, Ford? Where do you see the industry going?"

Ford looks at him in uncomfortable confusion. "The industry?" he asks, drawing the words out.

Trevor continues, "Yeah, do you think natural gas prices will continue to drop with enhanced fracking processes? I believe an infrastructure is being built that should facilitate distribution, and that will probably help bring costs down. What're your thoughts?"

"I dunno," Ford says. "I have to go back to work now." He gets up, quickly scoops up his dishes, and returns to the kitchen.

Trevor does not look at Sammy, who does not look at him. A moment goes by. Trevor reaches down and pets Jinn but doesn't get absolution from the dog. He knows he's an asshole, but some days it's just too close to the surface, damn it. He straightens up, looks at Sammy, "We need to figure out something for the walk-in cooler, too. Got any ideas?"

"How about converting the vault into a walk-in?" There is no obvious judgment about the Ford thing.

"Dude! Not only are you a genius in esoteric bizarre shit, but you are cool!"

"Pun intended?"

They are discussing health care costs and workers compensation funding when Mattie walks in.

Trevor sees she has changed clothes and thankfully, is wearing a tight-fitting western shirt that has several buttons undone at the top. He gets up and pulls out the chair next to his.

"Hey, guys." Mattie bends to rub the head of the tail-thumping dog sprawled under the table.

"Hey, Mattie." Sammy says. "Rough day?"

She nods, "I hate lawyers. Trev, would you get me a drink, a whiskey maybe?" reaches for her wallet.

Trevor stops her. "I have this, Mattie."

"Maybe another day, this needs to be on me." She hands him a credit card.

Expressionless, he takes the card, "Another round, Sammy?" Sammy nods and Trevor heads for the bar. While he waits for the bartender to fill his requests, he stands so that he cannot see his reflection in the mirror, keeping it blocked by some of the collection of boxes that are stacked there. He scoops up the three drinks and returns to the table where Sammy and Mattie are sitting comfortably but are quiet.

"Thanks, Trev, my being independent was a big deal to my Uncle Tony, my mom's brother," she tells this to her glass. "The one point of contention between mom and Uncle Tony was about my dad. Tony thought my dad really took advantage of my mom. He thought my mom was swept off her feet by my dad because dad bought her things and basically bought her out of her pants. That's part of why I have such a big thing about being independent."

"Okay, Mattie, here's to the power of self-bought drinks." Trevor tips a beer to her.

They talk about her family, how she isn't close to her sister, who liked to compete with Mattie for boys, and how Mattie often took refuge from the difficulties of her teenage years by hanging out at Uncle Tony and Aunt Dianne's house.

Ford shows up at their table to clear several rounds of glasses and bottles. His demeanor is reserved until he sees Mattie.

"Hey, Mattie!" He reaches to hug her.

"Hey, buddy."

"You guys know each other?" Trevor asks.

"Our moms were friends," Mattie tells him.

After two beers Trevor switches to Pepsi. Sammy continues with the beer, but at a slow pace, and Trevor sees no signs at all of intoxication. Mattie, however, is getting wasted.

"Hey, Mattie, we can come back tomorrow and get your car," Trevor tells her.

Mattie smiles at him and slurs, "Okay, I'm feeling pretty darn okay." Her voice is low and raspy and virtually screams, on some atavistic level, to a baser Trevor.

He nods. "Can I buy you a drink yet?"

"Still nope." She smiles. "Not tonight, I think. I want the glorious conquering of my head, and tomorrow's hangover, to be all my own doing. You may get the credit some other day, but today, not so much. How's the pub thingy anyway?"

Sammy and Trevor take turns telling her about their plans and share the details of their successes to date. They get some laughs out of Mattie as they explain a bait and switch maneuver with the building inspector. They had faked giving up an easy-to-fix item that wasn't to code in order to hide a harder-to-fix discrepancy. Mattie gives some good feedback on ways to sort through the job applicants to pick out the easier ones to work with. Trevor hears in this is a way to identify the potentially less morally pure girls.

Noticing droopy eye lids, Trevor asks, "Hey, Mattie, want us to get you home?"

Mattie looks at Trevor. He resists the urge to squirm, feeling that she is looking into him and rending his every lustful thought, of which there are many, bare. He's self-aware enough to know that he wouldn't be the first guy to confuse alcohol-induced behavior with actual emotions and can't decide if he doesn't care at all or just doesn't care mostly.

Sammy is talking about his experience at MIT. Eventually the discussion ebbs as Mattie's progressively huskier voice becomes more slurred and the bartender tells them Mattie probably shouldn't be drinking any more.

"Montana is fairly liberal, but I can still get my butt in a sling with the liquor control department over serving a visibly intoxicated patron, I'm already in a bind with the health department if I get caught letting your damn dog in here. So don't push it," she adds. Trevor returns to the table with three sodas.

"I'm ready for that ride home now," Mattie says as she slowly slumps over onto the table and rests her head on Trevor's hand.

When she looks up, with the easy emotional flexibility that can be found in a cup, she is smiling again. "Sammy, you mind driving my car while I ride with Trev and the dog in that piece of crap Jeep of his?"

~

"You doing okay?" Trevor asks Mattie as they pull away from the Dixie Girls.

"Yeah, I'm all not-barfing good."

"Not barfing is good. I'm not sure where you live, Mattie. You want to give me some directions?"

Mattie is silent for a minute as she rests her head against the flapping plastic window of the soft top door. "Is the rest of that bottle of Crown still in the secret stash in the dorm?"

Trevor snaps his head toward her, hoping she doesn't notice through the curtain of booze. She is, as far as Trevor can tell, not telegraphing any hints about her motives. "It is, I think that guy only drank one glass at the party."

"Can we go there? I don't feel like going home. I can stay in one of the bunk rooms."

"Okay, ma'am, to the airport." He salutes her and signals a left turn for the new destination, Sammy following close behind. As they pull up in front of J D AG, Trevor hurries a bit to scoot out of the Jeep and open the other door.

"See, chivalrous." She smiles at him.

Trevor can't help watching and admiring her ass as she wobbles toward the office. It's been a long time since a drunk girl has been dropped in his lap.

"Come on, gasbag." He tells Jinn as he holds the door a minute longer. Mattie lets herself into the building with only marginal fumbling and then the three males follow. She navigates to the upstairs without too much tottering. In the dorm, they discover the Crown Royal, still mostly full, in the hidden cubby.

Trevor pours three glasses. "I'd pour you a shot, too, buddy, but I can't imagine how that would come out of you so, sorry." He hands the two glasses to Sammy and Mattie and raises his glass to them. Having no idea what his toast will be, Sammy interrupts him.

"Et vinum ad gyrum, which is roughly: 'To the circle of life and booze'."

Trevor taps the other's glasses and drinks the smoky liquid. He reaches for a deck of cards that has been lingering on the counter. "You guys up for some cards?"

Sammy nods, Mattie shrugs. Trevor sits and shuffles and then deals five cards face down. "Five-card-draw?" They play through a few hands and then Sammy suggests they bet.

"Okay, y'all, the winner of this hand is exempt from dishes for a day."

"Okay, fine." Trevor looks at a very good hand and, thinking he'll likely win this round, raises the stakes. "Make it a week."

"So, if I win are you two going to come to my house and do dishes?" Mattie asks.

"We will not only come to your house, but I'll raise the stakes on this hand to two weeks, winner gets their dishes done." Sammy smiles at them.

Sammy wins the hand.

As they continue playing cards, Trevor concludes that Sammy cannot be beat. In frustration, he suggests they go straight to trying to stump Sammy at any card maneuver they can think of and the conclusion remains the same. He finally gives up. "Dude, what is this? Do you have x-ray eyes or something?"

Sammy laughs. "No, bro, I'm pretty good with the odds in my head. Do you want to play chess?"

Mattie lowers her head to rest it in her arms on the table and mumbles into it. "Trevo, can you show me a bed-o. I'm pretty much done, oh."

Trevor stands up beside her chair, rests a hand on her back. "Sure Mattie. I'll do you one better. You ready for a carry?"

Mattie tilts her head back and looks at him with partially lidded eyes and nods.

He squats down, and slipping an arm behind Mattie's knees and back, scoops her up in a smooth motion. He is thinking that she might be about one-half drink away from revisiting the barfing conversation and hopes for the best as he carries her to the only remaining dorm room with an open bed. He maneuvers her through the doorway and gently settles her onto the bed. She has passed out. His gaze travels up her fit body. The tight-fitting jeans leave no lingering gender questions, he looks at her for a moment, removes her shoes, then turns and is about halfway to the door when she surprises him.

"C'n you?"

Trevor can see that she is trying to manipulate the buttons of her Levi's.

"Mattie?" Still half passed out, she is not winning her half-hearted struggle with the buttons of her pants.

"Fucking pants. Will you help, please?"

"Undo your pants?" Trevor looks at her. Her eyes are closed but she nods as if she's reading his mind, yes, she really did say that. "You sure?"

"Uh huh." Another nod.

He looks at her face. There is a smile there, an inviting one. His eyes walk slowly down her form again. He has spent a lot of time thinking about that body. Another button has come undone on her shirt and he can see the sweet swell of her breasts. She nods again, eyes still closed.

A snore escapes her lips.

Chapter 9

WHEN TREVOR looks in on her in the morning, Mattie's eyes are tiny slits, barely open.

"Holy mother of God," she groans. "Please… aspirin, death, either."

"Yeah, hang on." He heads for the medicine cabinet, returns with several pills and a glass of water. He kneels down beside the bed. "Hey, I could only find aspirin."

Mattie opens a bloodshot eye and focuses it on him. "Do I hate you?" she asks.

There is a lot of flexibility in interpreting that question. "We stayed mostly clothed, if that's what you mean."

She nods almost imperceptibly, "Oh."

Is that disappointment? Sammy is moving around in the kitchen. "Let me know if you need anything." Trevor goes to join him.

Sammy looks up at him from the New York Times crossword he's working on. Is that smugness in that smile, is that one side slightly more off kilter than normal?

"Good night?" Sammy drawls innocently.

"In the sense that a slow and painful death by hormone overdose is good, it was one of the best."

Trevor wolfs down a quick bowl of cereal and then toasts a pastry. "For the condemned," he grabs a fork and a glass of orange juice and heads down the hall, looks in the door at Mattie's bloodshot eyes.

"I have food."

"Okay. Thanks."

None of the cheerful appreciation that he was hoping for. He squats down to her eye level, holding the warm pastry and glass of orange juice in front of him as an offering, or thin protection from a potential attack. "Breakfast."

Mattie opens her eyes and focuses on the food. She sits up slowly, pulls the sheets up to her chest, then looks down, sees her shirt, "Oh yeah," lets go of the blankets. "Breakfast in bed, wow."

Trevor hands her the plate and the fork and then stands. "I'll be in the kitchen if you need anything." Getting a responding nod, he turns and leaves the room, closing the door softly behind him. Trevor finds Sammy still in the kitchen finishing up the New York Times puzzle and realizes that another finished one is already on the table. He watches as Sammy quickly fills in word after word. "Dude, do you know what your IQ is?" he asks, fascinated.

Sammy shrugs. "Something over two hundred." He pauses, looks at Trevor, shrugs again and goes back to quickly writing in words.

Trevor knows that a two hundred IQ is estimated to occur roughly once in every twenty generations. He wonders again what Sammy gets from their friendship. "You ready to get some work done, bro?"

Sammy nods and speeds up his writing, finishes the last words and then looks up. "Mattie going to live?"

"That might depend on how you define life. I don't know if she's planning on working the office today or what, but she's a big girl. Ready to roll when you are."

~

They get to the end of another day of sheetrock sanding, phone calls, and scribbled notes and to-do list items. Trevor and Sammy walk down to the café for their first non-coffee food of the day. As they take a table, Sammy sets out the laptop and takes Trevor through the three-dimensional depictions of the plans for the building, asks Trevor what he thinks of the proposed changes. They consider and discuss it all and Sammy quickly keys it in on the laptop. He looks up at Trevor.

"Do you feel like you're doing all of the brain work in this, Sam?"

Sammy shakes his head. "No, it's not like that. Our friendship is not one-sided and we make a good team. I think that's good enough."

~

Later that evening as he opens his laptop on the large almost-finished bar counter. Sammy is in his room. There are a bunch of emails, but only one from the FBI. This one is short, even by comparison to the others. "G. Paxton, Special Agent Federal Bureau of Investigation. There is a substantial monetary reward for information leading to locating Samuel Houston. Please call 202-278-2000."

~

Another day of reconstruction ends with discussion about possible strategies they might use with creating microbrews. Trevor believes they will get to be in actual business someday and these possibilities are promising. They clean up using the newly installed, large industrial kitchen sink with its spring hung hose for showering. Trevor stands in his wet swim suit drying his hair.

Sammy looks around the corner. "What do you think about taking a trip to Stanley?"

They grab sleeping bags and packs, lock up, and throw their gear into the back of the Jeep. Sammy turns on the music and twists the volume as ACDC's "Dirty Deeds" blasts out. The Montana countryside rolls by as the old red Jeep rattles them along on the path, retracing their original journey.

After an hour, Sammy reaches and turns down the volume. "Do you know about the infinite universes theory?"

"I think I do. That's the deal where every choice creates two new universes, one for each of the possible options that could have been picked?"

"Yes. That's the theory. I keep thinking about the possibilities for where the Earth is going and where I am going. I keep wanting to ask Amy out, but that's what stops me."

"You're saying that you're afraid there is no future or you're just sure that she likes me more anyway?"

"No, I'm definitely hotter than you, but every time I run through all the scenarios, the ways the possible universes might shape up, I come up in a bad place." He's smiling, but Trevor can see that he is serious.

He looks at his friend, realizing the complications that Sammy's amazing mind can conjure up might be really terrifying and feels, for the first time ever, sorry for him.

Sammy goes on. "All the potential futures I model come up dismal."

"Sammy, maybe sometimes your smarts cloud the dumb beauty of humanity. I think we can collectively find a way to a better way. I think that if we can imagine it, it can happen."

"I hope you're right, dude." He reaches and turns up the music.

Many hours later they roll into the parking lot of The House Restaurant. Morning is not far off. Trevor looks at the bleary-eyed Sammy. "There are some great picnic tables out back."

As they climb into their bags on the sturdy wooden tables, Trevor observes the clear sky. "This sure is a beautiful place. I could make this home."

"Home later, sleep now," Sammy says.

~

With the lightening sky already disturbing his sleep, Trevor wakens to the sound of footsteps. Amy comes out the back door of The House.

"Hey," Sammy beats him to the punch.

"Hey yourself." Amy smiles back sweetly. "I didn't know if I'd see you guys again."

"Well, here we are." Sammy burrows back inside his bag.

"Good morning, Trev." Amy looks his direction.

"Good morning, Amy. Let's go in and make some breakfast. It's freezing and I am starved."

"He's shaping up to be a little difficult to inspire." Amy pries Sammy's sleeping bag away from his face.

"Oh, just offer him bacon. He shares my carnivorous side."

"Alright, bacon it is." She reaches and pulls the sleeping bag down farther, exposing Sammy's smiling face.

They go into The House and the three of them spend a few minutes catching up, then Trevor and Sammy return their gear to the Jeep, collect toothbrushes and clothing changes, and join Amy in the kitchen. She's at the large commercial grill with an array of pancakes, French toast, bacon and eggs spread out and cooking. Trevor leans against a doorway while they chat, switching back and forth between watching her cook, watching her ass and simply wallowing in the aroma of the simmering bacon. His stomach is churning.

Amy and Sammy are deep in a discussion about physics and dark matter. Trevor stops taking in the words and lets them sort of fall on him like rain drops, undefined but noticed in aggregate. He likes being with them.

Breakfast is ready, three plates are filled, and Trevor follows Sammy out to the dining room. Trevor sits down second, next to Sammy and wants to jump up and high five himself when Amy occupies the chair next to him, leaving a gap between her and Sam.

They go through a rundown of the recent months. Amy has been feeling stagnant in Stanley and has little to report. The bank building fascinates her and she questions them about it.

"And you guys still don't really have a name for it?"

Trevor and Sammy look at each other.

"Well, 'The House' is already taken. What the heck is left?" Trevor kids her.

"Let's brainstorm and come up with something, "The Billings Brewery? Sammy's place?"

"Hey! What's wrong with Trevor's place!"

"We could adopt Jinn and call it 'Odifors'?"

Sammy laughs and then, seeing Amy's confused face, explains about Jinn's reoccurring 'condition.'

Trevor takes a breath and without looking at Sammy, says to Amy, "We really are hiring." He smiles in a way that he hopes is not lecherous.

"What's the wage?"

Sammy looks at her, the wattage on the crooked smile notches up. "Good company?"

"So, not that I'm too serious about throwing my hat into the ring with you two itinerant wanderers, but if I was to think about working with you guys, or signing on as chief baby sitter or whatever, is there housing available in the area, cheap housing?"

"There are extra rooms in the Bank building. There's a little bit of a shower issue, but we'll figure out something soon."

"A shower issue?"

"Well, the shower works perfectly considering there isn't one. We've been cleaning up in the kitchen with the dish hose."

"You fit in the sink?"

"Floor drain." Trevor shrugs.

"You can bring a suit."

"Or not," Trevor adds, smiling hugely.

"Hey guys!" Claire walks straight toward their table. She approaches Sammy, wraps an arm around him and presses her head to his. She turns to Trevor and hugs him too. She finishes off the round with a sideways hug for Amy. "It's nice to see you all together again. Are you guys staying long?"

"No, sorry, Claire, just overnight. We have a ton of work left on a building Sammy and I bought and we really need to get back to it. But we'd love to help out for the day in the kitchen if we can."

She sits down at the table with them. "Sure, trade you a room and food? And what have you two gotten yourselves into with this building thing anyway?"

Trevor and Sammy give her a quick rundown on their project. They outline an abbreviated description of the months of work and planning and Sammy wraps up the narrative with an explanation of how the small stage will work in the rear portion of the room, relating how it can focus the band in toward the room or toward the rear, seasonal outside dining area through a roll-up door. "That's what we're planning anyway."

"That's an ambitious plan for a couple of young guys who were basically homeless not so long ago." She looks like they might be pushing their credibility. "You guys have this plan funded?"

Sammy's smile is comfortably in place. "Yes, ma'am. We're pretty sure we have it covered."

Wanting Claire to know they're legit, Trevor tries to shore up the weak spots in the thread. "It was a little bit of an alignment of the stars thing. I was thinking I wanted to be a pilot and worked all summer for an ag spray outfit that paid well and provided a free room. I bankrolled pretty much every penny I made, but I also discovered that I wasn't the gravity defying zealot that you have to be to spend your life that way. Then Dr. Houston here sort of sold a profitable patent thing to a mining company that expressed their appreciation with large bills. The rest was target of opportunity. Sammy found the building the day after it came on the market. It was being offered in some weird estate sale and they wanted to be done with it, so they offered great owner financing. The rest is going to be sweat and good Craigslist shopping skills."

Claire looks at them and Trevor wonders if she might prefer believing that their story is crap. He sees Sammy wait in that patient way which he has come to understand means that Sammy is letting you put the pieces together for yourself. Claire watches Sammy too. She turns toward Amy and her look shifts. Trevor understands then, they are here to take Amy with them, the unspoken obvious, and their story really is hard to swallow. He knows Claire sincerely likes them and understands her daughter-protection circuits are drawing heavy amperage right now.

Claire glancing at her watch, is surprised. "We have to open up in five minutes! You guys better do some work now that you are going to be the competition and have shot my morning down with all of this talking!"

Amy looks sideways at her mother. "Mom, they can hardly be the competition when they are five hundred miles away!"

"I'm not referring to the business."

Amy's face colors a little as she walks into the kitchen.

As the morning rush winds down, Trevor clears tables into the bus tray and Claire walks into the dining room.

She stops near him, looks directly into his face. "What do you know about Sammy? I had Alan search the net on both of you guys after the whole discussion about your pub. I hope that doesn't offend you and I'm sorry if it does. There isn't much about you, but there's a lot about Sammy. The reason I'm asking is that immediately after we searched Sammy's name we got an email from some hacker saying he was with the FBI and needed information on Sammy's whereabouts."

"FBI, huh? Some Paxton guy? I think that's a new scam I read about. It's going around right now. Just delete and ignore it. Everybody's getting them. I think I even heard about it on the news."

She put her hand on his arm. "Thanks, Trevor, that makes me feel better."

Claire turns away, smiling a little. Trevor watches her as she goes and wonders how he would feel if he had a daughter who was considering moving to another state with a brilliant Sammy and a guy who lies.

~

They finish out the day with a good-sized dinner crowd. Amy and Claire field a few comments from the locals about the boys being back and share in the disappointment that, no, they aren't staying. At one point Alan walks in and gets several ribbing jokes about how much better the food is tonight without him in the kitchen. He responds with how much better it is to be doing something that doesn't involve cooking for those who do not appreciate his skills.

After closing, they all fall effortlessly back into their choreographed dance to finish out the day and settle the restaurant in order to leave it locked and loaded for the next day. At length, after The House is put to bed, they gather at the back door, where Sammy had left the guitar and, with him in the lead, they all head to the sandbar.

The night is clear and cool and the stars are shining. Trevor works at getting a fire going. Alan brings two chairs for him and Claire. "You young and less achy types are on your own. Thanks for the day off, by the way. I got a lot done that has been on my... well... Claire's list for a long time."

"No problem," Sammy says. "I think we're good through late tomorrow afternoon if you want another."

Alan leans back in his chair and looks at the stars. Trevor notices this, sees Claire looking at Amy and feels like something heavy is waiting among them.

"Tell me about your project?" Alan asks without looking away from the sky.

They give another shared explanation, describe the building, the work and their plan for the pub's future. Sammy picks out quiet melodies as they talk. Amy sits between Sammy and Trevor, leaning against the same log.

After the fire is burning well, Alan asks more questions about the building and their plan. Trevor realizes again that he hasn't really given Alan the credit he deserves. Alan is a shrewd and intelligent businessman, if a generally understated person.

"So where did the money for the building come from again?" Alan circles back to this question. Trevor and Sammy have skipped by it twice without providing any real substantive information. Trevor is unsure how to respond. His part is easy; Sammy's is a little harder to explain. He waits a beat to see if Sammy will answer, then wades in and tells them about the summer with JD Ag, Jake, and frugal living, finishes with, "That was all my hard work. Sammy robbed banks or serviced old ladies or something."

There's a little laughter and Trevor wonders if Sammy is blushing behind his long hair.

"No banks or old ladies. I just sold some technology, a patent, to a mining company. I also helped them set up the modifications to their process. It worked out good for them and for me as well." He finishes off with a quick rift on the guitar and a shrug.

The implausibility of Sammy is pretty big sometimes. He believes Sammy is honest, just isn't sure that Sam's version of honesty is actually true. He thinks back to Claire's statement earlier in the day and ponders the possibility of his own naiveté.

"So, you know that sounds a little sketchy?" Alan asks without malice.

Sammy looks at them, his smile barely visible. "I understand how it looks," But does not add any additional explanation.

They share the rest of the beer and keep wood in the fire while enjoying the clear Idaho mountain night sky. Sammy plays a variety of songs, does a few new millennium country songs, and several requests. Trevor thinks the night is good, the beer and music are good, and the company is the most wonderful thing he can imagine.

Eventually Alan mentions that it's almost midnight and the restaurant will be probably packed in about seven hours. The group calls it a night. They kick the fire, scattering the coals and embers across the sand, and gather up the chairs. Claire gives everybody a hug and trails across the sandbar toward the house. Alan stands for a moment and looks at the remaining three, then reaches out a hand to Trevor, but instead of a shake, pulls him in and wraps him up in a hug. Alan turns to Sammy, does the same, then reaches for Amy and lifts her off her feet into a strong embrace, sets her back onto the sandbar and follows Claire toward the house. He lifts a hand over his shoulder without looking back, waves and says, "Six o'clock."

They walk silently back toward the motel, listening to the night as they walk. Trevor wonders, for the millionth time, what goes on in Sammy's head.

At The House, Amy turns to them. "Mom said to put you guys in the suite; nobody's in it tonight and she likes you guys, so there you go... big boy beds."

By the dim moonlight Trevor can see that she's smiling, and he will think a lot about that smile in the future. Those golden eyes are amazing, all the more by moonlight.

"I have the passkey with me and will let you guys in if you want to grab your gear out of the pink death there."

After Trevor and Sammy retrieve their backpacks from the Jeep and fall in line behind Amy, she leads them to a newer section of the motel just across the street from the restaurant and unlocks the door. Trevor walks past her and gets a hug and a kiss on the cheek. He steps into the room, turns in time to see Amy reach up on her toes and kiss Sammy's cheek, too. Trevor finds this disappointing. No kiss on the lips tonight for either him or his long-haired Texan friend. Amy closes the door behind Sammy, whose face is unreadable.

Chapter 10

THE SOUND of the Sunday morning alarm clock is unwelcome. Trevor starts the day by firing one of his pillows at the alarm, but the shot goes wide and bounces off the wall. He takes stock and realizes that he only has one pillow remaining and concludes the situation is critical, he may as well get up.

After showers, they head to The House. Claire is already there and Trevor finds it odd that Amy is not. This will be the first time they have gotten here before her in the morning. He heads for the sinks, having lost the best two-out-of-three 'paper scissors rock' game on the way across the street.

After the last of the lunch crowd disappears, Trevor pokes his head around the corner to where Sammy is cleaning off the grill, looks at him for a moment, then, "You ready to roll, bro?"

Sammy nods.

Sammy and Trevor stow everything in the Jeep for the trip back to Billings, then join everyone in the foyer of the otherwise empty restaurant. There is a round of goodbyes and hugs. Alan and Claire promise to come to Billings and check out the new pub. Amy gives hugs and promises nothing and then the two of them are out the door and heading for the Jeep. There are no kisses for either Sammy or Trevor. The drive is long and empty of conversation and they let the music drown out the noisy soft top for most of the night.

~

Pulling up in front of the bank building as the eastern sky starts to glow, Trevor looks at Sammy, who looks back, bleary-eyed and blinking. "You could have slept, you know."

"And miss the chance of being awake when I die from your crappy driving? No, thanks."

"Dude, my driving is great! What's up with the redhead chick anyway?"

"I don't know, bro." They climb out of the Jeep and stumble into the old bank building.

~

Later in the morning, Trevor is taping off the dining area when Sammy walks in. His long hair is matted and disheveled. "Staying up all night kicks my butt." He scratches his head.

"God, that does me wonders!" Trevor says, nearly laughing.

"Driving all night does you wonders?"

"No; seeing your superman-like self struggling does me wonders. I'll cut my gloat short here, though, you see anything that needs touching up before we texture?"

"Nope. Are you going to do a knock down or straight up orange peel finish on the walls?"

"Knock down," then, "Dude, what was our trip to Stanley about?"

Sammy shrugs. He looks around the room, not at Trevor, grabs a roll of blue tape. "To visit, I guess." Pauses, then, "I need to take a day or two this next week to head out to the farm. Some stuff is getting delivered."

Trevor's radar lights up on these statements. "I'd almost forgotten your crazy scientist side. You don't know what day yet?"

"Not yet, waiting for a call."

Trevor wonders if Sammy is hiding something and thinks about the general idea of trust, and his FBI emails, and looks at his friend closely. Trevor thinks about not believing Sammy, can't make that stick, but his dark side hasn't left the room.

~

Sitting at a table in Dixie Girls in the later evening, Ford brings them their dinners. Wiping his hands on his apron first, he shakes hands with Sammy and then Trevor.

"I cooked it! She is letting me be a cook! Donna said it's because I'm smart and I hope it tastes really good, because I cooked it myself." He's beaming. "Is Jinn okay?" Ford says. "Where is he anyway?"

"We haven't seen him for a bit. He's hanging with Jake somewhere."

"Will you bring Jinn in again when he comes home from being with Jake? Please?"

"We will definitely bring Jinn in again when we find him. You run interference with Donna when we do?"

"Donna says I'm not supposed to run." His brow furrows. "That doesn't mean you can't bring him in, does it?"

"No, buddy, it's all good. Trevor was being silly. We'll bring Jinn in to see you, I promise."

"Okay, I'd really like to see him. I gotta get back to work or Donna will kick me in my butt." Ford hurries back to the kitchen.

"What's the deal anyway? Amy's not liking us and Mattie hates me, because I did or did not sleep with her, I'm not sure which. Do Jake and the dog not like us now, too?"

"Let's head out to the airport tomorrow. We have the main lobby area all finished except for paint. My stuff hasn't been delivered to the farm yet. Let's duck in and see if we can get some free lunch."

"Okay. We'll plan that. This is a really good burger. Ford did great."

"I don't expect Donna is going to give him a raise any time soon."

~

After working a few hours in the morning, Trevor calls JD Ag. Mattie answers.

"Hey, Mattie, it's Trevor." He feels his pulse race as he waits for her to respond. The long millisecond stretches as he waits to read her tone.

"Hey, Trev! I've been thinking about you."

"Ditto," he says, confused and relieved by the response and trying not to sound eager. "Sammy and I were thinking about swinging by later on. You guys going to be there?"

"I will be for sure. I don't know about Jake."

"What's up with Jake? This is the slow time when he's supposed to be chilling around the hangar."

"Yeah, he's not doing normal work stuff. There have been some FAA guys here from DC," she tells him. "What time are you thinking of being here?"

Trevor wants to sound off hand. Telling her that he'll be there about one, they agree to go to lunch and he ends the call. He can't imagine what federal agents, FAA or otherwise, want with Jake and the coincidence between this and Paxton's emails is a nagging concern and pushes the Oh-Shit meter right up into the red.

He finds Sammy. "Hey, I just talked with Mattie. Jake is busy, but she's open for lunch. Want to go with me?"

"Is she still being weird with you about the other night? I don't know if I want to be in the middle of that. Besides, I have some computer things to do. I'll take a rain check."

"Thanks, bro, I was hoping to tap into your analytical mind and see if you could help me understand the female psyche a little. I still don't know what the heck that whole drunk night thing was about, but I'll try and dig a little and maybe come up with an answer. Thanks. I'll bring you back a doggie bag and a thorough description of whatever Mattie's bra looks like today."

"You still favoring the purple one?"

"It's all about the contents, not the packaging."

"Well, if you come back with knowledge of that, I don't think I want you to share."

"Okay. No kiss and tell." Trevor walks off to start painting one of the now-finished rooms.

~

Trevor punches in the code at the airport gate and rolls the Jeep through the opening and onto the property. He diligently straddles the yellow line, marveling again at how weird it is to drive on top of the line instead of to one side of it.

He finds Mattie in the office and can tell that Jinn isn't too far away, "Hey," he says as she looks up at him.

"Hey yourself, stranger, where have you been, anyway?"

Trevor is perplexed, having assumed she was avoiding him somehow. "Oh,

110

getting all of the sheetrock dust, wood splinters and paint splatters that I could ever want." He asks if Mattie is ready to get some lunch.

She is and offers to drive. "Not because I don't like your driving, I'm just not so hot on your car."

"It works well when Jinn is involved. Good air flow."

At the restaurant, they find a table and Trevor sits across from her. They chat about the pub project for a while.

"You guys settle on a name for sure yet?"

"Not really. 'The Bank Building,' 'The Vault,' we even thought about 'Sam's Place,' but Sammy really doesn't want his name on it anywhere."

"Is he shy or what?"

Trevor shakes his head. "He is shy, but his reluctance with the name is more like paranoia."

They talk through another half hour until Mattie says she has to get back to work and Trevor says he feels pretty sure that Sammy is tapping his foot and clock watching until his only minion returns. Mattie returns him to the airport and his pink Jeep and he watches her skirted ass as she saunters back into the building.

Halfway between the airport and the bar, Trevor pulls the Jeep over. He opens the smart phone and scrolls through his emails. There's another one from G. Paxton. "Mr. Tavish, please contact me," followed by a phone number. That's to the point.

~

Walking into their future pub, Trevor catches sight of Sammy wafting from the kitchen area. He is completely white, ghost-like and trailing sheetrock dust.

"The purple one again?"

Trevor smiles and shrugs, embarrassed. "I forgot to look. I was too busy trying to figure out if I'm still in hot water or not and why. I think I'll go work back on the store room area. How's that sound?"

Sammy nods. "What do you think about working on the stage? I was thinking that as the weather gets warmer we could start doing some open door jamming and maybe start getting some notice that way."

"That's a great idea, bro. I'll see what I can get done." They talk for a while about how the combination stage and loading dock would be configured.

"Other than being free of obvious lingerie, was your lunch good?"

"Yeah, it was nice."

"She doesn't hate you for not taking advantage the other night?"

"Not that she was willing to tell me about over sandwiches. I can't figure out if she was angry because I went along with her a little way and she ended up with no pants on or because I didn't go along with her enough and she ended not completely naked. It's confusing." He walks toward the back of the building to survey the site of the planned skirmish. Sittings on the stage, he sips quiet coffee and wonders what the future will bring. When the coffee cup is empty of both hot liquid and excuses to stall, Trevor grabs the sledge hammer and swings into the plaster wall. There is something fundamentally satisfying about destruction and the sweaty process of smashing and sawing in preparation for the installing the new roll-up door. The weather is, fortunately, clear and warm.

Toward the end of the decaying day, Trevor is finishing the platform at the back wall of the building when Sammy approaches. "Dude, check out your work. This is looking great." Sammy hops onto the combination stage and loading dock.

"Added cool touch," Trevor stands to the side and waves a hand out, "gear locker underneath. I spanned a couple of spaces so there's a place to stash the equipment. Look at this, though, I found a funky photo hidden in the wall where I was tying in some of the stage framing."

"Bro, I'm impressed, you got the whole roll-up framed, wow! Show me the picture?"

"We need to start looking for the rest of the band." Sammy looks down at Trevor from the stage.

"Yes, sexy chick singer would be a great idea!"

"Sure, we will get that on the list but it's music first, boobs second."

Trevor picks up the sepia-toned, grainy photograph, hands it to Sammy.

There are four people and a dog, facing the camera. The group, three men and a woman all have bandanas over their faces, bandit style. They are each holding a hand out with thumbs up.

"What the heck do you think that's all about?" Sammy hands the photo back to Trevor. "Keep it? We can research the building some more later to try and see what we can come up with?

After cleaning up they make the short drive over to the Naked Dixie Girls. Greeting Donna on the way in gets the predictable lukewarm, and mechanical response.

"She loves us," Trevor tells Sammy. "Beneath that crusty veneer is an even crankier person than the one we are normally treated to. She saves her good side for us."

After they sit down, Ford comes through the swinging doors from the kitchen area. His face beams when he sees them, but dims as he looks to the floor beneath their table. He walks up, sets two water glasses carefully down, then reaches out with a ceremonious air and shakes, first with Sammy and then Trevor.

"No Jinn?" He is worried.

Trevor shakes his head. "Nope, his owner, our friend Jake, is traveling and Jinn is with him. We haven't seen much of either one of them."

"Oh, okay. I would be a friend with you guys too." Ford's odd tone suggests it is a command that has been delivered into his head from a faraway place. He turns slowly toward Trevor. "You aren't still mad at me, are you?"

"What are you talking about, buddy?"

"You got really angry at me when I didn't know about your gas freaking pieces and infracture that was built to do something with distributors."

Trevor inspects the grain of the wood in the table, then Ford's shoes, last, Ford's face. "I, no. I would never be mad at you. I was maybe having a bad day was all. It wasn't you and you definitely are a friend already."

Ford pauses, his face clears and he nods slowly. "It's Okay Trevor. My daddy had bad rays, too."

Trevor clenches his fists a little. He knows all about shitty parents and he is hoping that maybe sometimes, the apple does fall far from the tree.

"Ford," Donna calls from the bar. There is a tone of threat in her voice.

"Oops," Ford says under his breath. Then, posturing formally, "Can I take your order please?"

Ford carefully notes what they have asked for on an order pad and then returns to the kitchen.

An hour and a half of laughing and talking about opening plans, media ideas, and names for their restaurant goes by.

"I'm going to stop in the kitchen and give Ford a tip, that way I know he will get it."

"Alright, meet you at the car. I'm not going to hang out with the always bubbly Donna while you fill up on Fordisms."

~

The roll-up door crew arrives after noon and goes to work on the new opening. After they install the large door and leave, Sammy and Trevor go back and play with the mechanism, marveling at how cool it is to have the big roll-up opened and the stage exposed to the back area.

"What do you think the deal is with the picture? That's a weird thing to do, stash a photo in a wall."

Sammy looks over at the dusty picture still sitting on the stage. "Got any theories?"

"Not really, some funky family photo, four bad guys and a dog. Maybe they were robbers and got caught and killed and are buried in the foundation and the photo was a memorial or something. Or maybe some kind of freaky time capsule, but it seems odd that you can't see who they are. What's the point if you can't make out the people's faces, it's weird."

Sammy agrees, it is weird.

Some further discussion leads to plans on finishing parts of the kitchen and then Sammy grabs his backpack and is gone. Trevor's options for the evening are limited as he's now without a car. Not that it matters, he was spending the evening working anyway, it's just a lot less fun without Sammy around.

Chapter 11

TREVOR'S IN THE KITCHEN, upside down and scooted under the counter area, putting the finishing touches on the drain plumbing when he hears a voice coming from the front area, Amy? He yells, "Back here." and wriggles to withdraw himself. He looks up to see her auburn pony tail bounce around the corner and stands up to find himself in her warm hug. Trevor wraps her up in his arms too, wonders if he can get her to kiss him, doesn't try, for now. He's not sure of the why of that, if that's got something to do with her, Sammy, Mattie, or even just himself.

"It's great to see you." lets him go. "Is Sammy here?"

Trevor wallows in those golden eyes for a beat, shakes his head. "He's out on 'Sammy only' business but should be back later today but I'm glad you are here and Sammy will be, too."

"I think I'm job hunting. Normally careful and pragmatic, now here trying to convince myself this is an opportunity I can't pass up or finding some other flimsy rationale that will make me feel a little more in control of an out-of-control situation."

Trevor smiles and wants to reach out and hug her again. "That's awesome! Let the wild rumpus begin. We will all see where this crazy ride takes us."

They walk around the building for a while. Trevor explains as they go what the different functions of the areas will be. He shows her through the unfinished kitchen.

"You guys built an apartment on the upstairs?"

"Yeah sort of. Four bunk rooms and a bathroom is it. Later on, those rooms will be something else but they are housing our butts for now. Our main focus is definitely trying to get done with the restaurant so we can start some incoming cash flow."

Trevor points to the commercial washing hose that hangs from above the sink.

"This is the shower until we get things more together upstairs."

"You just stand here in the middle of the kitchen and shower with this hose?"

"Yup, that's it. I'm almost done with the drain plumbing and then I have a little wiring to do." Wishing for a live wire that he could grab right now and stop thinking about Amy showering.

"How soon do you think you can open?"

"We're hoping in another month. How are you at construction anyway?"

"Dad has had me pounding nails and running saws since I was ten. I can keep up with you guys!"

"We'll be happy to put you to work then. I have it on good authority that the board of directors will be pleased to take you on, construction skills and all. Come and check out Sammy's favorite part." He leads her toward the back of the building.

Trevor hops up onto the stage and rolls up the door. "Jamming right here, outdoor seating there." Pointing across through the open roll-up door into the alley.

She joins him on the platform, standing close. "I'm impressed, Trev. The place is amazing."

"Thanks, Amy. I'm really glad you are here." Looks into those golden eyes again. "Hey, check this out. I found it built into the wall when I was tearing out plaster for the new door." He hands her the photo that they left on the stage.

"This is a little odd. Any theories about it?"

"None; the whole thing with the masks is quirky. The best we could come up with is that these guys are the original founders of the bank and this was some kind of talisman because, as you can see, they were bandits and they started their bank on stolen money."

"Nah, it's you, me, Sammy, and some stranger telling ourselves something from the distant past. Thumbs up, it's all good, right?"

"Yeah maybe, but isn't that also the ASL sign for poop, too?"

Amy laughs a little and then, after more small talk, heads to get her gear from the car and find space in a room. Trevor goes back to working on the kitchen. When she shows back up in the hallway, she has changed into work clothes, cutoff Levi's and an old, paint-splattered tee shirt that ends just above her navel. Trevor points toward paint cans and equipment.

By late afternoon Trevor has finished both the plumbing and the wiring in the kitchen. He is turning to walk toward the back of the building and catches a glimpse of movement through the frosted glass of the front door. Turning that direction, he finds Mattie, Ford and Jinn coming into the building.

"Well, hi, guys. What are you up to?"

Ford is wearing a backpack, carrying a very large instrument case, and looking distressed. He reaches a hand out toward Trevor, who is unsure at first if it's for balance or to shake. "Hi, Trevor. Is this your house? Mattie said it was." They shake hands and Ford keeps leaning forward in his peculiar, wide, all-Ford stance, incongruous and intense.

"Sort of, Ford. Sammy and I are going to have a restaurant here, and for now, we live here, too." He looks at Mattie with raised eyebrows.

"Well, Jake brought Jinn back. He was here for a day but is now gone again and Donna fired Ford for being slow. He needs a job, and..." she breathes out slowly, "a place to live. I think I've inherited him. He and I are besties."

Ford watches them closely, leaning in on the balls of his feet. Trevor would have read this as aggression from another person, knows it is anything but that here. Ford keeps up the scrutiny while Mattie talks. Jinn thumps his tail.

"Fired?"

"She said I was a food bar."

Trevor looks at Mattie for help. Gets none and shrugs. Wracking his brains and trying to work through the Ford code in his head, says, "There's worse things to be buddy. That probably means that you are wholesome and healthy, like granola mix or something. What instrument do you have there?"

Ford turns lovingly at the instrument case, giving Trevor the chance to look at Mattie. He silently forms the word, "FUBAR?"

Mattie gives him a combination nod and shrug of agreement.

"A cello."

"What kind of music do you play?" He points to an alcove where the instrument will be less likely to get painted, "You can leave it here if you want."

"Cello music." Flatly, then, possibly realizing what Trevor was really asking, turns to Mattie. "What kind of music do I play, Mattie?"

"Good cello music, Ford." She laughs.

"Our friend Amy is here from Stanley. Let me introduce you guys."

They walk together into the building and then toward the sound of singing to find Amy painting trim in the women's bathroom. "Holy crap, Amy! Where have you been all this time? You're a painting machine!" He introduces Mattie, Ford, and Jinn. After they chat for a moment Amy says it's nice to meet them and picks up her brush to go back to work. Ford and Mattie leave the room first.

As Trevor is about to follow them out the door, Amy leans toward him and asks quietly, "Is that purple bra girl?"

"Did I tell you about that?" he whispers.

"Yes, after several beers at the fire last time you were in Stanley."

Trevor nods. "Yup, her."

"You and her a thing?"

As Trevor shakes his head, he thinks about Amy's body pressed against him earlier and shakes his head again. She watches him closely as he follows the other two down the hallway.

Trevor gives Mattie and Ford the tour, explaining all the imaginary things that he hopes will be real eventually. Mattie asks questions about their plans and Ford asks Trevor to say a lot of things over again. Trevor is patient, even with the repeats. Happy that he is not having bad rays.

They all end up back in the stage area. Amy, who has finished painting, comes to join them. Mattie and Amy sit on either side of Trevor.

Jinn issues a quiet, "woof" and a second later Sammy opens the smaller door beside the roll-up.

"Hey, guys." He looks around and notices Amy and the rest of the group. "Hey, how are you doing Amy?"

Trevor watches as Sammy nods and goes to sit on the other side of Amy on the stage.

Amy explains again about being here because of their job offer. Jinn and Ford take this at face value.

"Besides, there was no music on the sandbar. I needed a fix."

"I could play you guys a song," Ford says in his flat cadence. "I know a lot of stuff, songs. I just don't know the names, not very good."

Trevor has no idea how to respond to this. Ford takes out his cello and is fussing with the tuning knob at the top. "Do you know 'Go for a Soda' by Kim Mitchell?"

Ford puts bow to strings, pauses like something is downloading and then plays the song perfectly. They all watch his performance with complete attention.

"Dude, that's weird!" slips from Trevor's lips before he can stop it. He sees confusion on Ford's handsome and vacant face. "Really good weird, amazing and weirdly beautiful!"

"Ford, can you play like that all the time?" Sammy asks leaning in and watching Ford closely.

"No, I can't play if I'm working or doing something else like washing dishes or cooking or pooping." Ford pauses as if collecting his few thoughts, "I got fired from the Naked Dixie Girls, so I guess I could play a lot now because I don't have something else to do like washing dishes."

"That makes sense," Amy agrees with damp eyes.

Mattie reaches over and ruffles Ford's hair, then pulls him in sideways and hugs him.

There is a special quiet for a moment. Eventually Trevor breaks the silence, "Did your network of minions come through on everything?" Unsure what he is really after right then, wonders if he is showing off his friend or trying to share his fears about Sammy's sanity with the girls. Maybe both.

Sammy flips his hair back over a shoulder and nods. "One crate had been opened, but nothing was damaged. The thing is, there's virtually no way anybody could understand what the parts are as a whole, so it doesn't much matter that it was opened. Even if all of it got stolen, none of the parts could do anything without the rest."

"Okay, we can't leave that unasked about. So, what are you building?" Mattie asks him.

"Well," the drawl thickens, "mostly a laboratory. I'm fixing to do some experiments with these theories I have about some particles and the Higgs field. So, I'm setting up an environment where I can do that. I've had some equipment made for me and I'm trying to make sure that it can't be used for anything bad. My goal is to be able to ensure that my research can't be weaponized."

Trevor listens to this mini burst of revelation and tries to check out the reactions of both Amy and Mattie as Sammy gives them a look into his world. Up to this point, as far as Trevor knows, Sammy has avoided sharing any of it with anybody besides himself.

Mattie is unsure, "You seriously think somebody would want to take your ideas and use them for weapons?"

"Yes, I do. I know it seems hard to choke down, but yeah, that's exactly what I worry about. It's why I left MIT."

Amy watches Sammy closely, "And you said that your research is about how the Higgs field affects time?"

Sammy nods, "Kind of like that."

Amy isn't quite ready to let that go. "So, you had science stuff built and shipped to people you found on the internet, who forwarded it on to you, your lab, and that is all to keep it from being weaponized? Really?"

Trevor tries not to be obvious watching as Amy has asks this question. He wonders how his friend is going to fill this gap. Sammy nods and smiles.

"The world isn't always as sane and predictable as you'd like to think. Our federal government is blackmailing about every university out there to make sure anything that has military potential will get to them with no delay, really."

"We need to round up some more musicians." Trevor hopes for a distracting redirect.

Sammy smiles at Trevor, with understanding but without apparent relief. "We need a cook and dishwasher, too." Then he looks at Amy. "To answer the question, I think you're asking, having the parts traced to me would be problematic."

Trevor looks at his friend, long hair gathered over one shoulder, and waits for more explanation, but it does not come. Amy doesn't exactly look satisfied, maybe more like she's nervous to dig further.

~

After Ford becomes an employee of The Vault, they toy with ideas for a band name, but no front runner settles out of the dust. 'The Friends of Sammy' is Trevor's contribution.' Sammy and the Dudes' is Amy's. Sammy tosses out, 'The Bankers' and 'Compound Interest.' Mattie's entry is 'Bull Market' and Ford's is "Thinking about it for a while." Amy gains the titles of accountant, wait person and Maître D, though Trevor thinks of her more as a maître A, due to cup size.

Later in the day, the group ends up back again on the stage. The roll up door is open and they sit with legs hanging off, facing the outside. The sky is dark and endless stars are shining brightly. The photo is now tacked to the wall. Trevor, Amy, and Sammy sip beers. Mattie has a glass of red wine and Ford is metering out bottled Coke. Mattie turns and leans her back against Trevor. Amy and Sammy sit near each other, but Trevor notices furtive glances at Mattie by the redhead. The evening air smells like freshly cut grass.

"I forgot to ask you guys. Are you up for sort of adopting Jinn? Jake is taking off on his weird government assignment and can't take Jinn and wants to know if you guys are up for the task," Mattie asks.

Trevor looks at Sammy, gets a subtle nod. "Yeah, we're up for that."

"Are Jinn and me both going to work for you guys?" Ford's face is shining with enthusiasm.

"That's what it looks like, buddy." Mattie turns slightly against Trevor so that she is leaning full on him and her head is against his shoulder. He's acutely aware of her soft, warm presence and electric existence next to him. He's also aware that Amy is glancing their way.

Seemingly an afterthought, Ford says, "I'd really like that."

"Us, too, Ford. We're really happy to have you, both of you," Trevor turns toward Sammy. "You heading back to the farm tomorrow or are you staying in the real world?"

"Sheetrock, plumbing, and painting being the real world, I guess I'm avoiding it for a day or so." Sammy turns to Amy, "Have you decided to stay?"

"If you guys need the help and have a place for me."

"Sammy is way past help, but I need you and we have real estate available. Mattie, you want to stay, too?"

Mattie's eyebrows twitch, she measures Trevor for a moment, then shakes her head. "I think my bed is a pretty good place for me to be sleeping tonight." Her eyes dart ever so briefly to Amy.

Trevor thinks there's emphasis on the word 'sleeping,' shrugs. "We do have space available."

"Sleeping alone is better for your soul."

"What lunatic ever said that? Walk you to your car?"

"Ford has his stuff in my car. You can come along, too, though. Ford, are you staying here?"

"Yeah, Mattie, I would like to stay. Is Jinn staying, too, and can he sleep with me?"

"Well, somebody should have some company tonight," Trevor says. "I'll catch you later, Mattie. Ford has guard duties."

Trevor watches as she takes Ford's hand and the two walk out of the roll-up door. She says nothing else to him and he wonders how the universe really works. Flopping himself onto the floor, he rests his head on Jinn's furry side.

After Ford comes back with a sleeping bag and without Mattie, Trevor closes the large roll-up door. "You guys want me to show you some bunk spaces?" He leads Ford, Jinn, and Amy up to the sleeping rooms. He shows Ford where he can bunk and leans down to scratch Jinn behind the ears. "You're too stinky," he tells the dog. "Amy, the girl's dormitory isn't done yet, but you can have this one all to yourself." He holds his hand out toward the last empty room. With no idea he was going to do it, he reaches out for her then and wraps her in a hug. "I'm really glad you're here. G'night, Amy." Not trusting himself or what he might do next, he steps across the hall to his own room.

~

In the morning, they all meet and walk to the nearby diner for breakfast. The three discuss finances with Sammy and Trevor trying to catch up Amy on everything that they've done so far. Sammy produces a notebook with rows of columns displaying planned expenditures versus actual. "We are currently under budget."

"That's because you're a slave driver and a tight wad bro."

Sammy nods in agreement. "The stuff we've found second hand is a big bonus. Especially the fryer, I budgeted five thousand for that and we got it for three hundred bucks."

"So, with you and the crazy card thing you do, how about we take some of the surplus cash and haul your skinny butt down to Vegas where you can take them to the cleaners and come back and live an easy life." Trevor thinks he's making a joke until the words are out there and then wonders.

Sammy smiles and shakes his head.

"Are you a card shark or something?" Amy asks him.

Sammy nods his head. "Something like that. I only ever cheat you guys, though."

Trevor looks at Amy. "Never play strip poker with him unless your intentions are to lose." He turns to Sammy. "Why not, though; what keeps you from taking advantage of people?"

"Is this a morality question? You really want to know my inner workings over breakfast?"

"Sure, morality aids the digestion."

"You'd really think I was crazy if I told you the whole picture of my principles."

"We already know you're crazy."

Sammy shrugs and looks between Amy, Ford, and Trevor. "I've lived my whole life with a belief in the goodness of people and that doing the right thing is always just that... the right thing to do. Now I'm trying to navigate through my life with this idea that I might actually be able to change the world, and suddenly changing the world is no longer the clear, right thing to do. Things like giving back extra change and stopping for the pedestrian crossing the street are important and easy. Cheap energy for the world is a much more difficult question."

Amy is watching him. "Okay, but can't you just stop? Can't you drop the research and dig a hole for the equipment?"

Sammy looks uncomfortable. "My theories are in my head all day, every day. I can't let it go. I can't not follow through. To me, that would be about the same as suicide."

~

That day and the next few are spent in a semi-organized frenzy of activity. After the completion of the painting, a load of flooring is delivered, and Trevor and Sammy sort out how to operate the air driven floor nailing tool. Jinn appears both fascinated by the device and terrified of it and looks toward it continuously. He will not approach closer than about fifteen feet from it, but won't let it out of his sight, either. He makes a wide detour across the room when passing it.

Ford earns his keep as a general laborer. Amy's plumbing skills are good and the remaining kitchen and bathroom work get turned over to her.

Trevor sees another email from G. Paxton but puts off reading it. For now, his focus is on finishing the pub, and Amy and Mattie.

Most evenings they end up back on the stage, after a shared day of hard work, sitting together puts a satisfying framework around their efforts.

Both Sammy and Trevor are flirting with Amy. Trevor is thinking about this when he realizes that Sammy has been talking to him. "Huh?"

"I asked what you think about us playing here next week."

"Brother, you can play anytime you like. I just wish I could play with you guys."

"And the mere distraction of learning how is not likely to get in your way." Amy adds, mostly without malice.

~

Sammy strums a soft chord on the Takamine and looks up at Trevor and Amy. "I'm going out to the farm tonight. I have the last delivery of my equipment tomorrow and the pieces that I had built for the reactors are coming."

Amy smiles at him. "Okay, Sammy the science guy, just button up that collar before you go."

"You're making fun of me."

"I played my cello with a lady once and I thought she was making fun of me, but she was not. She was a friend of my auntie's and came to our house to play with me. I don't know why but she did, but I thought it was fun and we played really well together I think. She said it was better than S E X. I asked her if that meant I wasn't a virgin and then she cried." He looks down as if checking this presentation of these facts against a distant memory. "She laughed a lot and that's why she cried, the laughing."

"That's pretty funny." Trevor gets up. "Did she ever answer your question about being a virgin?"

"I don't know, not sure. She said I had an old soul and a young heart and that she hoped I was always happy. That's all. Then she cried some more but without the laughing."

"Too much drama here! Do you guys want something to drink?" He steps down off the stage and heads toward the kitchen.

"Beer, please!" Amy asks.

Sammy echoes her request.

"Are you having a beer, Trevor?" Ford asks timidly.

Trevor stops quietly, turns, and looks back at Ford. "Yeah, buddy, I was thinking I might. You want one, too?"

Ford nods his head. "I would clink one with you guys."

Trevor wonders again about the wiring in Ford's head and about the oddly poetic homonyms it seems to randomly substitute. He returns with four beers and hands out the bottles and then, standing near the group, holds his bottle in toward them. "To us, a clink. May we live forever and never die."

The others raise their bottles. Ford raises his as well. Trevor sits back down and joins the conversation with half his mind on the banter and jokes, but part of him is pulled back and observing. He wishes they could stay like this, going around and around like fish in a pooled eddy of time, preserving this moment forever. The idea that the un-answered questions of the future are postponed is good because the outcomes of those potential futures rarely live up to the promises or hopes. He looks toward Sammy. "Are you ever going to let us come and check out your area fifty-one?"

"I thought we had established it's imaginary." Sammy rolls his eyes.

"Okay, yeah. That is definitely established, but we are sensitive and caring people and will humor you and call your bunny friends by any name you like."

Later, after the group has broken up for the night. Trevor is in his room staring at his laptop. He opens it, logs in and looks at his email. Paxton has written him. "Transformer, we know you are in Billings and we will have Sammy's specific location soon. You have two options. One is to cooperate with us and help us locate Sammy and take the reward money. The other is an obstruction of justice charge, a federal felony, when we find the two of you. Your choice. G. Paxton."

Trevor searches Sammy's name again, resisting the urge to hurry in case someone is somehow watching this happen in the cyber world. He finds many pages, doesn't read any, closes the computer, shuts off the lights, and lies back onto the mattress on the floor that he calls a bed. He says, "Bullshit," out loud and laces his fingers behind his head. You aren't even close, is what he thinks. It's got to be a ploy or something and he isn't even sure it's legit. That there is a real person, very likely Garwin Paxton, trying to find Sammy, he has no doubt, but it might not even be the FBI. Hard to say but Sammy's whereabouts is safe with him. The reward money, that is intriguing, though.

Chapter 12

WHEN SAMMY RETURNS in the middle of the day, three days later, the group is collected in the main dining area, having lunch.

"So, how is the fantasy life treating you?" Trevor asks.

"Great, the bunnies said hello. I got most of the equipment assembled. Everything fits like it was designed to. I haven't proven its functionality yet, but at least the equipment looks cool."

"I'm relieved. Rescuing humanity with ugly stuff would be unforgivable."

"I do my best to make sure all of my lab stuff is up to the highest aesthetic standards and whether or not humanity gets rescued is still up for debate. Did anybody come by or anything while I was gone?"

Thinking about the email, Trevor shakes his head and Amy answers in the negative.

Trevor can't quite let that go, though. "Are we worried about anything specific?"

"Not really."

There is a little tug of guilt. "Okay, good, back to work for me. Ford, are you ready to earn your keep?"

"Sure, Trevor. Can Jinn work with me?"

"Okay, guys, back to the finishing touches on the office trim. Come on, Ford, let's round up your stinky dog and get some stuff done."

As he climbs the stairs, Trevor looks down on the main dining area and sees Amy talking with Sammy. She is standing slightly behind him and he's looking away, but she is very near Sammy's shoulder, very close, leaning in, almost close enough to be touching. After she moves away, Trevor continues on around the corner and down the hallway to the office.

~

At the end of the day, Sammy has the Tak ready and Ford brings out his cello. Trevor trots down the hall and returns with an empty five-gallon water bottle. Mattie is there. He taps the side of the bottle, "drums," and sits on the floor with his water bottle between his legs. He turns to Sammy, "Are you going to give us more details about your real work?"

"I've got things assembled from all of the parts. I'm about ready for some trial runs."

Amy also sits on the floor of the stage, leans against a chair near where Sammy is sitting. Ford sits quietly in another chair, balancing the cello against his leg. Trevor is more or less in front of the others, facing them, and Mattie leans against a wall. Tonight, they are the only members of the tribe there.

Amy is looking at Sammy closely, watching. "Trial runs, as in… run your reactors?"

"Trial runs as in… the reactor has already been run quite a bit, it works perfectly. The trial will be with some of the Higgs boson field stuff."

Trevor is hoping they will all keep their mouths shut. Amy doesn't.

"Time stuff then?"

"Do you guys think we're ready to open soon?" Trevor very much wants to dodge this subject line, wants Sammy to dodge it too.

Nobody calls him on it.

Sammy looks at him with the patience of God. That makes him feel shitty. Not that it matters, they skipped the sticky spot.

"I think we are about ready."

The discussion segues back to a debate about which vendor to order supplies from. Amy will firm up a recommendation tomorrow. Sammy produces his notebook and reads from the list he has of the remaining things that need to be accomplished to have the business open. He tells Trevor that a guy from some government branch is coming soon and asks if Trevor will meet with him.

"Sure, it's not another freaking Health Department money grab is it? What time and how butt kissy do I have to be?"

"I don't really know. We should be all done with those. We just got an e-mail from the Federal Office of the General Counsel. I checked and the routing looks legit. I'm sure it's not a big deal." Sammy tells him the scheduled time, adds that he is positive they are complying with all of the state and city rules.

'Not a big deal' to the fairly paranoid Sammy is a pretty good seal of approval; he'd go with that. "So, if the guy is an asshole I can bitch slap him and we have no worries?"

Ford's head pops up and he looks straight at Trevor. "We can do stuff to the bad guys. Our bribe is really strong."

Trevor processes the likelihood of Ford understanding the concept of buying off an official. "Tribe?"

"Yeah, us." Ford has no self-consciousness about the words switch.

"You have that one right, buddy. We're a butt-kicking machine."

"Hey Sammy, are you worried about your tests?" Amy veers them back toward the ditch.

Sammy looks at Trevor again, still patient, before answering.

"Nope, I've tested the actual technology before. This is just a test of the latest version and the scale of the equipment."

"Well, the bribe has your back buddy." Amy reaches over to pat Sammy's leg. "We will keep you housed when your mad scientist stuff doesn't work out.

To Trevor's amazement Sammy throws back his head and laughs, a full, deep laugh. Sammy then raises his bottle and toasts, "A clink to the bribe." smiling hugely.

Ford looks confused but not uncomfortable. He is smiling.

~

Over the next few days, Amy establishes contacts and credit lines for food delivery and the new drummer is interviewed and signed on for some evening jams. They work hard and successfully as verified by Sammy's notebook and Trevor checks his email every day.

~

Collected on the stage, they are sprawling in chairs and on the floor of the stage. Ford solemnly hands out beers, pops one of his own, a local IPA that has become his favorite. The roll-up door is open and the Montana night sky is sharing its full complement of stars. Mattie's looks in around the corner from the alley.

"Hey, guys."

Trevor hops up and steps over to give her a hand up onto the stage and into the building. She gives him a hug, but it's one of those hip-and-shoulder things. Her body is turned slightly away. The worst part, he thinks, is when he notices that Amy saw the turned away hug. Damn it.

"So, how's the struggle?" Mattie greets the rest of the group.

Trevor watches her make her way through the group and over to sit down near Amy, noticing both that her ass is sweet, in snug fitting Levi's and that everybody gets the shoulder hip treatment.

"It's hard!" The smiling Ford tells her. "I really like these guys and they like me too. We really, really like each other, but we all wok hard, too."

"Are you happy here?" Mattie gives Ford a peck on the cheek. "I mean with the company and the job, not the Asian pans."

"Yeah."

"We are definitely burning through some calories these days. So, what's going on with JD Ag?" Sammy asks.

"You guys will have to show me around before I go," Mattie says. "JD Ag is closed up. Jake and the big air tractor are gone to Salt Lake City; he's teaching government pilots how to spray drug crops in armored airplanes. The other air tractor is in the hangar until he's back. I gather he's gone for a few months. I'm cleaning up the last of this year's accounts receivables. When is opening day here?"

Sammy opens his notebook and flips a few pages. "Next week for some trial runs. You want to come in and be a guinea pig?"

"Sure, I'll come by and see how your cooking plays out."

"What are you doing after the doors close at JD?" Amy asks.

130

"I don't know, you guys want a waitress for the winter?"

"You're on!" Sammy says, still consulting the notebook. "Show up and be patient with our chaos and we'll make it work?"

Jinn gets up from his place beside Trevor and walks softly to Sammy, rests his head on Sammy's leg and whines softly as he looks up to Sammy's face.

They talk for a while longer before Mattie says she's heading home but will be back again soon. Trevor watches her go, keeps watching for quite a while after she is gone. He gets up and pulls the roll-up door closed, tells the others goodnight, and heads upstairs. He turns out the lights in his room and kicks back in the bed.

~

Trevor is working on the kitchen when Sammy's head appears around the corner of the door.

"Morning Trev, I'm heading out to the farm. You got it all?"

"Sure bro, I'm good."

"Thanks Trev." Sammy disappears from the doorway without looking back.

A few hours go by and Trevor is still in the kitchen when he hears the front door open and steps out into the main area to see a thirty-ish guy, wearing a tailored suit.

"Hi, there, we aren't open yet. Sorry, just a few more days and we'll be happy to sell you some bad food."

The man looks at him with a fairly expressionless face. "Mr. Tavish?"

Feeling like a serrated knife has pierced his gut, Trevor sticks out a hand. "Yeah, I am he, and you are?"

"Grant Peterson."

There doesn't seem to be a desire to add an explanation to the name and the demeanor and body language look like cop. Trevor's Oh-shit-o-meter goes orange.

"I'm with the Department of Homeland Security."

"The Office of General Counsel? I hadn't made the connection to Homeland Security." Not the Mormon missionaries but not the FBI either.

"You here looking for radical extremist dishwashers?"

Grant shrugs. "That's government organization for you. General Counsel is over us. Would you mind if I look around? Someone at your business responded to an email request a few days ago."

"Not really; we're kind of busy getting ready to open, but you can snoop around if you like. There are two others here. Ford, somewhere doing something only he understands and Amy, who will be painting everything in sight, so be careful if you like your suit the way it is."

"Okay, it's just a formality, it's a new Trump agenda thing. With all the focus on emigrants, all field agents are tasked with a bunch of extra work." Grant starts walking toward the back of the building. "You are pretty young to be taking on something of this scale."

"Over achiever."

"Can I ask how you are funding your venture?"

"Crop dusting mostly. I had a really great butt busting summer, lived under a bridge, starved and saved like a crazy cat lady and bought the building cheap. I've done all the work myself so less cash out that way too."

Grant looks at him for a moment, those look like cop eyes. Trevor tries to go back to work while the guy wanders around but can't focus. It's too weird. He finds Peterson poking around the stage/loading dock area.

"Okay, so I have to ask, what exactly are you looking for anyway?"

"We aren't sure really, North Korean pizza machines full of special sauce maybe, or Dirty nukes duct taped under a table."

Trevor follows the agent through the building. The whole damn email thing is making him crazy. "Do you find anything with these, uh, checks?"

"Not really. No stray Jihadists yet. There's some extra wiring under your loading dock. What's that about?"

"It doubles as a stage. We'll have seating out back, food, music, drinking, and rocking out."

"What kind of music?"

"Well, it being the middle of Montana, country is pretty much mandatory. I think we'll have to feel out the crowd and see where we go with it."

"Who is in your band?" They have headed toward the stairs that ascend from the main lobby.

That bumps the meter back up to orange or should this all really be on the paranoia scale. "Some local kids. Nothing that is going to make the big time. Come and check it out when we open. We should be open in a few days."

"I might. Thanks for the invite. Do you have partners in the business?"

Partners in the business, no, just this crazy hitchhiker that handed over a bunch of thousands of dollars and may or may not be sought after by the FBI, or by you. "No, I have a friend from Idaho here helping and another guy, a disabled guy. Both are pretty much full time around-the-clockers." That sounded passable. "Once in a while I hire locals if I need extra hands."

They finish looking through the kitchen and, after another few minutes, Grant seems satisfied. Trevor shakes his hand as they walk out to the front lobby door. "Come back after we get things going and we'll give you a discount on a meal or something."

"I'll do that, Trevor.

Returning to the kitchen, Trevor attempts to go back to what he was doing but can't focus. The guy came across as legit. He bends and examines the diagram he's working with. Grabbing his box knife he strips the insulation off a wire and makes a deep slice through the palm of his hand.

A few minutes later, Amy stops at the corner of the kitchen. "That was a little weird."

"I'm guessing you aren't talking about the partial removal of my thumb?" Trevor holds up the wet red rag that he has wrapped around his hand.

"No, I was referring to Agent Grant but your self-surgery there does have my attention. You need stitches or anything?"

"Actually, if you have a Band-Aid or two, or maybe three?" Trevor thinks he really does need to stop the blood flow if for no other reason than the kitchen is currently being violated with his fluids.

"Hang on for a second and hold it up so it doesn't, pour out so much." She turns and heads upstairs.

Trevor returns to what he was doing, periodically wiping the blood off the wiring for the deep fryer.

Amy returns and hands Trevor some bandages. "Lime green."

"Wow, designer colors. What every socially conscious person uses when bleeding to death."

"Funny guy, a little wimpy on the bleeding to death thing though, want me to fix you up?"

"In the interest of not having to sanitize the place, I think a patch would be appropriate." He holds out the red-wrapped hand.

Amy unwraps it. "Christ, Trevor, you probably should get stitches. Hang on." She wets an unbloodied rag in the nearby sink, then wipes the wounded thumb and the inch-long slice. "Okay, I'm going to blot you dry and then try to bind you closed."

Trevor watches her work, willing her to look up so he can see those eyes. He breathes in slowly; her hair smells heavenly.

Finally, she does look up and into his eyes, their faces are very close. He thinks for a moment that she's going to smile, it twitches there at the corners of her mouth, he thinks that she is waiting for him to kiss her and he is going to when she stands up and steps away. Her movement is small, economical and doubles the distance between them to a foot and then four.

"Thanks, Florence."

"De nada." Looking away. "What do you make of the whole Homeland Security thing?"

"The name 'Homeland Security' has always struck me as very Natzi-esq. Like there should be a bunch of jack-booted guys protecting the fatherland. As for Agent Grant, I'm at a complete loss. Back to work I guess but thanks Ames. I appreciate the first aid. Maybe next time I'll be passed out and not breathing."

She gives him a look. "Yeah, maybe. I'll get Ford to do the mouth-to-mouth and I'll do the chest compressions. Will that work Trev?"

Not sure if that's a win or a loss but he likes her using a nickname for him. "Hey, you want to go get some lunch? I'll buy."

"Yeah, I'll get Ford."

The three of them walk to the diner. Amy is in the middle and Trevor is enjoying the sunshine and feeling her bumping into him. He thinks about calling Mattie and seeing if she can join them, sees the sun glinting off of Amy's auburn hair and decides not to.

Sitting through a nice lunch, Trevor enjoys the small talk. Ford's pleasant demeanor, as usual, makes up for the constant string of questions. He wonders what Ford's intellectual level really is, decides it doesn't matter anyway. He likes watching Amy's patience with Ford.

After lunch they return to the nearly finished pub. Back at his wiring Trevor realizes he has almost no idea what the conversation during lunch was about, just that Amy laughed a lot and the sound thrilled him.

Later, they all gather at the stage. Mattie joins them. Jinn thumps his tail as they settle in and discuss the day. Ford passes beers around. Trevor throws an arm around the middle-aged man's shoulders. "Ford, my friend, you are cool. We are going to keep you!"

A tiny bit of color creeps into Fords handsome face and he smiles as he looks at his own shoes. "Thanks Trevor. I like it here way better than the grope home too. I do."

The small door opens at the rear of the building and Sammy comes through it. Jinn's tail thumps furiously as the smiling Sammy walks into the room. His button-up shirt is fastened at the collar and wrists.

"Hey, y'all," Sammy says, beaming rays of his straight white teeth at the group. He grabs a chair.

They all talk through a string of subjects. Trevor is getting a sense of excitement from Sammy, like he's waiting to tell them something.

Amy tells them that some Department of Homeland Security guy was here today.

"Homeland Security?" Mattie is surprised. "What's with that?"

"What did he want Trev?"

Amy looks toward Trevor for an answer, he likes that. "It was about the email we got the other day, the Office of General Counsel? Apparently,

Homeland Security is under them. The guy said there was a program looking at new businesses. They want to catch all of the bad sandwich shop owners."

"Homeland Security, that is a weird one. So, did you guys feed him full of misinformation?" Sammy asks quietly.

Ford leans forward in his chair and conspiratorially lowers his voice. "We told him that Jinn is really a cat."

"That would definitely throw him off." Sammy laughs as Ford hands him a beer too. "Good job, buddy and thanks for the beer."

Mattie tells them she has to go home.

"You could stay here with the rest of the tribe. Nice and homey, comfortable and with good friends? Definitely a really good massage, not all cold and empty like your far away house."

"If I get desperate for company or a massage, I'll head the three minutes back."

"We will see you in a little bit then?" Trevor is trying to see what Amy is doing with this conversation.

"I'm sure we'll cross paths again." Mattie gets up off the floor, heads out the door.

Chapter 13

KEEPING THE CHOREOGRAPHY in step with the tasks on his notebook's "to-do list, Sammy is the organizer, but to Trevor's surprise, and enjoyment, the group, and Sammy, treat him deferentially. The Vault might have been Sammy's idea, but isn't he, Trevor, the one people gravitate to? Is he the power axis in their tribe?

The unofficial pub opening goes well with a large, friendly, and patient crowd showing up. Sammy is subtle and everywhere, answering staff questions with frequent references to what Trevor wants them to do. From his position tending bar, Trevor enjoys schmoozing with the crowd and feels great when they compliment his good ideas, even when he hadn't known they were his.

The band begins playing about nine. The night is warm and instead of dwindling, the crowd swells. By ten-thirty Trevor counts seventy-two people laughing, listening to the band, dancing and flirting. He collects seven phone numbers from a variety of cute patrons at the outside bar and he is thinking that this is all pretty damn promising.

"Hey, handsome." Mattie says into his ear.

"Hey, yourself." Trevor spontaneously reaches out and hugs her and in that one, frozen second of his life, realizes the deep draw of long-term friendship. Sharing with people you know and love is better than anything else there has been in his life, ever. "What do you think?" he asks, loud enough to be heard over the band and the boisterous gathering.

Mattie looks out at the crowd. Sammy is playing lead and smiling while he sings, his long hair is flying and his face is shiny. Ford is currently bowing the cello, looking down, completely focused on this task. The new drummer, Ted, is sweating and keeping the crowd moving with a great beat and enthusiastic percussions. A girl is playing the four-string bass. "I think you guys are the new 'in thing' for Billings."

"Aren't you part of the 'you guys'? You're definitely in the Tribe."

She steps up to him and rests her head on his shoulder for a moment then moves away, smiling. "You want some help tending bar?"

"Sure, yeah. Step right up." He walks away, flirting through the crowd.

After they close down the bar, the staff collect on the stage. Someone grabs chairs but Trevor sits on the floor. Mattie sits, leaning against a wall.

Trevor turns his attention to Ford who is on the edge of the stage, his back is mostly to the group. The bass guitar chick is sitting backwards in a chair, her tattooed arms resting on its back. She is wearing a shirt with a deeply plunging neckline and Trevor can't help notice that aside from her mostly exposed breasts, she could be attractive, if she'd smile. "Ford, what are you doing?"

Ford shrugs and answers without turning. "Sitting."

"I had a rough idea you were doing that buddy. But you're way over there and we're way over here and you don't usually sit way over there."

"I'm okay, Trev," still doesn't turn his head toward Trevor.

Somebody cracks a joke about an impatient patron and there is a good laugh. They talk about the successes and the remarkably few glitches and Sammy keeps giving Trevor credit. Trevor stays torn between giving it back to Sammy, where he knows it belongs, and wallowing in what he really wishes is his by right.

After a little while, without saying anything, Ford steps onto the lower floor and trundles off in his peculiar all-Ford gate.

"You aren't calling it a night yet, are you, Ford?" Trevor watches him shuffle out of sight without answering. Most of the rest of the happy group seems oblivious to Ford's unusual behavior. The bass chick is not taking part. Trevor gets up, says, "Too much beer." and heads toward the restrooms. He does not turn into the bathroom though, heads past it for the stairs. He knocks quietly on Ford's room door.

"You can come in," Ford's muffled voice tells him.

Entering, Trevor finds Ford's in his bed, lying on his side. He has the covers pulled up to his shoulders. His shirt is still on. Trevor sits on the mattress beside him.

"What's going on, buddy?" he asks Ford's back.

Ford is silent for a while and then he sighs. "She calls me the mandatory quotient baker."

Trevor rests a hand on Ford's shoulder. "Okay, buddy, I hear you. The new girl? Did she say the mandatory quota maker, maybe? I'm not even sure that I know what that means, a quota maker."

"It means you guys just have me here because I am retarded and get you a tax dedumption."

"Oh, Ford, that is so not true." Trevor feels a roiling burn of anger and a fierce protectiveness of Ford. "Buddy, if you trust me at all, trust this. You are a core part of the tribe. You are a very important part of 'us.' The girl who said that to you is not any part of any us. You are, she is not, straight up. You are not any sort of tax break, but you are ours and you belong with us. That's the way it is, Ford. Can you believe me?"

Ford's handsome, middle-aged head nods against the pillow. "I think I will sleep, Trevo. I'll feel better tomorrow. Momma always told me that."

"Okay, buddy." Trevor gives a soft squeeze and takes his hand from Ford's shoulder before heading out of the room. Seething, he heads back down to the main floor. Stepping onto the stage, he returns to his place against the wall, watching, looks at Sammy. The group keeps talking. Amy has put her feet in Sammy's lap and he is rubbing them. A conversational point comes his way and they pause briefly for his response, but he doesn't pick up the thread and they gloss over the gap. Trevor continues looking at his group of friends, and the one outlier.

He watches them talking, responding to each other, sharing threads of thoughts or completing ideas for each other. Almost surprised he's speaking, his mouth opens. "What's your name?" he asks the bass player. His tone is casual, calm.

"Lisa."

"Okay, Lisa, our band is going to be fine without you. You're an okay bass player, but not so hot with people. You should go." Icy cold calm, looking her way. His back is straight as he leans against the wall and smiles in her direction. The rest of the group is silent. Trevor likes that she looks scared right now.

Without another word by anybody, she gets her guitar and leaves by the small back door.

Mattie looks at Trevor. "What was that about?"

Trevor wonders if she thinks he was a jerk just now? Maybe he was, but with the multitudes of shittier things that he'd considered saying, he'd been a virtual saint.

"She was a total shit to Ford," Sammy answers, then turns to Trevor. "Thanks, Trev. I was trying to figure out what to do with that."

Trevor looks at Sammy, sees a pleased smile on his friend's face and knows he's done the right thing, but mostly it's because Sammy is pleased. It feels good to have his friends looking at him this way. "It's all about the tribe."

Mattie looks at Trevor and dramatically bats her eyes. "My hero..." she says in a deep southern drawl. "I have to go home and dream about y'all now." She drops the drawl.

"Alright, going home. Goodnight you guys." Mattie heads for the door.

The two girls leave after Mattie. Trevor, Amy, and Sammy are left on the stage. Trevor thinks Amy looks sexy as hell. Her hair is disheveled and she looks tired but incredibly attractive. Her feet are still in Sammy's lap. Trevor walks up to his room. He can hear Amy and Sammy following.

As he lies down onto his mattress, relieved to hear both Sammy's and Amy's doors closing, separately.

~

The pub is full, mostly to capacity, through every lunch and dinner. The bar is a hit and is packed until closing. Sammy's band jams every night. Their current name is The Wrangling Neutrinos, a Sammy and Ford collaboration, and they have a new bass player. The group all meet on the stage every night to laugh, make fun of the less pleasant patrons, share tips and life.

Sammy is sitting, watching as Trevor divides up the proceeds from his very full bar tip jar.

Mattie is in what has become her usual place at the wall near Trevor, too close for any of the waitresses to fit in between them, but no closer than that. "You are an amazing schmoozer Trev."

Trevor makes equal piles for all the employees. "I kiss a little butt and listen." He holds up a twenty.

"Flirting hard with the middle agers again, Trev?" Amy asks.

Trevor nods, smiles, and shrugs and continues counting and dividing.

"You should have another jar for phone numbers. I imagine it would be pretty full, too," Mattie says with a reserved smirk, leaving Trevor, as always, struggling to comprehend the enigma she is.

"Have we gotten any complaints yet?" Sammy asks the group.

One of the waitresses shakes her head and asks for her share of the cash, saying she has to work another job in the morning.

"I did hear a few complaints about possible gas leaks," Amy says. "An older couple stayed later after the band had started and Jinn was making the rounds.

"I think he's still a good addition though," The big dog comes padding over to Mattie as if he knows she's talking about him. He drops to the ground, plops his head onto her legs and sighs with deep dog contentment. "Nobody seems to mind him."

"Agreed," Trevor says. "Everybody enjoys him."

"Some of the short skirts get a little miffed with his investigative greetings," Jill, the brunette waitress adds.

Trevor reaches out to pet Jinn, whispers, "That's my dog!"

"A girl kissed my geek tonight," Ford says with a bit of a dreamy and distant smile.

"On the cheek? That's because you're a stud, buddy," Trevor tells him, barely noticing the misplaced word.

Jill gets up and walks over to Ford. She bends down and kisses him on the cheek. "You are a stud. Alright, guys, time for me to go to bed. Good night all." She turns and heads for the small door by the roll-up, then stops with it half open and turns back to the group. "I really like being a part of this. I've never had a better job than this one. Thanks for letting me in." She closes the door behind her.

"It is good," Trevor agrees quietly almost to himself. He thinks it's not only the best job he's ever had, it's the best anything. The group is tight and always welcoming. He feels more a part of something than he has ever before. The tribe is good; he thinks, I am happy. We have each other's backs.

"I like being here, too," Amy says.

"No, you guys all suck." Mattie tosses her head, laughing.

Trevor softly punches her shoulder.

Sammy closes his eyes contentedly and leans back farther in his chair, "I really enjoy being here too. I've never really told you about my research at MIT. I know I told you about the spying, but there were other reasons I left, too. The competitive atmosphere was ugly."

"You felt under the gun or something?" Mattie asks.

"Not that exactly, no. It's more of a quantum thing? Where the existence of the observer changes the outcome of the observed? The egos were messing with my results."

Amy's face scrunches up. "So, is that a scientist joke or are you saying that the pressure from your peers actually affected your research?"

"It's a little bit joke but not completely. Mostly I needed to get away from that mind set. Don't get me wrong, there was government spying going on like crazy, too, but the rest of the academic atmosphere was very oppressive and divisive. The worst part, was that I really had only one friend, Garwin Paxton. At least I thought we were friends, anyway, and then, after one disturbing visit by an NSA officer asking questions, I realized that Gar had to be giving away my stuff. Worse, after I called him out on it, he admitted that he actually worked for the FBI. He was a brilliant, spoiled, rich kid, but also an amazingly uncreative person. I'm pretty sure that by being a spy at the university, he could pretend he was at the top of the food chain. He was a big part of what pushed me to disappear."

Ford leans in toward Sammy, "Are we helping?"

"You are helping a lot. You and your cooking and table bussing and especially your music is really helping a lot, but mostly your friendship, Ford. All of you are helping

~

A week after they open the pub, Sammy takes Trevor aside after the lunch rush subsides. "What do you think about all this so far?"

Is there subtext there? "Dude, life is kicking ass. Do you think we're ready to start scouting for another location to carry on with our franchise?"

Sammy's smile tilts slightly. "I'm heading to the farm tomorrow. I think I'll make it a two-day thing. Are you good with that?"

This isn't a good time for Sammy to be going. There is a lot of work to do here and they are just getting things figured out. "Okay. You have world saving to worry about. I haven't forgotten. I was kind of hoping that maybe you'd give up on that shit and focus on the chicks and guitars. The value of the human race is highly overrated."

"Don't I know it. But what do you do?" Sammy shrugs. "I know you've got everything here taken care of and I appreciate you covering for me."

"What are you doing out there right now anyway?" He hadn't really intended to ask that.

"Right now, mostly just a ton of calculating, kind of a crazy big velocity and trajectory thing, but when it gets closer to some action I can take you out there. That work?"

Trevor nods, hopefully hiding his resentment. "Sure, bro, all good."

~

Right before closing time, Amy approaches Trevor in the kitchen. "Hey, Trev."

"Hey Amy. Is everything okay?"

"I think so, maybe. Do you know anything about Sammy and his farm?"

Crazy timing for that question. "Pretty much zero. I was going to ask you the same thing, see if maybe you had a take on it."

"I don't and I'm a little worried. The whole story is a lot to choke down."

"Are you thinking he is full of shit or something?"

"I don't know Trev, it's a lot to believe."

That's an understatement. "Yeah, I know it."

"Are we still getting together after closing?"

"Heck, yes." Trevor walks off to finish closing up, wishing the after-work get-together could number just two.

After the doors are locked and the main dining area lights are off, the tribe minus Sammy, assembles in the back. Amy is in a chair, Ford is against a wall with his cello in an open case in front of him. Jill and another waitress are reclined near each other and Mattie is on the floor in front of Trevor helping him separate the bar tip jar into equal piles.

"Hey, Ford, you want canned music tonight or do you feel like being a solo act?" Trevor asks.

"Canned music?"

"Sorry buddy, canned music is a goofy phrase for playing recorded music."

"It's funny, like they stuffed some tiny musicians into the stereo."

"It would be funny like that." Trevor separates the last of the money from the bar tip jar, scoops up a portion and hands it to Jill, reaches another pile over to Amy, then hands one to Mattie and one to Ford.

"Pretty generous, handsome," Mattie says.

Trevor assumes she is referring to him not giving himself a portion. He smiles at her. "I'm so generous that I would actually even share my body with you."

"You've mentioned that before."

"I might have brought it up once or twice."

Amy looks at Ford. "Are you up for requests?"

"If I know it, I'll play it for you."

"How about "California Dreamin'" by the Mamas and the Papas?"

Ford picks up the cello and begins to bow. His tempo is slow, but gradually increases as he plays the large instrument.

Mattie stands as the last of Ford's mournful rendition echoes in the large room, "I gotta run, guys. See you all tomorrow." heads quickly out the door.

Trevor watches her go, sexy as hell and more confusing than that.

~

Later, after everybody has gone, Trevor slips out of his room and pads barefoot down the hall. He heads down the stairs to the main dining area, slips into the walk-in cooler and grabs a Corona, which he dutifully marks on the sheet Sammy has placed there for the employee perks that get consumed. He is about to close the heavy door when a quiet statement drifts from the empty dining room.

"Me, too."

He looks out into the gloom, raises his beer in answer. He's feels something warm and conspiratorial as he reaches for a second beer.

He hands her a Corona and she leans back, her freckled legs stretched out and her arms crossed across her chest. He thinks she's just wearing panties as he sets the bottle on the table near her, then pulls out a chair across from her. "You can't sleep?"

"No, and beer means pee, which doesn't bode well for the rest of the night either." She reaches for the cold bottle. "I'm wondering where my life is going." She takes a drink, sets down the bottle, and then reaches back to lock her hands behind her head. "And how to fit all of this into it."

The light is low, but not so low that Trevor can't see the small outline of her nipples in the fabric of her tee shirt. He puts on a crappy half smile. The dark should keep it from being too obvious. "Whatcha mean, Ames?"

She leans her head back farther and ups the ante on the torture with further tightening of her shirt.

"I'm really lost. I love you guys and this whole pub thing is a ton of fun, but it's not exactly furthering a career in geology."

Trevor looks away so that he can actually think. He wants this to be a

145

come-on, but beyond the perky boobs and his own internal wishes, he knows it's not. "So, you're saying you can't decide between staying here and having fun and getting out of Dodge and joining the corporate world somewhere?"

"Yeah, kind of like that. I love this," she waves her hand around at the room, "but it has no place in my life's plans. At least not the plans that I made before."

"Is that kind of a people versus the pressures of the real-world thing?" Pretending there is no hypocrisy in that statement

"I guess it comes down to that. I love the Bribe, us, the group, but I've planned on being a scientist for my entire life. It is a conflict."

He takes a breath and still looking away says, "I wonder if it doesn't come down to simple trust. I think that if we knew we could really depend on each other to always be here and that we'd always have a place with this group, we'd just do what we're doing. Isn't this the real stuff of life, belonging to each other? The trust part is the weak point. We know the whole thing could fracture and fall apart and then we'd be left with nothing in a society where having nothing means we'll be essentially cast out. It is a big deal and the truly shitty part about living in the twenty-first century."

Amy lowers her arms and looks hard at Trevor. "Where have you been hiding that?"

He shrugs. "I don't know. Maybe I picked that up tending bar." He smiles at her and tips his bottle her direction. "Think I'll head back to bed."

She taps her bottle to his. "Always good to share a clink."

"Thank God for Fordisms. G'night, Ames."

Chapter 14

TREVOR IS DRYING GLASSES at the kitchen sink and wondering if he'll hear from G. Paxton again. The easy thing, would be if he never does. The last email had mentioned a hundred thousand dollars. That's a lot of money and especially to a kid who grew up broke, an unfair amount of money. It would mean the end to the tribe but he'd survive that. That's a weird one too. This is some of the best stuff of his life, but it's all going to be even better, he's going to make it better still. Mattie comes around the corner and pats him on the ass.

"You look a little spacey."

"Can an employer sue an employee for sexual harassment?" He steps closer to her and she doesn't back away. "Or should we go for a quid pro quo approach?"

"What're you guys doing?" The handsome Ford's vacant face is peering around the corner at them.

"Nothing, buddy. Mattie was telling me what a good job you were doing, that's all." He lifts the crate of bottles and moves around Mattie and Ford, heads toward the bar.

"Really? I'm doing good?"

"Definitely good, she says you're the best."

~

Trevor turns and flops on his back onto the stage, reaching up, he cradles his head in his hands and relaxes, staring up at the ceiling. Ford puts his bow to his cello and begins playing a mournful song that Trevor doesn't recognize. The rest of the group collects and settles in. One of the newer wait people hands Trevor a beer on her way by. Mattie sits near Trevor and lies back, rests her head on his leg. Amy is smiling as she mirrors Mattie's position on his other side so that he has auburn hair spilling over one thigh and jet-black hair spilling across the other.

Ford finishes and one of the girls asks what the title of the song is.

"It doesn't have a name. It's just a made up one."

"Wow, that's really impressive." Trevor looks at Ford. What the hell is in there?

After a bunch of random chat and Ford's occasional playing, the group calls it a night and drifts away. Trevor keeps to his spot on the floor where Amy has fallen asleep with her head on his leg. He feels Mattie roll toward him, lifts himself up, catching her eyes. He raises his eyebrows in question, mentally broadcasting the idea that tonight would work fine either with or without Amy.

Mattie gives him a very subtle head shake and he lies back down, smiling and unsurprised. After a little bit, Mattie gets up and goes around to Amy, reaches over and shakes her gently.

"Hey, sleepy head, you're missing all of the fun."

"I am. Wha' fun?" she asks groggy and sleepy.

"We were having sex with Trevor; it was really great. Well, in his mind it was, anyway."

"Oh, okay." Amy's eyes are still closed and she rolls sideways, nestling her head against Trevor's leg. "Musta been good, 's why I'm so damn sleepy."

"Come on, babe." Mattie shakes her again. "Or I'm gonna leave you here on your own with wolf boy and who knows where that will go."

"That would be okay." Amy hangs on the edge of awareness.

Without looking in Trevor's direction, Mattie shakes her again until Amy sits up. "God, I'm tired. Heading for bed." She hops off the stage to shuffle through the building toward the stairs.

Trevor watches her go, "Long drive home."

"Yeah, that grueling three minutes is murder."

He wants to ask what she wants, but either she doesn't know or, more likely, she'll just lie to him.

Trevor reaches out a hand. Mattie helps him up and he walks her to the back door, gives her a hug and watches her disappear into the alley. He closes the door and heads off to the vast open real estate of his own, empty bed and the intrigue of his laptop. G. Paxton of the Federal Bureau of Investigation has written him again.

"Transformer, if you cooperate and provide credible information about the research that Sammy Houston has taken with him from MIT, as well as his location, I am authorized to compensate you in the amount of two hundred-fifty-thousand dollars. Think about that really hard. This is pretty much your last chance. Contact me by phone or text any time at the following number.

~

As the lunch crowd winds down, Trevor is walking down the hall. Sammy is in the kitchen. The sleeves of his button-up and is elbow deep in the soapy water helping Ford.

"Hey, dude."

"Hey, bro. All good?"

"Oh yeah, making money hand over fist and having a ton of fun. Definitely, definitely all good. How was the mad scientist gig? Do you glow now or anything?"

Sammy looks at Trevor, smiling for a moment, shakes his head. "Not yet; soon, though."

"Okay, glad to have you back." Trevor returns to his bar. A few minutes later Sammy pushes the bus cart out into the dining area and begins clearing tables.

Later Trevor finds Sammy in the pub office going over receipts. He leans in the door for a minute watching Sammy punch numbers into a computer. "You back that up, right?"

"I'd hate to be a hypocrite," Sammy says.

"You ready to open another pub?"

Sammy turns, and looks up to Trevor. "You're serious?"

"I kind of am. We have an amazing thing going here. Like maybe we have the ticket. Applebee's must have started some place like where we are now. I think we've stumbled onto a good recipe, no pun."

Sammy is still looking at Trevor. "We could kick it around I guess. What exactly are you thinking?"

"I dunno, maybe start scouting out another potential location?"

"It would take some bigger money this time around. We'd have to pay for all the work that the two of us did on this one. I don't think we could afford to be away from here that much and still expect it to keep rolling smoothly."

"Yeah, I've been thinking about that, the money aspect. I was thinking we could hit Vegas." He has been thinking, a lot and hard. Having the two-fifty K hanging out there does put ideas in a guy's head.

Sammy laughs, "Guns and masks?"

"Not that, I have a better one; I know this guy with this amazing talent with cards."

The smile slips from Sammy's face. His neatly combed, long hair is in a perfect pony tail. His shirt is buttoned to the collar. The sleeves are buttoned as well. Trevor would best describe the look on Sammy's face right now as the one you would have if you were trying to answer the question of whether or not you'd shit your pants. "Just a thought. Let's kick it around some anyway?" And turns to walk away. Sammy will work through this. If not, there is always the reward money. He is going to fly his parents out here and rub their noses in both of his successful restaurants.

Over the next few days, Trevor brings up the potential for opening a second pub several times. Sammy seems to have an odd desire to please him. He also doesn't seem interested in opening another business and is clearly resistant to the idea of scamming the casinos at cards. He still thinks Sammy will see the light.

~

Later, during a lull, Sammy is helping dry glasses at the bar, "You think we can get away with it? Going to Vegas and taking money from the casinos?"

"Dude, I don't see how it could be anything but that. We both play, I lose, you win. We cut it off below fifty grand at each place and then waltz home.

Not a problem. Net five hundred thousand and come back to Billings and start shopping for another building; easy stuff, Sam."

Sammy looks at him in that way that makes him feel transparent, like his every thought is open, which is bad because he knows a lot of his thoughts aren't all that great. Might even be that some of them are actually bad.

"We have a good thing here, Trev. It would be okay to let it be, enjoy it, as is."

"Okay John Lennon. I do get what you are saying, I ...I need this success." Sammy is obviously being greedy about his farm and his research. He'll get back to all of that.

"I know you feel that way, Trev. I get that." Sammy puts a gentle hand on Trevor's shoulder. "Let me give it some more thought, okay?"

"Yeah, sure. When is your next farm visit anyway?"

"I think I'll go again next Sunday."

"And your experiments are going well?"

Sammy nods. "I'm still powering the farm and there is a ton of excess, so that side is a definite win and I'm almost done with my calcs for the, the other stuff."

"You are getting close on your time, shit?" This is becoming a conversation he'd rather not have.

"Yes." Simple answer, crazy complexity.

Sammy possesses the power to change the world, right here and now as they stand at the bar of their insignificant business? It's too insanely implausible. Okay, impossible. "What next?"

Sammy has that deep seeing look again. It's like X-ray eyes that don't light up bones or flesh but soul. "Prove, right or wrong, that my other theory works on a larger scale. That's what's next — PTFB, push the fucking button and see what happens."

"See what happens," Trevor would kind of like to barf. "Okay, bro. This is the Higgs field gig? You are my best friend and business partner and if you disappear off to some other place or other time, what do I do with that? What are you doing?"

Sammy's smile is enigmatic and sideways. He looks at Trevor for a quiet moment. "It's not snake oil, Trev. Can you give me a little bit longer to prove it out and then I'll spill my guts?"

"Okay, why later?"

"Mostly because, if it doesn't work, we can have a much easier conversation and a good laugh over a beer. If it does work we will need a good sit-down mind meld and a much longer talk."

"Okay, bro, okay." Trevor thinks that of the nine billion people on the planet, he still can't understand why Sammy wants this friendship. "Have you sorted out the ethical thing, the moral issues?"

"I haven't decided for sure. I have an answer that might work. I'm still working out those details, too."

"All right, bro, for now. I do want full disclosure at some point, though, okay?"

"I'll fill you in Trev, I promise."

~

Later in the day Trevor finds Sammy back at the sink helping Ford. He ducks in and settles with his back against the counter. "You give any more thought to my idea about the extra grub stake?"

Sammy smiles as he scrubs dishes. "Can I give you an answer when I get back from the farm?"

The fucking farm and all of the weirdness are really grating on him, not to mention the two days a week that he has to pull the extra load.

"I'll take that. You are on the hook, you know, you now owe me both a trip to the farm and an answer about Vegas."

~

After the rest of the tribe is gone to their homes or is asleep, Trevor turns on the laptop and opens the email that he knows will be there: G. Paxton. He reads the content, nothing new there. They are definitely still fishing. He heads out barefoot toward the walk-in cooler, writes down two beers on the list and settles at a table.

He can hear Amy's shoe-less footsteps coming down the stairs, looks up and smiling. He points to the beer on the table. "Hey, Red."

"Hey, yourself." She slides into a chair across from him.

"If it's the future keeping you up again, Sammy's working on some sort of time something-or-other. Maybe he can shoot you forward to have a look."

"That is keeping me up a little."

"Anything I can do to help?"

"Where is your future taking you, Trev? Is this your end game? Are you happy with this, the pub?"

Not the direction he was hoping the conversation would go. "No, it's not my end game. I dig it, running things, the success and the staff. It's all pretty awesome, but I need more too."

"More success?"

Trevor nods.

"Best friend, good friends and…" She trails off and opens her arms, welcoming.

"I need success, Ames."

She nods and crosses her arms back across her chest, holding her elbows. She's quiet for a moment, "I hope you get your success, Trevor."

The staff continues meeting every night, often Sammy and Ford play, but mostly the time is spent chatting and laughing. On Sunday, right after closing, Trevor notices Sammy and Amy talking. Their heads are very close together. He watches their body language, wonders if he's missed some kind of shift.

~

Mattie walks up behind him and lightly pinches his butt. She stops and leans on his shoulder. He can feel her breasts pressing against his back and wonders which of the lacy, teasing bras she is wearing today.

She talks quietly into his ear. "What do you think they're talking about?"

"Probably Sammy's ridiculous farm. I think it's making us all a little crazy, wondering if it's even real, and if so, what the hell he's really doing there."

Mattie leans harder into him. She turns her head and takes his earlobe into her mouth, nibbles, turns away. "Everybody loves some mystery."

Speak for yourself. Sammy has moved away from Amy and is making the rounds like he always does before he disappears. Trevor beats him to the punch and, telling everybody good night, walks towards his room although that's not where he is going.

Trevor slips out of the front door and makes his way to his Jeep, starts it and moves down the block to another parking space, shuts the motor back off and waits.

After about ten minutes, Sammy's pickup comes around the corner. Trevor lets it go by. Following him discretely would be impossible in the rural area. As soon as they are out of town, Sammy would see he was being tailed. Trevor knows the address.

After sitting another quarter of an hour, Trevor starts the old Jeep and drives off in the same direction Sammy has gone.

He finds the address his GPS guides him to. The driveway to the mystery farm. Shutting off the lights, Trevor turns down the gravel path, drives the winding route through a few curves in the hilly terrain. He stops when he can see light reflecting off some small trees, gets out and walks toward it on foot.

It doesn't take long, Sammy has not been conservative, the place is totally lit up. Trevor stands, trying to keep to the shadows and looks over Sammy's farmhouse. His truck is parked there and is the only vehicle. He sees Sammy walk by a window, doesn't see anybody else and there are no curtains or shades.

So this much is true anyway. Sammy is really coming out here and alone. After standing for another minute, Trevor trots back to the Jeep, turns it around with the lights still off and rolls back out to the main road. That half of his quest is done anyway and it will make him a little less likely to get shot with phase two. Knowing the homeowners are away is essential to breaking into a rural Montana dwelling without being killed.

Trevor is relieved that Amy doesn't seem to have insomnia this night and is not sitting in the dining area as he slips back into the pub. He carries his shoes as he walks quietly to his room.

Chapter 15

TREVOR FINDS SAMMY standing in their office. "Hey Sam. Would you mind if I took off for a little bit this morning? I talked with Jake on the phone and he asked if I could check on the hangar."

"No problem bro." He turns to face Trevor. "I've got it. I know you've been working your butt to the bone. Is everything good with you?"

"Couldn't be better."

Sammy puts a hand on Trevor's shoulder. "Okay, see you whenever. No worries, I've got it."

"I'll be back in a few hours." Reluctant to walk away from that hand. Trevor grabs the jeep keys from the office wall and walks out toward the door, passing Mattie in the hallway.

"Where are you going handsome one?"

"I talked to Jake and he asked if I would check on things at the hangar."

"Sammy is overlord for today then?" She leans slightly toward him.

"He is." He can smell her perfume and he thinks he can see, out of his peripheral vision, that she has that damn purple bra on.

"Okay, I will be a faithful minion. See you later?" It would take very little movement from either of them to close the distance for a kiss.

He isn't going anywhere near the minion thing right now, nope, or a kiss.

"See you later." Turning away, a little slowly, he heads out of their building.

He wrestles the sticky door of the crappy old Jeep, climbs in and starts the motor. It has run perfectly without any other work ever since Sammy fixed it that forever ago day in Oregon. He puts it in gear and heads toward Ingomar Road.

~

Sammy is a neat house keeper. Granted they all keep the pub shiny clean but some part of that was arguably because they were not supposed to be living at the business and any messiness would make getting caught worse. Here though, and left to his own devices, Sammy is a total neat nick. Not that there is much keep cleaned up, this is definitely a minimalist theme.

Not sure what he hopes to find, Trevor wanders through the old farmhouse. He assumes that, if Sam's story is on the up and up, there would be some science stuff to see. There is not. There is a computer on the table, password protected when he tries to turn it on, some clothes in the closet and a stack of notebooks on the kitchen table. There are a few veggies in the fridge and some canned goods in the cupboards along with some granola cereal but no science stuff.

Remembering Sammy telling him about getting a shipping container, Trevor looks out the back window. A container could make sense as a lab for his experiments, if there were experiments. As far as he can see though, there are zero shipping containers. There is an old barn back there but it's front doors are open and Trevor can see that there is no shipping container inside of it either. He scans a little more, there could be something behind the barn but from this vantage point, Trevor can see that the only trail curves off to the right and does not go behind the barn.

Trevor turns away from the window and sits at the kitchen table with the large stack of notebooks and books with academic titles. Shuffling through the stacks, he is a surprised to find that one of the piles teeters when disturbed. There is something in the middle it. Reaching in with his fingers, he finds the point where the object is, lifts the material off the top of it.

There is an ID badge on a lanyard. The name on the badge is, "Garwin Paxton, MIT, Faculty."

The photo, below the title, is pony tailed, white teeth gleaming, Sam, Samuel, Sammy Houston.

What the fuck?

Trevor sets the stack of papers onto a bare spot on the table, reaches for the lanyard. The badge looks real enough. There is no evidence of splicing. None, it looks like, as far as Massachusetts Institute of Technology knows,

Sammy is G. Paxton.

Sammy, you fucking liar. Trevor looks out the back window, watches the tall grass wave in the breeze. It's been a very long time since he has wanted to cry. I believed you brother. I believed in you so much.

He puts everything back on the table as he found it, stands, eases the chair into its original place and walks slowly out of the room, out of Sammy's house and gets into Shawna's stolen Jeep.

Trevor turns the vehicle around without looking at the farmhouse. He stops at the main road. There isn't any traffic out here.

The Jeep is facing south, a right turn would be west. A left turn is toward Billings. There isn't much for him west, parents, Grants Pass, an airport he used to hang out at that he now knows he doesn't belong at. He isn't sure how much there is for him in Billings either.

He turns left.

Chapter 16

THE DAY AFTER LEARNING who the real G. Paxton is, Trevor tells Sammy that he has something to finish for Jake. It's okay if it sounds ridiculous, he doesn't even care and pays no attention at all to how Sam reacts. Driving to the town of Laurel, he meets with a realtor. The structure is not as old as their bank building but has an equal appeal of its own. It was originally built in the early nineteen hundreds as a feed store, Trevor thinks they could create the same kind of ambience here as they have in Billings. The layout has good possibilities to be modified for function as a restaurant and the traffic pattern of the area streets seem good. After an hour walk-through he takes the agent's card, thanks him for his time, and promises to talk with his partner and get back to him soon.

On the drive back he debates the possibilities, he and Sammy could trade off which restaurant they managed, maybe a week at a time, to keep things fresh. maybe they could set up a second band to jam at the new building. Even though they nailed it pretty good to start with, they still learned a lot at The Vault. Christ, they make a good team, even if Sammy is a lying sack of shit.

~

When he walks into the crowded pub, he can't help but smile at the crowd. The place is packed. He greets many of the patrons by name. They are definitely building a following of regulars and he knows a lot of these are the same faces he sees hanging out around the band. Winding his way to the bar, he looks around the corner to where they stash the booze and other necessities. Amy is sitting on some boxes. On impulse he steps into the alcove and relaxes onto a box across from her. "Hey, Amy, what are you doing?"

She seems a little surprised. "I'm just thinking; it's the only relatively quiet place. What have you been doing?"

"Checking out a property for another pub. I feel like we are doing amazingly well here and I want to grow."

She nods slowly. "To feed your need for that success?"

Trevor looks at her eyes. "Yeah, mostly."

She looks at him for a moment, stands up and leans over, putting both hands on his shoulders and lowering her head to him. She rests her forehead against his and then leans in farther, kisses him full and lingering, on the mouth. Moving away, she smiles. It's a small smile. "Okay," She walks away.

After a few minutes, Trevor gets up and wanders into the kitchen where Ford is washing dishes.

"Hi, Trevor." Ford smiles. "I was thinking about you and Sammy. I sure like working for you guys and hagging out here. That's good, isn't it?"

"Hagging out? The best. We like you being here, too, Ford. I'm really glad you like being here." He smiles without feeling it, continues to the bar where he greets Tom, the new bartender, claps him on the back. "Doing good, buddy? Swimming in the tips?"

"Yeah, Trevo, not so much as when you're in here schmoozing with the chicks and blue hairs. All my tips are from regular, old guys."

Trevor smiles distractedly. He was going to relieve Tom, changes his mind. "Hey, you want to stay on the clock? I still have some other things to do if you're up for more here."

"Sure," Tom says. "I'm good for the rest of the night."

Trevor turns and goes out the front door. His intention is to walk around the building to the back where the Jeep is parked and avoid Mattie and Amy. There is some thinking that needs to go on in that category. Taking the top down on the Jeep, he heads for an area of town where he knows there are car dealerships.

Trevor returns to the pub driving a new Dodge pick-up truck. Feeling good in the shiny new machine, he knows the pub isn't returning enough money that they can afford the excess, but that success is just around the corner. Back in to a busy restaurant, he heads unhurriedly for his place at the bar, sees Sammy turning the corner into the kitchen area. There is a twinge of guilt, but he likes the feeling of knowing he has a shiny new truck parked out where the shitty old jeep used to be. It's definitely time for a better standard of living.

The band starts up around nine, after the dinner crowd thins out and shifts to the drinkers and the younger segment of the Billings population. Some of the bar crowd dances to the music. The waitresses hustle, tossing drink orders at Tom and Trevor.

Eventually the crowd goes home, the doors are closed, and the remaining staff collect in their usual spots on the stage.

Standing next to Trevor, Sammy says, "You're looking kinda smug, bro."

Trevor thinks about telling them about the new truck. "Just happy to be with the Tribe. I'm checking out early though. Good night." Trevor makes his way upstairs toward the sleeping area. He is not surprised to find another email from "Garwin Paxton." Better still, the reward money has jumped to one million. *What the fuck is that about Sammy? Are you really that desperate to test me?* Without turning off the computer, he falls asleep.

~

The pub is full the next day. Business is getting busier. After the lunch rush, Sammy walks over to the bar. "We've cleared enough money that we should be in the black within a month. That's virtually unheard of for a new restaurant."

This is an opportunity sent straight from God. "We have nailed it, bro. We make a good team." *They do make a good team.* "I found some great buildings, one in particular I'd really like to show you. What do you think about making a run with me and checking it out?"

"Sure, dude. Is now good?"

Surprised, Trevor lets out the breath he didn't know he was holding, "Yeah, now is perfect."

Sammy turns around, "I'll go tell Amy that she has command," walks across the pub. Trevor watches as Sammy takes a winding path that puts him in contact with all of the staff in sight. Greeting each and getting a smile or laugh from most. *Whatever else is going on, Sammy might really be their gravity.*

161

"Where's the Jeep?" Sammy asks as they approach the shiny red Ram truck.

"Oh, traded it in. The red one is my new ride."

"Wow, nice." Sammy doesn't seem at all unhappy.

Except for the new car smell, the air-conditioned comfort, and lack of the crazy flapping soft top, the drive to Laurel is a lot like the first day Trevor picked Sammy up in Oregon. Trevor is surprised at how nice it is to have it be just the two of them without the many distractions of the business, other friends, and staff.

They talk mostly about the pub and the possibility of the new business. Eventually the discussion works around to Amy. Sammy looks at Trevor. "She is really trying to figure out what to do. I think she is pretty lost right now."

"I do get that waitressing wasn't the plan from four years of college."

"Yeah, it's always struck me as weird that we have built this whole society that contradicts itself in so many ways."

"Like?"

"We have this huge pressure to 'succeed' and to buy stuff and all of that at the expense of what really counts, each other."

"You think that's where she is at? Stuck between what she thinks she should do and staying with us?"

Sammy looks around the new truck, "I do think that."

He wonders if Amy will ever kiss him again. "It does look like that."

Sammy looks up as they roll up to the grange building in Laurel. "It does look cool. Are we going in?"

"Yeah, I noticed a key above the door when I checked it out last time."

"So we're breaking and entering?" He is smiling.

"Dude, no breaking in, I know where the key is. Just entering, which will obviously have reduced jail time."

"We could always call the realtor?"

In the building Trevor tells Sammy about the floor plan and where the kitchens, bar, and various equipment could be situated.

"Okay, I get it. It's definitely a solid idea and there's potential, but there's a lot of work that would have to get done and there's the money thing."

"Dude, we can do this. We need this success." Trevor doesn't consider the irony of the 'success' part of that statement if Sammy's reactor claims are real.

Sammy only nods, "Okay."

Chapter 17

THE GROUP MEETS on the stage after closing. Amy is sitting in a chair beside Sammy. Connie, one of the regular attendees of the tribe gatherings, stands behind Sammy, braiding his long hair. Ford sits, smiling and hugging his cello. Two of the other regulars have chairs and Tom, the bartender, is flat on his back in the middle of the group. Mattie sits against the wall with her legs against Trevor's legs. Jinn makes the rounds, visiting each of them. Trevor has already handed out beverages, mostly beers, with sodas for Amy and Ford.

"Did you guys catch the one chick flashing the band?" One of the waitresses asks.

Amy looks at Sammy. "You got flashed?"

Ford's head begins nodding and his face turns very red. "She had doobies."

Trevor looks up, torn between laughing and translating. Struggling, he watches Ford's highly entertaining red face and nodding, relents, "You mean boobies, right, buddy?"

Ford's nodding slows. "Yeah." His face remains red but he is smiling hugely.

"Hey Ford, it's alright buddy. Sometimes, it's all about the boobies, guys just like them, nothing wrong with that."

"Okay, Trevo." Ford is quiet for a moment, his handsome face relaxing toward it's normal slackness. His flush fades and then he looks up at them. "Sammy, do you take anybody to your farm with you? I'd really like to go and see your labertory where you live."

"I will take you soon, Ford, I'll take everybody out there soon. I don't live in the laboratory though. My actual lab is in a metal vault that is buried in the hillside behind the house in an arroyo."

"What's that, a royal?"

"It's a kind of washout, like a ravine. It curves out behind the farmhouse. You'll see when we go out there, buddy."

"Okay."

~

The next day, during a lull in business, Trevor catches Sammy in the office. "So, I hear you're spending a few extra days at the farm?"

"I'm really trying to wrap up this phase."

"Wrap up, like in… done?" Trevor asks, surprised.

"In a way, yeah. I'll still go back. I have an answer that I want to try. Like I told you, I'm done with the initial experiments and I want to complete this phase."

"When are you coming back then?"

Sammy shrugs. "I'm not sure exactly, maybe four days."

"Do you care if I follow up with the realtor?" Oblivious to the emotional blackmail.

"Okay." Sammy turns the office chair so that he is facing Trevor directly. "Do you think that will work for you Trev? A second pub and that chartered flight for your parents?"

"This is the first time in my life I feel like there's something within my reach."

Sammy looks like he is going to follow up with that but doesn't say more about it.

They discuss figures and agree on what offer Trevor should make and what financial limits they should not push past for the new building. Trevor's about to go back to the bar and turns to Sammy, "Are you ready to come out of the closet on this one? To be a partner on paper too?" He can't help but wonder if the reasoning behind this has more to do with Sammy's legal identity. Maybe, he is Paxton and not the other way around?

Sammy ponders for a moment. "Not yet? I'll think about where we are going to go with all of that, too, during these next few days at the farm."

Chapter 18

THE TRIBE IS COLLECTED on the stage after closing. Amy looks in Trevor's direction and pets Jinn. "A reporter was here this evening."

"Like in… reporting and not just for a meal?" Trevor asks her.

"Yeah, like that. He asked who owned the pub and things like that. I really didn't have time to talk, so I told him to come back tomorrow during the day and look for you."

"Okay, any weird vibe or anything?"

"Nothing that I noticed. He seemed straight up, looking for the human-interest side of things, the young, handsome, hardworking guy thing."

"That couldn't hurt business I suppose, to get some more exposure," Trevor shrugs.

"That could be great for the ego," Mattie smiles smugly.

Trevor is annoyed by this, both for the fact that it's a deliberate dig and that he knows it's the truth but lets the irritation go, looks to Mattie. "Food, this starved ego needs because some chick keeps messing with it."

Grace, one of the now regular members of the staff and tribe smiles and says, "Yeah, Mattie, poor Trevor."

Despite the sarcastic tone, Trevor has the impression that she would be happy to help shore him up in this regard, or any other.

"What does Sammy do at his farm?" One of the newer waitresses asks.

Amy answers, "Sammy is sort of a professor. He kind of works remotely with a college. When he goes away he's doing research and writing papers for them."

"So, he telecommutes? Like that?" She ruffles Jinn's fur.

"Yeah…" Trevor adds to Amy's response. He would use the girl's name right now, but can't remember it, "like that." wondering how soon they can head down to Nevada and go to work on the new pub. Mattie gets up and asks him to walk her to her car. Surprised by the request, he agrees and stands to join her.

As they step out, she points in the direction of her car and puts her arm through his, wraps her hand around his bicep. He can feel her breasts against him.

After they've walked some of the distance, Mattie turns toward Trevor, "You think of Sammy as your friend?"

This strikes Trevor as an odd question. "You know I do; why do you ask?"

"Because I think he is that to you, a good friend. Like, he's family and maybe you don't really get it."

"Maybe he is Mattie, I'm not sure. Where are you going with this?" He is enjoying the walk.

"Because…" she pauses. "Because I think we all love you and I think you really don't understand any of that."

"Okay."

"Okay?" Mattie is not looking up at him.

"Yeah." They arrive at her car. Mattie fumbles her car keys out of a pocket and opens the car. She gets in, not looking his way, and tells him good night. "Thanks for walking me out." Closes the door and starts the car without waiting for any sort of response.

Trevor is left standing on the sidewalk, smiling and turning the watch in his pocket over and over, shifting his weight from one foot to the other and wondering why he is so God damn angry right now. Eventually he turns and goes back to the pub through the small door. He has remembered the waitress's name: Grace. He sits down near her and picks up where he had left off with his Corona.

A little while later there's an odd whooshing, rippling sound followed by a small but very real earthquake. The overhead lights sway and dim dramatically.

"Fracking, it's that damned fracking thing. It's busting up the earth," Tom pontificates.

A lively debate ensues about the evils of fracking as Trevor tries to remember the last time he felt an earthquake.

~

The next days seem slow for Trevor. Things go well with the pub, the crowd is good during the days and the bar stays full in the evenings, despite the lack of a band. Trevor continues to be occupied with customers and the staff. Grace launches a full-on flirt campaign, which Trevor sort of ignores, but enjoys, while he tries to figure out what to do with Mattie and Amy.

Trevor wonders if there is any truth to an FBI reward for information on Sammy but realizes that doesn't make any sense if Sammy is Paxton. What in the hell was that about anyway? If they don't go to Vegas soon though, he will make a call. Maybe the FBI is looking for Sammy anyway, then again, maybe he is just an escaped crazy.

~

"Hey, bro." Sammy says from behind. It's afternoon. Trevor jumps, startled.

"Dude, Sammy. Christ! You scared the shit out of me! How did things go?"

Sammy smiles his normal crooked smile. "My stuff is solid. I'm done for now. All the data and equipment are shut down and ready for whatever happens from here."

"So, are you saving the world this week?"

Sammy's shakes his head. "Nope, probably going to be a barkeep and lead guitarist."

"Really, no world saving? Just, done?"

"Mostly like that."

Trevor is wondering what in the hell that means but forgets that with Sammy's next question.

"When do you want to go to Vegas?"

"Whenever you are ready."

"Sure, okay, tomorrow?"

Sammy nods. "Yeah, we can head off in your fancy red truck."

"Awesome!"

"Okay, I'm going to catch up with some of our books and stuff. I'll talk more with you later?"

Trevor reaches out and claps Sammy on the shoulder. "Alright, dude. Later." He turns back to the bar and finishes stacking glasses from the clean dish tray. Seeing one of the regular patrons, he gives the guy a high-five and picks up a conversation they'd been carrying on thorough the guy's many visits to The Vault. Trevor drifts along with the conversation well enough, but his mind is on the trip to Las Vegas, the new building and mostly, on his shit head parents. The current version of the fantasy has him sending a private jet to the Grants Pass airport and enjoying the slack-jawed look they'll give him when they get here. He, of course, will send someone else to pick them up in Billings; he'll be too busy himself.

Later that night when the staff gathers on the stage, Mattie does not stay. Trevor has decided her statement about loving him is crap anyway. He has put that idea in the file titled, "There's-A-Sucker-Born-every-Minute."

Trevor samples these thoughts as he listens to Sammy laugh with the group. He likes the Tribe, his people — Sammy, Amy, Mattie, Jinn, Ford — and the rest, okay, really likes them, but there's his future to think about, too. He gets up to find a quieter spot to call Mattie.

She answers after the second ring. "Why are you calling me, handsome?"

"I didn't call you handsome, but I have, on occasion, told Sammy I think you're attractive and mostly that your ass is amazing."

She laughs but doesn't say anything else.

"Why didn't you stay, Mattie?" Trevor tries, mostly successfully, not to sound petulant.

"I don't know, tired, I guess."

"Tired of…?"

Mattie laughs again. "You are perceptive."

"And I want to get in your pants, but I can't decide if that's part of what you're tired of or not. Besides that, why didn't you stay?"

Another chuckle. "Maybe one of these days we'll sort that out."

"I'm struggling right now, Mattie." That's a weird gush of honesty. "Are you coming back?"

"No, maybe tomorrow night; tonight, I'm still a little stung."

"Oh." He wants to say that he's sorry, knows he isn't. "I think Sammy and I are making a run to Las Vegas tomorrow."

"Vegas? What are you two going to Vegas for?"

"Just a quick business trip," loving the sound of that.

"Whoa, that's a new one. Do you want to tell me more about this?" Mattie asks.

"I'll tell you all about it when I get back."

"Okay," she pauses, "Are we good?"

"We are, Mattie. We'll sort this all out soon."

"I guess we both have some work to do."

"Yeah we'll talk more about it later. Goodnight."

Trevor returns to the stage area and walks in to a laughing group debating the potential truth in a recent Cosmo article claiming that women prefer men who eat pineapple because of the way it makes them taste during oral sex.

"Wow, that's an interesting conversation to walk into." He looks around at the smiling group, sits down and insinuates himself back into the flow of conversation. He enjoys the comradery and acceptance, but can't keep his mind off Mattie even while he is looking at Amy. After a while, he makes excuses, double checks with Sammy that they're on for the trip tomorrow and heads off to bed.

Chapter 19

THE NEXT MORNING, Sammy walks in to the bar area. Trevor is brewing espresso drinks.

"Hey, dude."

"Morning, sunshine." Trevor hands over a cup. "Americana, as you like it."

"Thanks, bro." Sammy sips the hot liquid and through his long hair, watches Trevor.

"You ready to rock?"

"Yeah, unless you're willing to let this all go and be content to make our living slinging hash and serving up drinks right here in this one place."

There is appeal in that but there is this growing need in him that won't go away.

Trevor walks out to the truck and Sammy joins him a few minutes later. Without speaking, Trevor turns up the music and pulls away from the curb while Sammy sips the last of his Americano and looks out of the window.

They intend to drive straight through to Vegas — making the whole thousand-mile trip in one day — set up in a motel, hopefully spend only one day in the casinos and then drive home the next.

They've been on the road for an hour or so, rocking out to the sound system without talking. Trevor reaches over and turns down the volume. "You and I really haven't had much time to catch up for a while."

"It's not too late to shit-can this Vegas idea so that we can go home and catch up all you want."

Can I ask you who you really are? That would be some real catching up. "Dude, let's roll on, gather up some funds, and go home."

"Yes, easy."

Trevor catches the sarcasm.

"So…" Sammy responds, waits a half minute, and then continues, "your plan is to hit the casinos one at a time, cheat them at cards until we skim, what did you figure, about forty thousand per gig, then we move on to the next one?"

"Assuming you aren't too hung over then, yeah, fifty-thousand is what I'm figuring. Ten or twelve hours and we should have half a million or so and we call it a day and head north. That's the gist of our plan."

Sammy shrugs. "Okay, hit the blackjack table. You have enough cash to get started?"

"Yup, twenty large, unmarked bills." Trevor says this in what he thinks of as a Chicago gangster voice. It comes out sounding like a Dutch immigrant with a speech impediment and a bad cold.

Sammy laughs a little at the failed impersonation. "Alright, dude. We'll do what we can to help you find resolution and maybe get you into your new pub."

"Our new pub, brother!" At best, a fuzzy truth.

Sammy takes the Takamine out from its case in the back seat, puts his stockinged feet up on the dashboard and starts picking at the guitar along with the music.

After about an hour, Trevor looks over at his friend. Sammy's head is tilted down and he's looking at his fingers while they play. His long hair is hanging over his face. Trevor watches for a while and finally says, "I've been thinking that since you're going to take me to your farm after we get back, maybe you could tell me some more about what you're working on?"

Sammy stops playing, turns down the music and looks up at Trevor. Flipping his hair out of the way with a head shake. He shrugs. "Okay, sure." He appears slightly taken off guard. "What do you want to know?" He takes a pocket watch from his pocket and checks the time.

Trevor's attention is caught by the watch; it appears identical to the one in his pocket. He's surprised that he never noticed Sammy had an exact match to his watch. Did he buy that one after they found Trevor's at the farm in Oregon?

"What are you really doing at your farm?" He desperately wants to ask about Paxton, saves that for the return trip home, after the money.

Sammy nods, like he might be clearing his head before he begins to talk. "You remember that the reactor is powering the farm?" Sammy asks, looking to Trevor for confirmation.

Trevor does.

Sammy nods, "Like I told you before, it works. The power source is a cold fusion reactor. The farm is running on free energy out of a twenty megawatt, non-polluting, three-hundred-pound machine. The prototype cost me about twenty thousand bucks to build as custom parts."

"So, they could be mass produced for a lot less?"

"That's about it," Sammy nods. "I roughed out an estimate that they could be produced for about one thousand dollars each in lots of a half million or more. That's including enough palladium to run them for a lot of years and works out to be about three hundred dollars per house for electricity for around a thousand years and zero emissions."

"Three hundred per year? That's amazing!"

"No, Trev, three hundred bucks for a thousand years' worth of electricity. Thirty cents a year. There aren't any moving parts even. Nothing to wear out."

Trevor thinks about the magnitude of that change, holy shit. "But you still don't want to release it, your technology?" Thinking Sammy is insane.

Sammy's crooked smile tips up an extra notch. "No, I don't think it's the right thing to do."

"Holy shit, Sam."

Sammy shrugs but the smile doesn't slip.

"And that's how you have resolved your whole save the world, or not, debate? Just say no?"

Silent for a moment, "In a manner of speaking, I think so."

"In this time Trevor, I believe that what I have created would do more harm than good."

"I wish I really understood what you are talking about." I really wish I believed you were on the up and up. If you were telling the truth right here and now, we would be talking about more leverage than the world has ever seen in one man. Free energy and nope, we are going to keep that to ourselves?

Sammy shakes his head. "Trevor, you are my best friend. It will make more sense after I show you everything. How about we go straight to the farm when we get back?"

"Serious, you are letting me go to the farm when we get home?"

"Okay, so the reactor thing is a home run." It is so odd that he and Sammy have shared so much of their lives with each other while also being so successful at avoiding this topic almost completely. "You haven't said much about the other experiment, the time thing. Is it a win?"

"Out of the park. I've been messing with the Higgs field and its effect on particles and I have a way to copy something and send it through time."

Trevor thinks he still hasn't seen a single tangible thing to support any of this and sweet Jesus, this is too far out there. Besides, all he needs is to keep Sammy from imploding or something for just one more night. After that, things will be a lot more flexible. He does not say anything else about Sammy's farm, looking for whatever measure of comfort and sanity he can find and willing to accept silence if it's the only solace available.

Eventually Sammy goes back to playing the guitar.

It's almost midnight when they roll into Las Vegas. The city is, as always, alive with people. Traffic is backed up as they leave I-515 and turn onto Las Vegas Boulevard. Trevor imagines there's no other street in the country that has gridlock in the middle of the night. They pull into the Stratosphere's parking garage, lock up the new Dodge, and grab their small bags to hunt down a room for the night. Still feeling slightly queasy, Trevor works hard on forgetting Sammy's claims and bizarre explanations.

He even wonders, briefly, if he should start thinking about finding some new friends when they get back to Billings. He shrugs off the thought as they turn the corner into the hallway, thinks it doesn't matter. He's never had anybody treat him like Sammy does, even if Sammy is bug-shit crazy. Impulsively, he reaches out and puts a hand on Sammy's shoulder. "All good, bro?"

Sammy's smile stretches a bit. "All good, dude." They walk into the lobby and pay cash for a room, something that can only be done in the quirky world of Nevada.

The room is one of the endless, nondescript, two-beds-and-a-shower-now-go-gamble rooms that Vegas offers cheap. Trevor flops onto the bed, sighing. "God, I'm tired." He looks sideways at Sammy. "Goodnight, dude."

"Night, Trev."

~

The next morning the alarm clock knocks Trevor out of a troubled sleep. He opens one eye. The clock reads five AM and there is acid in his stomach. He knows Sammy, as always, will come through and they'll get the money they need from the casino douche bags and go. Running his fingers through his black hair, Trevor steps out of bed and softly bumps the other queen bed on which Sammy is lying, inert.

"Wake up, dude," Trevor tells Sammy, not without sympathy. "Time is wasting and Montana needs us back. We can still catch the sleepy dealers before they go off shift."

"You suck, Trev." But Sammy doesn't really sound like he is still sleepy. He swings up without looking and smashes a pillow into Trevor's head, then bounces up and pads toward the bathroom. "I'll be out in a minute. Breakfast downstairs before we begin our crimes?"

"It's less criminal if you're robbing the robbers, dude. It's a little realignment of the rules. We move the money flowing from the marks, pour a little into our pockets, then it goes right back to flowing into the dragon's lair again, barely a bump in their world of greed to feed ours. They will never know, and yeah, breakfast before we begin." He walks to the window and looks out on the glitz and glitter of Vegas. The acid in his stomach asks him to settle for a teeth-brushing and in the name of expediency, skip the shower. He agrees with the burning fluid and a few minutes later, he and Sammy head out for one of the dining areas in the casino.

They sit eating and watching the crowd. Trevor's amazed at the variety and number of people who are gambling and playing slot machines this early in the day. He's also quite pleased by the proportion of women dressed in slinky clothes and enjoys the abundance of cleavage and exposed thighs as he eats his French toast.

They discuss the casino goers. Trevor finds material in plenty of them to joke about. Sammy laughs in all the right places and Trevor thinks he enjoys the mostly critical jokes, but he doesn't feel like Sammy's heart is really all here.

After a little more discussion about strategy, they decide it's time to hit the tables. Trevor goes first to one of the cashier windows and trades out eighty-five hundred dollars for chips. Sammy goes to a different teller and exchanges nine thousand two hundred dollars. Any cash transaction over ten thousand dollars requires an IRS form to be filled out and, so far, they're under the radar and ready for Sammy's skills to pay off.

Trevor gives almost all of his chips to Sammy, keeping under a thousand dollars' worth. He sits down beside his friend at the blackjack table. They begin to play and fairly quickly Trevor falls completely silent as Sammy's stack of chips grows and within an hour, he has amassed a sum close to the fifty thousand dollars they had agreed would be their limit. With Sammy going to three cashiers and Trevor going to six, the chips are exchanged for cash and they head toward the next game.

On the street, Trevor can't contain himself as they walk. "Dude, that was amazing!"

Sammy's thin smile is his only response.

Bouncing on the balls of his feet as they wind through the other pedestrians, Trevor eventually says, "Maybe I didn't really think it would work." He snaps his fingers. "Fifty grand and out the door in one hour and fifteen minutes." He shakes his head, once in thirty billion people a two hundred IQ happens, occurring only every few generations on the planet and here is Sammy Houston, right here beside him. Sammy Houston who might really be able to solve a lot of the world's problems. He snaps his fingers again; going home soon with enough money to start another pub — wow. He realizes Sammy has said something. "What's that, bro?"

"We could call it quits right now Trev. Go home, pay off that shiny truck, and enjoy our days."

Trevor smiles. "We could do a few more and roll right on out of town tonight with a whole bunch of cash and own that second pub in no time at all."

Sammy smiles and nods as they turn into the Circus-Circus. One hour and twenty minutes later they walk out with an additional forty-nine thousand, eight hundred dollars in Trevor's back pack. They repeat the plan at two other casinos. So easy.

They make a detour to Trevor's truck in the parking lot and stash the current load of banded bills under the seat. Trevor feels a little better as they walk away knowing that at least some of that sweet, amazing cash is safe.

As they head back toward the strip, Sammy looks at Trevor. He reaches out and puts a hand on Trevor's bicep as they walk. He is trying to smile, "Call it a day and take the money and run?"

"Quit now? You have to be kidding. Watching you take the money from them like candy from a baby is just too good, dude."

At the Silver Nugget they pick a table with several other players. Sammy chooses an empty chair between an elderly lady and a straight-faced middle-aged man wearing a tuxedo. Trevor takes the remaining chair across from Sammy and begins his chatter about his friend's lucky streak and their big time on the town.

Sammy strikes up a conversation with the elderly lady. He smiles broadly as his neighbor reaches across and whispers into his ear and then, to Trevor's surprise, busts out into a full-blown belly laugh and then throws an arm around the woman and uncharacteristically, hugs her to him. Trevor has no idea what they have bonded over so quickly. He can't help smiling, though, as the two continue carrying on while Sammy places bets.

As Trevor watches and loses his thousand dollars in chips, Sammy's pile grows quickly. Trevor is able to catch a few snippets of their quiet conversation and hears "… the grands…" and as he listens further, between chatting up the other players and the dealer, catches some talk about, "the damn cancer…"

Sammy pushes his chair back and as he scoops up his pile of chips, he pushes about half of it over in front of the lady. She beams and then stands, hugs him, and swishing his long hair aside with a finger, kisses him on the cheek. Sammy gets up and heads toward the cashier's cages.

"Dude, what was that about?" Trevor asks Sammy as he catches up.

Sammy smiles. "That was Sadie, she's from Kansas City. She has a great sense of humor, nine grandkids, and terminal cancer. She wants to take them all to Disneyland before checkout time."

"That's cool," Trevor says without much emotion. Then adds, "Did we have to give her a bunch of money?"

Sammy's smile broadens. "No, Trev, we didn't, but it was the right thing to do. A thing that is sometimes worth doing for no other reason than just because it is the right thing."

"Okay, bro. One more of these places and we're out of here. We can definitely make up for the lost cash."

"I'm ready to be done with this," Sammy says as two large men bump into them.

The men flank them on either side, pushing into them and forcing them together. It becomes immediately clear that there they have no choice but to go along. They are forcibly channeled toward a bank of elevators. They are clearly in deep shit. Though the men are dressed in jeans and tee shirts, their build and demeanor leave no doubt they are all business, and not the kind that happens on Wall Street. Trevor looks toward Sammy and is shocked to see him smiling.

Thinking that his friend, for all his amazing brilliance, doesn't understand what's going on, Trevor is about to open his mouth and try for a scene or distraction, when the man beside him simply opens a large hand and shows him the small hypodermic he has palmed. Trevor looks past the man and notices a very subtle shake of Sammy's head. He feels a tiny glimmer of hope that maybe he's the one who doesn't really understand. Maybe Sammy knows where this is going and it isn't as bad as it looks. He can still feel the weight of the backpack and wishes they had taken the time to go back to the truck again and lock up more of the cash. Maybe it is as bad as it looks and it looks really bad.

The elevator door opens as they arrive, even though neither the up nor down buttons were pushed. There is no conversation as they ride up. Trevor tries to catch Sammy's eye, but one of the men has moved and positioned himself between them and he cannot see Sammy. After a dozen or so floors have descended beneath them, the elevator opens and Trevor is forcibly propelled out and they are marched to a set of double doors at the end of a short and expensively finished hallway. Afraid to even look around, Trevor tries to monitor Sammy's progress with his peripheral vision. The double doors are opened and the two of them are thrust into a large room.

The thug on the right says, "Mr. Rand will see you now," very sarcastically.

Oh fuck.

"Good day, gentlemen." A slightly built young man sits behind a large desk. Their escorts had followed them into the room but have now stepped back, leaving Trevor and Sammy standing alone together. Trevor is trying to figure out what happens next and how in God's name they're going to get out of this with the cash.

"Where's your father?" one of the men asks. His tone sounds mildly surprised.

Looking sulky and petulant, the young man answers, "He is, as always, off with one of his teenage bimbos." He looks at Sammy and assumes a serious face. "We've been watching you rip off our casinos."

Trevor sees the guy twitching noticeably and thinks he looks like a strung-out junkie.

"Nick, your father should probably handle this," the quiet thug offers in a tone of respectful warning.

"He's not fucking here! I fucking told you he's off fucking his fucking little bimbo! Again!" screaming shrilly.

The man holds up both hands in a calming gesture and Trevor has a glimmer of hope. The situation might yet be salvaged, but when the junkie stands up, he has a pistol in his hand.

"Do you think you are fucking smart?" directed straight at Sammy. "I want to know how you did that, the cheating. I watched the tapes and I want to know." With slightly jerky footsteps, Nick approaches them.

Trevor thinks he's the poster child for a spoiled brat addicted to meth. The downside is, this brat is carrying a gun, bad combo. "Sir, Nick? My friend here is a genius. He did it for me; I put him up to it. I kind of blackmailed him into doing it because he really is a super genius and he did it by counting cards and running odds in his head. I'm really sorry, sir." As an afterthought, a reach for sanity, he adds, "Maybe we should talk with your dad about this?"

"You stupid fuck, my dad is NOT here and I am and you will deal with me!" He screams, spit flying and turning a brilliant, apoplectic red. Nick closes the distance to within a few feet of Trevor and suddenly and with amazing speed, kicks Trevor full on in the balls.

The pain is excruciating and Trevor drops, like a sack, to the floor, and Nick kicks him again — in the head. Trevor hears the quiet thug try to calm the junkie. It doesn't work. The kicking continues until there's a brief break and Sammy speaks calmly.

"Nick, it was me who ripped you off. I'm sorry, but you can stop kicking Trevor. It wasn't him."

"I forgot," Nick says, panting and still shrill, "you are the genius." The last word comes out as a sneered insult. "What is your IQ?" The insane young man continues screaming, but Sammy does not answer. "What's your fucking IQ, you moron!" Nick screams again.

"It's a little over two hundred," Sammy drawls quietly.

"Your fucking IQ is not two-fucking-hundred. My IQ is so high it can't," he emphasizes each word with a kick to Trevor... "be" ... kick ... "measured!" ... kick.

Trevor tries, mostly unsuccessfully, to cover his face and head, but he is able to force his eyes open and see a little bit through the blood but can't really understand what he is seeing. The junky, red-faced and shaking Nick, is pointing the giant revolver at Sammy's head. It is just inches away from him.

"Nick no! Your dad will not be okay with this!" The other thug says loudly and quickly. The gun goes off.

The kicking resumes, but Trevor no longer tries to cover his head as he lies on the floor. He watches the pointy shoes strike his face and abdomen. He watches the entire half second it takes for Sammy to fall dead to the floor.

"Nick! Give me the fucking gun," the thug demands but goes silent as the druggie turns the weapon on him.

Sammy's inert form is on the floor next to Trevor. Trevor sees the back of Sammy's head; a large mass of Sammy's long hair, skull, and that amazing brain, are no longer contained in Sammy. Sammy's soul has left the building. Trevor hopes the gun will be turned on him, but it's only kicking. It continues until the accumulated blows to his head finally drive him to unconsciousness.

Chapter 20

TREVOR SLIDES FROM OBLIVION into a gray semi-wakefulness. He becomes aware enough, through crusty, barely open eyelids, that he is lying in the desert and there is sage brush in his field of view. His mouth is parched and caked with blood. As he slowly opens his eyes, to the extent his injuries allow, he recognizes the back of Sammy's shirt and the memory of the shooting comes screaming to the forefront of his brain. He manages to move to a painful semi-sitting posture, supported on one hand and turns, in a fashion, toward Sammy. The position change brings the rest of Sammy's body into view and the truth slams into him. It's way worse than the pain. They did not bring the back of Sammy's head with the rest of his body. A stunning fog of screaming darkness, utter despair and desolation, descends on Trevor, blanking out the physical pain, blanking out everything, but unable to blank out the knowledge of the death of the best friend he has ever had in his life. Sammy is gone. The kind and brilliant friend of many, the young man with the ability to literally change the world, is dead.

Trevor falls back to the hot, rough surface of the desert, lies inert and inanimate, wishing that he, too, would please, please stop living. In total despair, there is nothing left but this death wish, but it won't be granted, will it. Like everything else about him, that's stupid. As much as he deserves it, he can never wish himself dead. He has no idea what to do. He doesn't know what to do with Sammy's body, or with his own. He thinks he might have a concussion and internal injuries and doesn't care.

At some point, he realizes that night has fallen and the thought occurs to him that scavengers will be here to visit his buddy sooner than later. While he loathes himself enough to allow them to eat him as well, he doesn't think they will do that — live shitheads not being a choice menu item for coyotes or vultures — and watching nature take Sammy back is more torture than he can stand. Eventually, he decides to simply walk or crawl if he has to. He doesn't have a direction to go to, just something to go away from, away from what used to be his friend Sammy.

Trevor can't bring himself to look at Sammy again, can't even stand the idea. It isn't the condition of his body, not that at all. It is the shame that torments him.

Before he can leave Sammy — and without even really thinking about it — Trevor keeps his face turned away and reaches out for the chain holding Sammy's pocket watch. By braille, he removes the watch from his dead friend's pocket, puts it in his own pocket, and slowly stands up. He trundles away in a zombie-like shuffle.

He stumbles for a while, eventually working out enough of the kinks to the point that he can more-or-less walk in place of the shuffle. Several hours pass, walking and trying to block out everything else. He tries to feel the pain of his injuries, to feel anything besides being alive. Sammy is not. Eventually his feet take him from the desert onto a paved road.

He can see lights in the distance, he must be walking toward the city. South, he thinks. I'm heading south and this must be US-93.

An hour later he comes to the interstate highway and his thoughts are confirmed. He knows where he is; shitty luck. He will have to trudge in the desert again. Friend-killing fucks are not allowed on the interstate.

He follows the fence for a few hours and, as daylight arrives, Trevor comes up onto a sidewalk. He leaves the desert behind and continues into the edges of Las Vegas, eventually encountering a homeless looking guy on the sidewalk. He doesn't realize how bad he must look until the disheveled man looks up at him and visibly cringes. He points the way Trevor is walking, croaks, "Hospital is about seven blocks that way and two blocks off the Strip."

Trevor nods and realizes that his eyes, while open enough to see through, are not actually open in the normal sense. He reaches up and touches his face and finds a lot of swelling and lumps. He probes at his body and comes out of his fog enough to realize that he hurts, badly. For the first time in the twelve or so hours since he woke up beside dead Sammy, he gives his body enough attention to realize that, when he stops to think about it, he really hurts. He also realizes that while walking on auto pilot, some deeper and more self-preserving part of him has made a plan.

The Stratosphere's parking garage is ahead and to the left. He starts to reach into his pocket to check for the keys and is stopped by pain. He lifts his damaged hand, looks at it, some person, Nick he assumes, stomped on it. He can see the outline of shoe treads in the inflamed tissue. He gingerly feels through the fabric of his pants with his other hand and is amazed to discover that the fob and keys to the new truck are still there. The bad guys have either towed it or it is still in the garage.

He continues his shuffling trudge into the building and is amazed when he discovers the truck still sitting where he, and Sammy, had left it. For a brilliant junkie/strategist like Rand, not too much thought has gone into that one. Trevor reaches across his body, and doing a wiggling extraction technique, fishes the key out of his pocket. He manages to open the door, crawl in, and slump, exhausted and in pain, in the driver's seat.

Trevor sits, thinking about the day he met Sammy. His mind goes through a sort of repeating loop of complex emotions, pain, anger at Rand, anger at himself, anger at Sammy for letting himself get talked into Trevor's stupid scheme. On some level he realizes the outright wrongness of blaming Sammy and on another level, refuses to let it go for the relief it gives him for this to be Sammy's fault, not his. The truth is too large and too ugly. Sammy is dead and it is entirely Trevor's doing. He continues sitting, waiting for inspiration to come, for some epiphany to float to the surface of his mind like methane gas farted out from the scum at the bottom of the pond to give him guidance. No guidance comes.

Eventually, left handed, he stabs the key in the ignition and lets his reserve self navigate the vehicle out of the garage and down the street. He drives, continuing to a destination he doesn't know and about which he does not care. Billings with Amy, Mattie, and Ford and Jinn and the pub crew, the Tribe? He thinks he really couldn't stand the searing heat of having them see him. He doesn't care if he dies, but he doesn't think he can face them. He can't endure seeing through their eyes the miserable failure that he is.

In a more lucid moment, Trevor finds it odd, as he drives, that he is simultaneously functioning and not functioning. He thinks he remembers stopping to eat at a diner and he obviously gets fuel now and then. He hasn't run out and there's currently three quarters of a tank, but he has no more than the vaguest recollection of doing any of this. He is going somewhere, although he doesn't know if he has changed directions or has

185

been on one continuous track. The truck's digital compass says east. Cool, the currently-in-residence Trevor thinks, what the east will bring?

Trevor tunes back in, slowly becoming aware of his surroundings. He is under a full moon and sitting, painfully, at a picnic table. He is cold. He looks around, it is sort of a park. The surrounding countryside is desert. He is cold and shuffles toward his truck, unsure of whether he has additional clothing or not, but hoping. It looks like the Trevor-bot has continued to do okay in his absence. There's an unfamiliar new looking bomber jacket mixed haphazardly with a pile of other clothes in the back seat. He puts the coat on, grabs other clothing and piles it on the seat as a pillow. He lies stiffly down in the front seat and is immediately asleep.

In the morning, the heat wakes Trevor. The sun is fairly high in the sky. Extracting himself from the hot interior of the truck, he looks around. It is a park, though it is definitely not meant for overnighting. It also doesn't look like it gets visited much by anybody. He thinks about Sammy and slowly takes stock of himself. He is sore as hell, something past sore that painkillers would mute, but he is not immobile. He maybe likes the pain anyway. If death isn't going to make this easier, at least he has the pain to keep him company.

Something inside the truck glints in the sun. A pocket watch hangs from the mirror, Sammy's watch. With his tender right hand, Trevor feels through his pants. The other watch, his watch from Oregon, is there, too. He looks away from the truck. We will leave that shit alone for right now, thank you very much. A trail runs from the park area into an arroyo. That seems simple enough. He gets out and begins walking toward the gap cut into the surrounding mesa.

Trevor treks slowly for about twenty minutes until he finds himself standing in the bottom of the wash, staring up at an elaborate ancient pueblo built into a large cave. He has read that ancient people built these dwellings in about one thousand AD. Trevor stares at the pueblo, noticing the stucco and the remaining thousand-year-old paint and thinking about time. He turns and shuffles toward his truck and the gold pocket watch hanging from the mirror.

~

At two-thirty a.m., Trevor sits in the dark. He's parked in front of the pub.

He has run through the whole sequence of events on the drive, letting it play out over and over again in his mind. He has been trying to force some forgotten tidbit to float to the surface that will let him off the hook. That tidbit is not there. His greed has cost his friend his life. Trevor wishes again that he could trade his own life for Sammy's. He stares through the windshield at The Vault. This is going to suck.

It's three a.m. when he opens the door and steps out of the truck. Trevor shuts the door of the truck and trudges toward the pub. He is surprised when his key opens the pub door. It seems somehow, like a very long time since he had been here last, like they should have changed the locks.

He tries to be quiet as he lets himself in at the back of the building. He walks past the stage where he and Sammy and the others have spent so much wonderful time. He walks slowly past the kitchen and the former vault, now walk-in cooler. Sammy seems to be everywhere in the building, and so incredibly absent. Trevor's self-loathing is at a life-time high as he reaches the stairway and is about to turn to go up.

"Nobody's up there right now. Ford and Jinn are staying with Mattie." Amy is seated at a table in the dining area.

With his nerves already stretched, Trevor is startled. He jerks away from the stairway, says quietly, "Hey, Ames." She does not respond. It's hard to make her out in the very dim light. She is sitting with her arms crossed over her chest.

"I shouldn't make it easy for you, but he wouldn't want that. I already know. I think you should go away, go stay at the farm or something."

He knew this was going to be rough but still doesn't know how to process what Amy has just said, doesn't understand what she is thinking, is terrified to tell her about his tiny glimmer of hope. "Okay, Ames."

"Don't call me that. In fact, don't call me anything. I know he wants, would want, me to forgive you and I am not him. Right now, I don't know what to think. I'm sorry."

Trevor gets close enough to see that she has been crying, is still. She might hate him, and that makes two of them. He desperately wants to tell her how sorry he is but turns silently and walks away. He retraces his steps toward the back of the pub wondering how Amy already knew about Sammy.

Trevor leaves the pub and its universe full of memories. His hand is in his pocket, on the gold watch that matches the one hanging from the mirror of the truck that he now hates. He misses the good feeling it had given him to get into the new vehicle. He misses everything about his world of five or six days ago. Now it just reminds him, like most things, that he really hates everything — most of all, himself. He punches the address into the guidance system. The truck tells him to go north on Montana road 87.

The sun is becoming visible over the eastern hilltops as Trevor turns down a driveway. Weary to the bone, he follows the rough gravel road as it takes him on an arc to the right and ends at the simple but solid-looking farmhouse. He is not surprised to find the door unlocked, even if there isn't any scientific shit going on here anyway. Sammy, for all of his bullshit lines, because of his bullshit lines, was way too trusting.

Trevor makes his way through the house to the kitchen area with its oak table, plain but functional chairs and the pile of notebooks and papers still stacked there. He notices the whole stack lies flat now, there is no id card and lanyard interrupting the symmetry of the pile.

Trevor sits and thumbs through the endless volumes of Sammy's calculations and notes. Most of it is incomprehensible gibberish and Trevor loses interest. It's not quite getting light yet as he shuffles into Sammy's bedroom. Unsurprisingly, the bed is made with military precision. The single pillow is centered exactly at the top of a taut, smooth wool blanket. Trevor lies down on that bed and is almost immediately asleep.

~

He wakes up a few hours later feeling unexpectedly refreshed and actually a little bit good. He's surprised that it wasn't too weird to allow himself this comfort even with the irony of him being in Sammy's bed. He definitely feels less achy and realizes that his body — at least — is going to recover.

Trevor looks around the simple room, opens the single closet door and is surprised to see several six guns, in holsters, hanging from the back wall. There is also clothing hanging there. Several complete sets. Everything is in pairs: pants and shirt, then a space, pants and shirt, and on it goes. There are four sets that all look like costumes from a play straight out of the 1850s. Trevor wonders what that is about, finds it weird, but very Sammy-like, he probably contracted the sewing to some distant person through blind drops.

Whatever is to be found here, besides the museum displays in the bedroom, will be in the storage container thing. That will be the final answer one way or the other, all he has to do is find it, if it's here. He remembers Sammy telling Ford about having the container in an arroyo somewhere on the property. It' time to put the rubber to the road. He fingers the watch in his pocket and knows he is stalling. Right here, right now, not knowing is the safer path. If he's right, there is real hope. If he is wrong, everything really is lost, everything. Thinking about Amy refreshes his despair and impossibly, deepens it. Being hated by her is what he expected, but not what he hoped for. He wonders how he would feel toward her if she was the one who had killed Sammy instead of him.

He glances back through the house from the kitchen and seeing nothing that piques his interest, steps out the back door and walks down the short stairs to the flat ground. He follows the path to the grey, weather-worn barn.

The dusty interior of the barn only turns up one anomaly in the form of a series of letters carved into the main support beam of the old building: S T A F. Somebody couldn't spell, graffiti from the last century. The barn is otherwise unremarkable and Trevor heads back out and continues down the path into the small canyon.

The ravine takes a sharp turn and narrows to less than a hundred feet. The day is warming slowly and threatens to be hot. A minute later, Trevor sees what looks like the back end of a shipping container protruding slightly from the vertical wall of the yellow/brown rock. As Trevor approaches, he sees an odd, industrial electronic combination lock on one side of the stout, double doors.

He has no idea how they could possibly have maneuvered the large metal box into the solid rock side of the canyon but there it is. With Sammy there is always a way. There was always a way. He sees that concrete was poured after the box was installed, effectively sealing the opening around it to the surrounding rock. He is no expert on shipping containers, but these doors and locking mechanism seem like a different category from the normal metal box strapped to the back of a truck. This setup looks worthy of a large-scale bank or the military. Okay, maybe Sammy wasn't so trusting, or really has something to hide. The combination lock mechanism has a digital display.

"Okay, dude." Six dials, numbers one through ten. Trevor wonders what ten to the sixth power... only a million possibilities. It could be Amy's birthday, when is that? June, the twenty-sixth? That would be first. Sammy might have been the smartest man born in generations, even the smartest man born ever, but he was, after all, still a man. Yes, Amy's birthday first. Then what... Sammy's birthday, maybe? That would have a nice symmetry to it. Trevor dials in Amy's, then Sammy's. He waits a second, breathes and looks around, then tries the doors. The display reads 'invalid code,' the handles won't budge.

Trevor starts to sweat. It's not the heat; he loves the warm weather. If he can't figure this out, he has no idea what comes next. He tries to freewheel his brain, waits a little longer and then, in that way that our multi-layered human minds work, allows himself to realize that he has a pretty good idea what the last three digits will be. When he asks, 'What would Sammy do?' he knows the answer.

He dials in the last three digits — his own birthday — and feels the click of the locking mechanism moving from within the thick steel of the door. He reads the display: 'Howdy.' Trevor breathes as the door relaxes against the seals.

As he pulls the heavy doors open, the interior lights come on and Trevor looks into a perfect, Sammy neat, brightly lit room. The air wafting out is cool and welcoming. Stepping in, he closes the doors behind him. The laboratory is an exercise in military-like simplicity. Painted clean and white, it is definitely unlike the interior of a shipping container. About half the length of one wall is lined with a three-foot wide, stainless steel shelf. There are several desk top computers, monitors and two laptops spaced out neatly on it. One of the laptops has a sticker on the lid that reads, "Tutorial." A large metallic machine sits in the middle of the room's open space and, incongruously, there is a leather chair in one corner. Everything else is very laboratory like. For a crazy guy's props, these are pretty good ones. It's getting hard to hang on to the idea that this is all fantasy.

On the back wall of the room there is what looks like electronic cabinetry. There is also a bundle of wires running from a rectangular box set toward the rear of the area but mostly, in the middle, there is the weird-looking thing. It is shaped roughly like an hour-glass made from two large, metallic cones, one is pointed up and the other, which does not look like it is actually attached, balanced maybe, is sitting, pointed down. As a whole, the thing looks like a large Christmas tree ornament or very abstract yard art.

Trevor walks past the device. From Sammy's descriptions, he has a rough idea that the fusion reactor is the box at the back of the room. He has less of an idea what the other thing might be although, there is a glimmer of familiarity. He wishes he had tried to get more out of Sammy back before time didn't seem so short.

The box is about the size of a regular gasoline powered generator set. There are multiple cables coming out of it, most of which seem to be carefully routed along the walls of the building. Some of the wires clearly go to the outlets and lights but others are routed into an opening in the floor. If Sammy was all straight up, those must be wires supplying the rest of the farm. He admires the high-tech carbon fiber enclosure but even with the woven black look, the box does not seem like much.

But if it's producing all the power for the farm, it's amazingly simply for the fact that it is this small and powering the entire farm but when you throw in Sammy's claim that it doesn't need fuel for a thousand years it seems beyond crazy. Here is this little box, sitting in this lab, ready to scoop up with a hand truck and take away. The answer to all of humanity's energy needs right here and now, about the size and weight of a large sewing machine, and probably worth more money than any other single thing on the planet. Home run, you had that right Sammy. Knocked it out of the park and the town the park is in. This bat and ball connection is at escape velocity, accelerating at thirty-two feet per second, per second, right off the fucking planet. He is staring at the reactor and his eyes are stinging.

He turns to the enigmatic merry-go-round, whatever-it-is, in the middle of the room. It would be easier if a lawn gnome was discreetly lounging somewhere on the weird sculpture. Absent the joke defining gnome, he is struggling to maintain his equilibrium. If these things, Sammy's creations, are real, it is beyond huge, a ten on the Richter Scale. The pressure is compressing him, he, who, through simple, stupid greed, killed off the best friend in his life and one of the most amazing people ever born on planet. That's too big, the weight of it is going to crush him. Later he will give in to that weight, maybe even take the easy way out, but right now there is a chance, a slim one, that all is not lost.

He examines the round thing, walks around it. He can vaguely see his own reflection in the surface of the metal it is machined from. A cable, larger than the others, runs from the reactor across the floor and into the lower portion of the device. As he moves nearer to the thing, Trevor realizes there really isn't anything between the two cones, nothing obvious, empty air. He moves in close, puts his eyes right up to the space, sure as shit, you can see right on through to the other side. The gap is about a quarter inch. He reaches for the top cone, gives it an experimental wiggle. It does not move, zero flex. He puts his finger up to the gap between the cones and feels a tingle. What kind of amusement ride have you built here, Sam?

Trevor takes a small knife out of his pocket, opens it and leans in toward the point where the cones meet. Poking the blade slowly into the gap there is no resistance at all. It slips into the gap with the same resistance as the air… and disappears. Trevor looks at his fingers, still held about a quarter inch apart, the width of the knife handle. The knife is not between them. It hadn't exactly been plucked from them, it just became insubstantial… and then was gone. Maybe he will not poke his fingers at the gap again. He really doesn't care about living, but he does have a healthy respect for the manner of dying. He looks around the room, moves to one of the laptops on the counter and punches the on button.

The machine takes the usual, painful eternity until the startup logo appears. There is still tremendous pain inside him and there will be a lot of sorting in his future. Maybe that future will be short too, but for now there is that one tiny glimmer of hope, however small and ridicules it is. Until that is resolved, motion is good.

"Password" comes up on the screen. Trevor types in "Amy," pushes enter. The screen responds with "Log-in failed." Trevor tries his and Amy's birthdays. The login screen comes back this time with an addition, "This computer will self-destruct in ten minutes if the correct password is not entered. This is not a joke." A steady beeping comes from the small machine. Sammy! Trevor thinks, what is this shit?

Trevor types in MIT and the date that Sammy earned his PHD. The machine responds with "Incorrect password. Detonation in six minutes."

The beeping comes out louder and at slightly more frequent intervals.

Trevor notices that a digital counter has begun running on the screen. It currently tells him that he has five minutes and some tenths and some hundredths of some seconds and then he is shit out of luck, and who knows, maybe dead. He is going to die sweaty then.

The screen tells him he has two minutes. "Sammy, this is ridicules, dude!" he yells at the insanely racing numbers.

One minute and thirty seconds.

"Shit!" Trevor smacks his hands onto the gleaming counter top, runs his sweaty fingers through his hair and then leans over the key board. He types T H E T R I B E.

The screen changes to an image of the sandbar at Stanley. He is in that image, with Sammy and Amy. The three of them have their heads back and are laughing, or maybe braying at the moon for all he cares, it's a wonderful picture. He remembers the laughing. Claire must have taken the picture. Seeing it now makes him feel like he is going to tear in two. Being there, on that sand bar with Amy and Sammy was everything he ever wanted. He looks at the screen, at the happy faces. That's it, everything, heaven. Here though, not that he's felt far from horrible ever since Las Vegas, he has just moved to the far end of the spectrum, the other end, closest to hell, or maybe in it. At least the beeping has stopped.

"Hey, Trevor," the speakers say to him. "I need to make sure you are you. Please say, out loud, the name of the town where the inbreeding coefficient would be too high to conduct proper research."

After the initial shock of hearing Sammy's voice coming out of the machine, Trevor takes a breath. He knows it's silly, stupid even, but right now this feels like Sammy is somehow still alive. He says, "Emmet."

"Cool, dude. Just one more and we'll have a chat. I know you think I'm paranoid," his dead friend tells him from the computer speakers, "but I come by my distrust honestly. What was the sign along the road when we met at the beginning?"

Easy for you with the amazing memory. He wracks his brain, the reference has to be to the rat shit road he was sitting on when Sammy strolled up out of nowhere, and then he remembers. He can see Sammy, lean and goofy-looking in that damn cowboy hat, walking past a Bonneville Power something sign … sun or something … power production, the sign said. Trevor shakes his head; close but not right. Bonneville Power Automated Substation. He blurts it out.

An image of Sammy's face replaces the sandbar scene. "Hey, Trev," the image is looking right at him. "If you're seeing this, there is probably some explaining to do. Take this laptop and sit down in the leather chair and get comfortable."

Trevor takes the laptop with him, sits in the leather chair, deliberately not thinking. Thinking, right now, is the enemy.

"I know you've heard some of this story in parts, I'm going to try and weave all of the pieces together in this video. Hopefully this will close all the gaps. I apologize if I miss anything, I can't be sure, as I set up this program, what exactly happened to end up with you sitting with this laptop now," Sammy drawls through space and time and a laptop computer.

Trevor's hands are shaking. "Oh, Sam, you have no idea what I have done to you," he moans to the empty lab.

"So, I want you to believe in me for a minute Trev. Take whatever time you need so that you are all here and chill and ready to suspend your disbelief while I unwind this story for you. Just hit enter when you're ready to go on." The image on the screen is replaced again by a still picture. This one is of the Tribe. They are sprawled out on the stage at the pub. Mattie is leaning against him, Ford is bowing the cello, and Amy and Sammy and Jinn are lounging in a big pile against a wall.

He knows that whatever message Sammy left him, it won't let him off the hook for his murder. He is willing to postpone it for a moment. Show me your stuff, Sam. He punches the "enter" key.

"Okay, Trevor, I'm glad you're with me. I know you have your suspicions about my credibility and I understand where you're coming from with those concerns. What I'd like is for you to be prepared to think outside the box. I'm about to prove to you that I am not crazy. I have found a way to travel through time."

Trevor was pretty sure this was coming. It still floors him.

"I know we talked about my research using the element palladium, and

194

specifically, its potential in creating and sustaining a controllable fusion reaction." The on-screen Sammy has been replaced by a series of calculations and weird chalkboard scribbles. "This is where that thinking took me. Before I left MIT, I had built a clunky, but workable, cold fusion reactor." Sammy's thin face is back on the screen. "What I came to theorize with this work is that the real reason palladium can catalyze this kind of reaction is in its unique properties, but while on the surface, it looks like the properties of the element make the difference, it's actually the way one unique element interacts with the Higgs field, and that is the exciting stuff. I built a small-time projector before I left MIT." This statement has an element of confession to it. There's a brief image on the screen of a small, metallic, hourglass looking thing, possibly the object that Sammy had thrown into the river in Idaho that day so long ago.

"The crazy part was that I had completely forgotten, until you asked me about throwing the thing into the river, that there was enough design data left on the CNC machine at MIT to reverse engineer that version of the projector. I apologize Trev, but the time I told you that I had to go see my parents, I actually went to MIT to delete that info. The funny part of that was that I the only way I could gain access to the campus was to pose as somebody. I made a fake ID in the name of the guy that sold me out."

Paxton? That was the story with the Paxton ID?

Trevor rubs his hands over his face. This is some crazy shit.

"It's a long story, but the shortened version is that I was able to identify the effects of the Higgs field and ultimately realize that the field can be manipulated." The image of Sammy looks intensely at Trevor. "I set up a series of experiments that led right to the threshold of actually moving an object through time but stopped there. I was getting way too much scrutiny and I knew Paxton had sold me out. The government was watching everything I did. That's when I decided I had to cut out and I was able to take my rudimentary projector with me when I left. The reactor was too big and I destroyed it before leaving."

He looks like a religious zealot, and Trevor supposes that might be exactly what he is. This little computer thing is way beyond weird now anyway. Trevor rubs his hands over his face again, runs them right up onto the top of his head, and wishes he could twist off his own neck.

"I know you, bro." An image of Sammy points a finger at Trevor. "You are doubting my sanity and I think that's mostly because you doubt yourself but this is true and it's real."

"The day I met you in Oregon, I had just conducted my first ever test. I had been carrying the projector around for a while, both while I tried to lose any possibility of being followed and until I got to what I felt was a rural enough place that I couldn't hurt anybody if it really went wrong. That, and I needed some place to get a lot of power. The substation near where we met was the most remote, unmanned substation I could find. That's the real reason I was out there. Not that the rest wasn't true, it was and is, that one little snippet I didn't really elaborate about. I hope you understand."

Trevor most certainly did understand. Sammy had been his friend for a long time now, was co-owner of his business but then, in the middle of Oregon, if that Sammy had told that Trevor any of this, it would have ended right there. Yeah, I get that.

"If you need to stop for digesting or peeing or whatever, just hit the enter key and I'll chill until you push the key again."

Trevor does that. Hits "enter" then gets up and walks to the door. He opens it and looks, squinting into the hot Montana landscape. Same old shit out there. He looks back in. There is sure as hell some wild stuff in here. You have to be kidding, Sam. Okay, dude, on we go. He returns to the leather chair and the laptop.

"So, I assume you're struggling to believe this, but the best part is, there is proof. I think it's in your pocket. You've probably been carrying it all of the time."

Trevor's fingers trail across his shorts to define the shape of the pocket watch through the fabric of his pants.

"That watch we found in the old farmhouse in Oregon. I sent that copy, right before I met you. Take it out now and open it up."

Trevor takes out both watches. He opens the original one that they had found at the old homestead. He sets the twin down on the arm of the chair. Both watches are shiny.

"If you take something sharp, a knife or a small screwdriver, and slip it around the inside of the rim of the cover, you should be able to pry off a sort of cap. Go ahead and hit enter and do that. Start me up again when you have it off."

Trevor complies. Since he no longer has a pocket knife, he gets up and finds a screwdriver set neatly placed in a drawer under the long counter top. He takes a small screwdriver and slides the sharp end around the perimeter under the watch cover and pops off a thin, aged cap. Underneath it is a very small computer printed picture of Samuel Houston, underneath that photo is a date. There is more computer printing: "To my beloved boy Sam who has earned his PHD. I am so proud of and love you, Dad." And then the words, "Tempus Fugit." Time flies, Sammy. Funny on multiple levels and you never said a word about me literally stealing your gift watch.

Trevor thinks back to when they found the watch. It had been right around the corner of the little shed. It was possible that Sammy had planted the whole thing, he had clearly placed the false cover inside it with the intent of doing exactly this, removing it or having it removed, as proof. That could have been true whether it came through time or was placed there more recently. Still, nothing had been disturbed at the homestead for a long time before they were there. Sammy had been weirdly specific suggesting they poke around in that exact spot. If he had the ability to send something across time and space, he could have sent his pocket watch back one hundred or so years to a different place. He would have needed the exact coordinates, not unimaginable with Sammy's brain. Trevor thinks back to the strange rippling sound and earthquake a half hour before he had met the straight-laced Samuel Houston for the first time. Had it been that, the launching of his watch? Did shooting things off through the Higgs field cause earthquakes? Why not, all bets are off in the weird wake of Sammy's world.

"I do have another bit of... not quite evidence... to offer up." Digital Sammy looks uncomfortable. "When we all went into Mack's house in Stanley during the fire — the first time around, you and Amy died. In the second round, I did."

What?

"When you and Amy went toward the back of Mack's house, the roof collapsed on the two of you and that was it. In that version, I finished my gig with the palladium mining and then bought this same place and ultimately sent a copy of myself back to Mack's house. That was a version of me they found after the fire. You and Amy encountered that copy when you first went toward the back and that me told you to turn around. I also gave myself a note and sent me the other direction as well. I don't know if that constitutes proof, or even how much you remember from the fire but it changed my outlook on things."

Trevor pushes the "enter" button and just breathes for a moment, terrified to hope and unable not to. He hits "enter" again.

"My second projection will be my last. I obviously don't know what happened but if you are seeing this, then at least one more version of me has gone missing from the universe. I would guess that only leaves the remaining projection who should be right here, at the farm you are on today, but in the year 1862 and is hoping you will show up." Trevor refuses to touch the "enter" button. It would be hard to see through the tears anyway. "So here's the deal; the funky machine sitting in here is the Higgs field projector. The green laptop on the counter that has the "tutorial" sticker on it is the trajectory calculator, the controller for the device. The machine I used in Oregon was much smaller and cruder, hence the pocket-watch as the parcel of choice; it slightly exceeded what that machine could do, to the point that the manipulator was damaged with the launching of the watch."

Trevor lets his eyes wander over the machine. The projector? He feels a little nauseous. This is definitely all a little rough on his ability to suspend his disbelief but impossible to let go of. He takes the second watch, the one from Sammy's pocket, and removes the cover from the inside of its lid as well. It is, down to some fine scratches on the lid, an exact copy of the other. He holds them up together, identical twins.

The electronic Sammy picks up his half of the one-sided conversation. "It's about to get a little weirder."

Trevor thinks weirder than this is not possible and wonders if puking will make the whole lab smell. If it comes to that, he thinks he can make it to the door.

"One thing I discovered while I was testing my code is that my program for controlling the manipulator's trajectory can also give me a kind of feedback that shows me where an object or person will be at whatever point in time I plot. It's a little vague but, as far as I can tell, is accurate. I discovered that no points exist for me after Las Vegas. I don't know how or what, but it looks like that's the end of the line for that version of this hombre. I suppose I could have just not gone on the trip but in a way, it gave me the excuse I needed and I let it happen, whatever it is. The good part is that it lets me off the hook on the moral thing. I really do believe the world is not ready for the changes that would happen if I release my technology, not by thousands of years. I destroyed the first reactor before I left MIT. What's in this lab is all that is left of my work. All copies and research documents are in this room. I know that I could just not release my designs, but there are so many pressures from the world that I don't believe I could keep it all secret. Something would leak out and then all bets would be off. My biggest fear truly is that I believe it would be the final straw for the world." Screen Sammy holds up a hand, palm out.

In this pose Trevor thinks Sammy looks remarkably like Jesus.

"The world is not ready for free energy and time travel. Not all of it and not any of it. Not now, probably, not ever. So, I let whatever fate had for me in Vegas happen."

Trevor can't decide if he feels betrayed or used or guilty or hurt. "What the fuck, Sam."

"The other part is this; I have repeatedly calculated that 1862 is about the optimal point in the human progression for making actual change in the path we're on. I have taken that on as my goal and in that universe, I might be able to make a difference. I'm going there to try."

Trevor wipes his eyes.

"I've left the coordinates and programming for you to come, too, should you decide to do that. I don't know what happens, happened to me in Vegas, but I do know that your path could be plotted after there and mine couldn't. Whatever it was, I hope it was quick and easy."

Trevor reaches out and pushes "Enter" again. He sits, staring at the wall of the lab, trying to sort out the mess of thoughts. Sammy is dead here, but not dead somewhere… or some time. Would Sammy have left this information if he knew Trevor had all but pulled the trigger himself? In the end, it doesn't matter; he knows exactly where he's going. He reaches for the "Enter" key.

"There is also a way for the others to come, too, if that's what you all want. I left codes that only you could know so I'm assuming this is in your hands only, Trevor. The one thing you will all have to understand is that the machine does not send you anywhere. It only sends a copy. The copy is exactly the same. All the memories, everything is the same. Every hang nail and booger and the shit stain in your shorts are all copied but the other you, stays right here and that makes for some complicated decisions."

"There you go my friend, you now have the whole package. The pub, the reactor, the time field generator, all of the design information, and all of the plans on the laptop are yours and yours alone. You can be ruler of the planet or the richest man on earth or both. You can elect yourself king and benevolent dictator or just sell off the plans and information and buy yourself an island, say, Australia. There's no limit here, Trev. It's even all legal, there's a complete will on this desktop and it leaves everything to you. You own it all. No one, not even your parents, can ever look down on you again. I have also left a way to make the reactor extremely destructive. Those instructions are on the laptop as well. You've been the best friend I've ever had and I hope to see you again and with that, I'm signing off. That's all I know and from here it's up to you. Good bye for now bro." The screen blanks out, the machine shuts itself down and Sammy is gone again.

Trevor sits back in the leather chair sifting through everything Sammy has just told him. It seems inconceivable, all of it, but here are the two watches.

He looks around the room, the amazing room with the mind-boggling shit that a one in fifty generations brain has filled with potential. He knows that he, of the average IQ will never release any of this to the outside. He runs his hands through his short, black hair and gets up and walks around the yard art that he can't bring himself to call a time projector. He walks around it twice, checking the size and thinking, then turns toward the door.

Chapter 21

TREVOR CAREFULLY SECURES the locking mechanism and checks that the door is secure. He walks a few steps away and then comes back, tries the handle again. This isn't the same place it was when he first got here. It is everything. It's his lifeline to Sammy and maybe, to himself.

He trots back to the farmhouse. Ignoring the half-healed injuries and aches, Trevor walks through the house and goes straight to the six-guns in the closet. Pulling one of the shiny brass and blued metal pistols out he breaks it open, looks in the cylinder. It is loaded with six rounds. He replaces the big iron into the holster and walks out of the house to his truck.

He's on a new kind of auto pilot on the trip back into Billings. He's not uncertain where this is going to go but is less sure about the route it's taking. Unconsciously he presses on the accelerator. Trevor pulls up in front of the pub, walks briskly in the front door of the pub and, mostly oblivious to the curious looks of the wait staff, strides through to the office. The door is closed but not locked and bounces loudly off the stop as he bursts through it. Like an addict hunting for a stash, Trevor jerks open first one cupboard door and then another, riffling through files and office supplies, he comes to his goal. Trevor takes out the old photo he had found during reconstruction.

Sitting in the office chair, Trevor stares at the photo of the four people and a dog. As he remembered, they have bandanas obscuring their faces. They are all giving a thumbs-up. He puts down the photo, picks it up again. Three men, one slim, one thicker, and one nondescript and slumped shoulders. One woman, one with long hair. The dog is sprawled, dog fashion, between the thin man and the stocky man. Maybe things are going to be alright. He turns, Amy and Mattie are in the doorway looking pissed off or ready to cry.

"You can kill me if you want to, but if you aren't going to do that, will you come in and close the door?"

"What are you doing, Trevor?" Amy's words are clipped.

"Will you two come in and close the door?" Jinn walks in, straight to Trevor and rests his head on a leg, then looks up at Trevor with ancient, wise eyes. "I missed you, too, bro." Trevor gives the dog a good rub behind the ears. "Please, you guys. I need to talk to you."

The women enter the office and Trevor turns the chair enough to see Mattie close the door. Amy folds her arms across her chest and leans against the far wall. This is exactly the farthest point possible from him in the tight quarters. Mattie posts herself at the door, leaning against it, holding the knob in her hands behind her back. Trevor is not sure if this is a slightly more trusting positioning than Amy's or slightly less. He takes a deep breath. "I can take us all to Sammy." Amy slumps back against the wall in her farthest-from-him position. Tears are running down her face.

"You stupid, selfish fuck."

Trevor braves a slight glance in Mattie's direction, but doesn't get much from that. She looks unsure of his sanity. She doesn't know what to believe, but weirdly, does not look hateful. Deciding he will think on that later Trevor blurts out, "He's dead and I'm not fucking kidding or crazy, he is also not dead. I'm not completely positive, but I'm very sure."

"Trevor, you're a jackass. What are you talking about?" Amy sprays the words at him with pure vitriolic hate.

Trevor hands her the picture. "This is us, four of us and Jinn. Sammy, Ford, Amy and Jinn. You must be taking the picture Mattie. Sammy left us a time machine." He looks up at Mattie. "A fucking time machine. I know where he is and how to get there."

Mattie says the first words to him that she has spoken in weeks. "How can that work? Sammy is dead."

Trevor rubs his face. "I don't know. I think it's a paradox Quantum thing. I think that when you get blasted through time with Sammy's machine you also don't get blasted. You get copied and the copy gets sent."

"You are either crazy or a pathological liar. You're saying Sammy left a machine at the farm that can take us to him in a different time? What time, when?" Amy looks something, scared or angry, or maybe like how you'd look if you meant to fart and got more than you bargained for while at the prom and in a white suit.

"About 1860-something, I think. He left instructions, but I don't remember the exact time he said we'd be going to." Trevor looks at them; Jinn wags his tail and the two women stare back.

"What kind of instructions?"

"He left a video on a laptop that explains the whole thing. Remember the fire at Mack's? That was a version of Sammy, Ames. You and I died in that fire the first time around. We lived through the second round and the bones they found were Sammy's!"

Amy's is crying freely. "His shoes! I knew something was messed up! He didn't have the right shoes on when he ran out of the back room! Is this all really true?"

"Yes, I think so. It seems a lot less muddy than anything else has been for a while." He smiles at her with a hope that is deeper than anything he has ever felt in his life. "He left us a way to meet up with him. All of us."

"This machine Sammy left will fit all of us?" Mattie asks.

"Have you ever sat in the lap of a lawn gnome?" Trevor laughs.

Amy looks at the door. "Do you know a Paxton guy?"

Oh shit. "Why?"

"He's the one who told us you had killed Sammy. He wanted us to call him if you showed up." She looked at her feet. "I called him right before I came in here."

Oh shit! "I didn't kill Sammy, but we have to go right now! Paxton is with the FBI; he's the guy who sold out Sammy at MIT. They are offering a reward for Sammy."

"We have to go right now. We can't take anything with us, zip and we have to go! Meet me at the truck as soon as you can. Leave everything here. It'll sort itself out. I'll get Ford." He reaches for the door and dashes toward the kitchen.

Ford is at the sink.

"Hey, Trevor!" Ford steps over with an outstretched hand.

Trevor pulls him into a surprised hug. "Do you trust me buddy?" Trevor asks hurriedly.

"I heard about Sammy and cried a lot. That Paxton guy came to us and said you guys might be bread. Sammy was for sure and yeah, I trust you."

"It's hard to explain but everything is going to be okay. Are you up for a trip tonight? We're going out to Sam's Farm right now. We are even going to leave the rest of the dishes, we have to go. Will you get Jinn and meet me at the truck really quick, like bunny quick?"

Ford looks at him in a weirdly knowing way and waves a hand in the general direction of the sink. He smiles at Trevor and walks into the hallway.

Trevor realizes that for the first time since Sammy got shot, he has gone five or more minutes without thinking about him being killed. He feels, not just hopeful, he feels completely fucking elated.

Turning toward the rear of the building, Trevor notices a black Suburban pulling up to the curb. He doubles his pace, almost breaking into a run, desperately hoping that Mattie, Amy, Ford, and Jinn are somewhere near the back of the building. He is crushed when he finds the stage is empty.

There is a prayer of sort, going through his head; he knows he doesn't believe in much, but right now it can't hurt. Please God, don't let me fuck this up. Slamming the door open, he sees his shitty new red truck in the alley. It is empty.

Turning back toward the front of the building, things have gotten worse. There is a man in a suit standing on the curb and talking on a cell phone. The phone call might buy extra seconds, but the guy has to be an agent. Not that he has any idea at all what he's going to do anyway. He slows his walk, the agent can see in through the windows as well as he can see out. He figures movement is okay, fast movement would be less so. His grip on the stair banister is white knuckled.

Voices are coming from Ford's room. Trevor should have known this was coming.

"I can't, Mattie." Ford's strident voice carries into the hallway.

Trevor hears Mattie and Amy both talking at once, but can't make out the rest of what they're saying. It doesn't matter, he just formed a plan. It's not long term and might only get them five minutes into the future, but that's five minutes toward a salvation that has to happen. Slamming open the door, he rounds the corner into the room. "It's okay, buddy, you can take the cello for now, but things have changed a little." He locks eyes with Amy. She's startled, but she'll go with it. He glances toward Mattie and doesn't see outright resistance anyway.

"We have to go, right... right now, and we have to go out the back window. The FBI is here." He grabs the bed clothes and shakes out a sheet from the rest. "The fire escape." Picking up the cello, he looks at Ford. "You can do this, buddy."

Ford has his normal dreamy smile back on his face. It's unsettling, but he's cooperating. Trevor urges the group toward the back of the building.

Looking out the window over the alley, they don't see any obvious government vehicles, yet. Trevor throws open the window and works the ancient fire escape mechanism, thankful they had spent the time to re-work and lubricate the components. The ladder lowers to the ground. "Amy, here's the truck keys; we can't send Jinn this way. He and I are going to run a bluff right now. If we aren't at the truck in five minutes, just go somewhere, I guess. Things are pretty far into the weeds right now but there is no turning back."

As Amy starts to climb out of the window, Trevor puts a hand on her arm. "I love you guys. Go, I'll be with you soon... I hope." Amy throws her leg onto the platform and starts to climb down. Mattie is staged to follow and Ford watches closely as Trevor knots the ends of the sheets. "I'm going to lower it down to you. That work?" He is relieved that Ford nods. He knows that ultimately there's no way the time machine is going to accommodate the cello, too, but for now he doesn't believe Ford will go along without it. He ties the sheet to the neck of the instrument as Ford watches closely and suspiciously and then climbs out of the window. Trevor dutifully lowers the cello to the group in the alley, thankful that the weather is cooler and the back area is not in use. Letting go of the sheets, he hurries toward the front of the building and the stairway, quietly calling to Jinn to come with him. What in God's name is going to happen next?

Grant Peterson of Homeland Security walks through the front door as Trevor and Jinn start down the stairs. Continuing toward the lower floor, Trevor furiously tries to figure out what his next move will be. He sees Paxton looking up at him. There's a slight smile on Paxton's face as he reaches into his jacket.

"Grant Peterson!" Trevor is quite loud as he steps onto the dining area floor, loud enough that patrons look his way. He holds out his hand to Paxton. Paxton's smile has slipped and he's about to speak. "It's good of you to come back, Grant. We've been hoping to see you again." Trevor holds a hand toward a table. "Sit down, we'll have you a menu in a second." Paxton turns toward him. He's holding a badge.

"Trevor, my actual name is Garwin Paxton; I'm with the FBI. We need to talk."

Trevor takes a breath, nods and turns toward the office. His eyes are almost closed. Absentmindedly, he pats his leg and Jinn follows. They walk into the small office. Trevor turns and puts his back to the file cabinet. Paxton sits in the only office chair, and Jinn sits on Trevor's feet.

"I'm sorry about the subterfuge with the inspection. We have been looking very hard for Sammy and info from your business license got a ping because of your age. It was really a shot in the dark, but now we know it's the real deal. We came up with the inspection as a way to check you out and see if we could find him. It wasn't until his body was found and we went back through video feeds in Vegas that we realized you really were with him."

"Agent Paxton, are you arresting me?"

The man in front of Trevor purses his lips for a moment. "Trevor, Sammy was the most important person the world has seen in a long time, since Einstein, at least. The government is desperately looking for his research materials and we are willing to go to any length to get that information."

"And you think I know where his stuff is?"

"I have a pretty good idea that you might."

"Do you know he thought of you as a friend and that your betrayal was completely devastating and the real reason he left MIT?"

Paxton looks at him dispassionately. "It's not about me, this is big Trevor. Let me make this simple. Several carloads of agents are heading this way. The last private moment of your life will coincide with their arrival. This is very serious shit. Frankly, this is so serious that your safety is not guaranteed. And there's enough video that we can put you on trial for Sam's murder. I hope you get the drift here, Trevor."

Trevor lets his shoulders slump a little. "If I show you where his stuff is, I mean if I knew, would the reward money still apply?"

"I'm certain that if you cooperate, you will both have your life and money to live it with a high standard. Think about that and take the easy route."

"The easy route being the one that takes you personally to whatever it is you are looking for? Before the rest of your agent buddies get here?"

Paxton shrugs and Trevor thinks that is the real reason Paxton is here before the troops, he must have the idea that he can get control before the whole thing gets blown open. It dawns on Trevor that there is only one way for this to go if he is going to get out of it. "Okay, Sammy left some notes about how to run the process. You get me the five million dollars you offered on the last email I saw and I'll get you that notebook, how's that?" Trevor thinks he's nailing the performance, but the reserve of his acting skills is pretty much used up. "How much time do we have?"

"A few minutes, maybe ten."

"Do we have a deal?"

Paxton nods. "We have a deal."

"Okay, I want that money. Sammy did a lot of his work in the basement. The way there is back by the stage." Without hesitating, he reaches for the office door and purposefully strides toward the back of the building. Greed will get you every time brother, knowing he is the expert. He hurriedly leads Paxton back to the basement door. Trevor signals Jinn to stay, and still without even glancing back, pulls open the door, hurries straight down into the gloom. The door to the old back up vault is open, as Trevor hoped it had been left. Through the opening a spiral wound book with Sammy's handwriting is plainly visible. "That's one of them," Trevor points toward the doorway. "Tell me how I will get my money and I will get you the rest of his notebooks."

Paxton walks past him toward the book, "I have definite authority in this circumstance Trevor, to get you your money. You are doing the right thing by turning Sammy in. It's the right thing to do."

Trevor slams the vault door shut and reaches for the round metal pin from Sammy's lab that is sitting on an old crate near the vault door. It slides perfectly into the hasp. Paxton hammers on the door. You are right about that Garwin Paxton, this is the right thing to do. Trevor heads back up the stairs.

Jinn's tail is thumping as Trevor bolts out of the basement door. Together, they hurry, almost falling into the alley and to Trevor's infinite relief, the red truck is right behind the building, the motor is running. Three heads are visible, no other cars are in sight. The tires spin as Trevor mashes the gas pedal and points the truck toward Sammy's farm.

Chapter 22

THEY PARK IN FRONT of the farmhouse, under a clear sky and a setting sun.

As they enter the house, Jinn trots to a dog bed set in the living room, obviously familiar territory. Trevor takes Amy by the hand for no reason other than that she is closest. He's pleased that there's no resistance as he leads them to the kitchen and shows them Sammy's notes.

They are standing side by side at the table. Their bodies are close, touching each other on either side. Ford is on the left, Mattie, then Trevor, then Amy. They stare at the notes for a little while, but no one reads anything. Mattie breaks the silence.

"You really think we can all go?"

Feeling more confidence than he could ever describe, Trevor tries to share some of that. "Knowing Sammy-who-thinks-of-everything, he wouldn't have even let it be a possibility if he wasn't certainty it would work. That's our Sammy."

Amy nods, "You said 1862? That's the year where his calculations say the world is still... what... malleable?"

Trevor shrugs. "I don't remember his exact words, but that's the gist of it, yeah."

"You're going for sure?"

"There is nothing that will keep me from going. Are you?"

Mattie looks away. "I don't know, Trev. This is so fucking weird. Are you really going to do this, Amy?"

"I am. I'm buying into this version of Sammy's save the world plan." She shrugs. "This seems more real to me than wandering through my life trying to find friends as I move around pursuing my career. Ford, are you in, buddy?"

Fords nods his handsome, vacant, middle-aged face. "Sammy said my place was with the tribe and that I shouldn't be scared. I'm going."

Trevor turns to Ford, "Sammy said you shouldn't be scared, of what exactly?"

"I dunno exactly, Trevo. He said that if you came to me with a crazy pan, I shouldn't be scared. This is your crazy pan right Trev?"

Trevor reaches out and, for the second time in both his life and this day, hugs Ford. "This is definitely a crazy pan buddy."

Trevor picks up one of the smaller spiral-bound notebooks and glances through some pages. Sammy's handwriting is on the front, it's about indigenous plants in the area, but it's hard to read even up close. Yup, that's the one. He leads them out through the back door toward the barn but stops as they are going by it.

"Hang on right here for a second? I have to find something." He trots into the barn and goes to a very old shelf built at the back. The shelf is cluttered and dusty but Trevor find what he was looking for, an old metal pin.

Staying close together, they follow the trail that takes them down the narrowing arroyo and eventually to the locked doors of the former shipping container. He punches in the code and the large industrial locking mechanism opens smoothly in his hands. The rest of the group stands silent and a little bit mind boggled, watching, in their own thoughts. The air is still and silent. The only sound Trevor hears, besides his pulse beating in his ears, is the soft swishing of the retriever's tail. He pulls open the insulated door and cool air wafts out over them.

The lights come on as they enter and Trevor moves aside to let the others in, closing, and locking the door behind Ford. Trevor gives them a minute to adjust to this reality. The lab is impressive with its quirky neatness and utilitarian look.

They all look at the device. "Yard art," he says. "The thing in the back on the right is the answer to humanity's energy needs. That's Sammy's reactor." He turns to Mattie. "You knew about that, right?"

She nods her head. "Amy told me most of the story after Sammy was... you know. Before you came back."

"Yup. I do know." Trevor nods. I sure as shit do.

"If you guys want to sit somewhere, I'll start the laptop."

The three of them head to the overstuffed chair. Amy sits down on the seat, Mattie settles herself onto one of the arms and Ford moves to stand next to her. Jinn positions himself alongside the chair as if he understands perfectly what the group is doing and so he can watch, too. Trevor grabs an industrial looking suitcase from under the long counter and sets it in front of the chair, table style. He then puts the laptop on it, opens the screen, and sets it up to play.

The group watches in silence as Sammy comes on the screen. Trevor mostly watches their faces as they listen to what Sammy is saying. They all sit silently through the presentation and continue in silence for several more minutes after it has stopped.

"Quantum twins," Ford says, breaking the silence.

"What do you know about that, buddy?" Trevor asks him.

"Nothin'. Sammy just talked about it some while we were washing dishes and stuff. I like it when Sammy talks to me. He said I get to be one, a twin. That's pretty cool since there was only one of me borned and now there's gonna be two."

"So, let me get this out before my head explodes," Mattie croaks. "We send a version of ourselves, to eighteen-sixty-two and where in eighteen-sixty-two, does that version, what, land?"

Trevor nods uncomfortably. "I don't know Mattie. I'm trusting that Sammy has it right." He tries not to mention the most compelling evidence that supports this theory, the apparent two dead Sammys. "This is all I've got, this little laptop telling me he might be alive in 1860-something and I can join him."

Mattie lifts her chin and stares at Trevor for a second before speaking. "And what happens to the version of us that stays here?"

Trevor rubs his whiskery face. "I think the reactor is going to be set to destroy itself and this." He waves a hand at the metallic disc. "And us."

"A twin goes back," Ford sounds weirdly confident.

Trevor is relieved that Ford is, at least on some level, making his own choices.

"Sweet Jesus," Amy says.

"I have to send these first. I have to have them at the pub to lock up Paxton." He holds up the pin and the notebook. "And then I'm going to send my copy to wherever Sammy has set up for us to go. You guys have to decide for yourselves, but this is the only shot at it. After this train leaves the station it ain't gonna stop here again."

Mattie looks at Trevor, her face is tight. "You aren't really going to let Ford do that are you?"

Before Trevor can answer, though, Ford answers for himself. "Sammy and I talked a lot about it. I know what it means and I want to go. I know you guys have to decide, but me and Jinn have to go. I want to and Sammy said I could." He is almost defiant and certainly the most assertive that Trevor has ever seen him.

"Okay, dude." Trevor holds out his fist. Ford bumps him and then goes back to sitting patiently.

Mattie looks back to Trevor again. "Tonight?"

Trevor nods. "Yeah. After we change. I have to go as soon as possible. I believe Paxton was telling the truth about the bad guys bearing down on us."

"It'll be all bright," Ford tells her.

Trevor takes the "tutorial" laptop and sets down against on the floor, leaning against the wall. After he enters the password, Sammy begins walking him through the process of sending copies of the pin and the notebook to a few days ago and to their respective places in the pub basement.

They all watch when Trevor hits the key stroke that, in theory, sends a copy of these things. The machine begins to hum slightly. The sound builds very quickly to a crescendo and then stops. There is a small, rippling earthquake and then nothing. The pin and the notebook are sitting on the yard art.

"Well, there was the earthquake. That's no small deal."

Looking terrified, Amy stares at him. "I get it." She points to the notebook and the metal pin that are still on the machine. "That's the part that I'm struggling with, that we can go and stay, at the same time."

"I don't know, Ames. Nothing that I've seen in the tutorial or any of Sammy's other crap addresses that question at all. It's clearly possible for there to be two of you or else Sammy wouldn't have been able to save our bacon and die in the fire. He said he gave himself a note."

"I can't do it."

All of them turn toward Mattie.

"I can't, I can't…. magically create another me and kill one or leave one or commit suicide or anything else. I adore you guys but I'm out." She looks relieved.

Amy steps toward her and puts a hand on Mattie's shoulder. "That's why you aren't in the picture. You don't go." She is silent for a moment and then turns to Trevor. "I think I'm going to stay too. The thought of leaving my parents childless is a little more than I can bear."

"But Amy, you gotta go. You are in the picture!" Ford's logic has an odd symmetry to it.

Amy smiles at him. "It's okay, buddy. I will still be in the picture. I'm going to go too. We will try the twin Amy's theory I guess."

Trevor's head is swimming and he wishes briefly there was some way to sneak sideway out of here, disappear and forget this whole thing. He looks at the three of them and knows that he wouldn't, even if he could though. If Mattie doesn't go, she will still be part of the tribe, that's the way it is and Sammy is waiting, a hundred and fifty some years ago.

~

In Sammy's closet, they find the sets of clothing. Surprising Trevor, Amy strips and swaps into the western clothes right there. Trevor and Ford shuck their modern clothes and don the period canvas jeans, heavy weave cotton shirts, and wool coats as well as the gun belts. Ford takes one gun belt and fastens it on his hip. Trevor takes two, his and Mattie's, though both are right handed and he ends up looking more stupid than Lone Rangerish. He puts the black hat on his head, slips on cowboy boots, and straps on spurs.

Amy shakes her head. "This is so weird."

"Can we go see Sammy now?" Ford asks with mild urgency.

"I'm just going to wait here for Amy." Mattie is crying.

Trevor turns toward her. "You guys have to get as far from here as you can, as soon as Amy shows up, get in the truck and go." He reaches in and pulls her to him. "I'm sorry it never worked out with us Mattie. I wish you were going but I understand where you are at."

Mattie tilts her head up and kisses him full on the mouth. "Have a great life handsome boy."

They make their way out of the house and retrace their steps to the lab.

"Do we all just stand on the thing?" Mattie asks Trevor as they are looking at the machine.

"I don't see how else we will fit."

They spend some time carefully going back over Sammy's instructions, including finding the file for setting up the reactor. Trevor opens a control panel on the machine and looks at the LED indication under it, as well as the other switches that had been covered.

"Wild," he says, mostly to himself. "This thing is putting out point-zero-seven percent of its total power." He pauses a second as he reconsiders briefly, again, the potential about to be lost to mankind, maybe forever, shakes his head and goes back to what he was doing.

"So, this is the code to override the protection programming." Amy shows him the screen of the laptop she has been holding. A long string of characters and numbers are across the screen. "There can be no more than thirty minutes from the time we enter the sequence."

"Okay, and we have all of Sammy's coordinates plugged into the machine. Ready?" he looks at Ford, "are you all ready, buddy?"

Amy and Ford arrange themselves on the metal disc around the upward pointing cone of the time projector. Jinn insinuates himself in between legs and the cone, a bizarre tableau. "You guys look ridiculous. I can still fit, right?" He punches a long string of characters from Sammy's instructions into the laptop, looks at Amy. "One last number and enter and that's it. Are you ready to make a run for it?"

Amy nods. "Is there a way to separate the functions. Like, launch the projections and then pause before setting up the self-destruct separately?"

"I just followed Sammy's instructions to the literal letter and this is the way he set it out, all or nothing. Besides that, I am at least a little worried that the FBI is going to get here. As far as I know, once the last button is pushed, it's a done deal." He scans their faces. "Ford, you are still sure?"

"Yeah, Trevo. I'm sure. I want to go be with Sammy."

"Alright you guys." He clicks in the last number and then steps onto the time projector. "Okay Ames. Just as soon as the earthquake is over you are off and out of here, right? Don't even change your clothes until you guys get as far as you can go."

She leans over and kisses him, nods.

Almost unconsciously he reaches for the hands to his left and right, Amy's and Ford's. There's a slight humming and then the earthquake begins.

Thirty seconds go by before the ground stops shaking. Trevor looks at Amy. "Okay Amy, go. Lock the door on your way out and then…try to have a great other life." He smiles very weakly at her.

"This is so fucking weird Trevor. Goodbye."

Have they just made the last error of their lives? He is vaguely nauseous and clock seems to be clicking by incredibly slowly. He smells a strong ozone and wonders if he could make it out the door and run far enough to survive the explosion. Ford is sitting calmly and Jinn's tail is thumping rhythmically.

"I wish I could have brought my cello."

"I know, buddy, I think we can find you one when we get there, though." He cringes at that, this is a very weird thing to say since "they" as they are sitting here right now, will never get anywhere else but here. Check out time is very near. The other they, is already there, one hundred fifty some years ago.

The smell of ozone gets stronger. The reactor is starting to hum a little. Trevor reaches for Jinn and runs his hands through the thick fur of his mane.

Chapter 23

AS THE FIRE DIES DOWN, Sammy picks up his banjo and starts playing a version of "Go for a Soda," Kim Mitchel's song that will be from nineteen-eighty-four.

Trevor bursts around the corner of their tent, laughing. He leans against the wagon and puts his hands on his knees to catch his breath as he chuckles. He has been laughing often in the month since they made their reunion with Sammy. "I didn't want to miss the rock and roll splits!"

Sammy and Amy laugh too. Not getting the joke, Ford smiles with his friends just because it feels good when they laugh.

Sammy shakes his head, "No splits, Sorry brother. This weather just reminded me of that night on the sand bar."

"I was ready to call it a day anyway. It's getting too hard to see and damn it, I still miss having electric lights!"

"Me too. I keep thinking about introducing some form of portable electrical generation but it's so hard to guess what and when will do good and what would do more harm than good."

Amy looks up from the work she is doing on the harness for the wagon. "We haven't talked about it much but could you build a fusion generator here, with what's available in this time? I keep thinking about that. It seems like there is the potential to stop so much damage from being done."

Sammy is picking the banjo quietly. "I keep kicking it around too. I could build one but it's the same set of risks as before and I worry that, if we introduced it now, we'd be setting the world up for a worse mess than last time around."

Trevor is looking up at the stars beginning to become visible in the sky and, out of the corner of his eye he is watching his friend. "We are sticking with the plan then, to spread the word? Do you really think we can change the course of all that, by educating the world about population explosion and greenhouse gasses?"

Sammy's fingers are rolling across his banjo. "I do. So the real question, Trevor, is are you ready to save the world?"

Trevor nods and looks around at the tribe. "Ready, bro."

Chris Allen Lynch is a fifty-eight-year-old guy who lives with his wife on a ten-acre hobby farm in the Cascade foothills of Washington State. He likes flying airplanes, hiking, and discussing the inner workings of the universe with the family's complement of wise Golden Retrievers.

Please check out his web page at: www.ChrisAllenLynch.com.

If you liked *Side Road to Nevada*, please, please, please write a review! This is the only way to let me know if I should keep writing or maybe put the computer away and think a little harder about whether to plant the corn or squash.

I know Side Road isn't very genre-fitting, but if you think others might enjoy it, please let them know. I knew about this cumbersome fit issue when I was writing the book, but I felt that Sammy's and Trevor's stories just needed telling.

So, there you have it. If you think the story was compelling, please go to Amazon.com and add your thoughts!

Thank you very much for sharing the journey with Sammy, Trevor, Amy, Mattie, Ford, Jinn, and me!

Chris Allen Lynch

Made in the USA
San Bernardino, CA
03 November 2018